Goy Crazy

Goy Crazy

a novel by
MELISSA SCHORR

Hyperion New York

Printed in the United States of America

First Edition
10 9 8 7 6 5 4 3 2 1
Library of Congress Cataloging-in-Publication Data on file.
Designed by Elizabeth H. Clark
ISBN 0-7868-3852-3
Reinforced binding
Visit www.hyperionteens.com

In loving memory of Clara

*To my beloved patron, Gary,
and my forgiving parents, Seymour and Thelma*

chapter 1

THERE IS NO WAY I'm dancing with Howard Goldstein.

That's the only thought running through my mind as I sit, alone, at the head table at my brother Ben's bar mitzvah. The bandleader has just launched into yet another excruciatingly slow song and is feebly encouraging everyone to get up on the dance floor. I am hiding at the table, picking over my salad, hoping no one will notice me.

So far, it's working. My mom's working the crowd for gift envelopes like a stripper stuffing her G-string; my dad's micromanaging the maître d' to make sure he's not scrimping on the smorgasbord; and my brother and his prepubescent friends are picking partners for those prehistoric party games like Musical Chairs and Coke & Pepsi, the same ones played at bar mitzvahs since Babylonian times.

Hard to believe only two years ago, at age thirteen, I was up there, too, on the bimah, singing my heart out like a complete dork, marking my entry into "womanhood," as is customary—no, make that mandatory—in my Jewish faith.

My own bat mitzvah was replete with painful memories. Bad hair. Bad skin. Questionable fashion judgment. True to course, on bat mitzvah morn, I woke up with a huge red zit on my cheek that my mom vainly tried to cover up with Lancôme bronzing blush. As if that weren't humiliating enough, later she insisted the photographer airbrush it out of the pictures.

Then there was my outfit. In a moment of temporary insanity, I chose to wear a frilly Snow White dress that better resembled one of the lace doilies sitting on my bubbe's coffee table than a garment emoting, "Man! I Feel Like a Woman." Now, of course, I don't wear any color but black, to my mother's constant chagrin. Brown, maybe, if I'm feeling cheerful.

At least my voice didn't crack during my reading, like most boys in my grade that year. But I still cringe when I think of myself at the reception, dancing away to the Chicken Dance, chin jutting, elbows flailing. What a nightmare. I've tried to block out the images, but even if I could, they're all right there, recorded for posterity by the videographer my parents hired to immortalize the blessed event.

Naturally, my annoyingly perfect brother hasn't had any of those issues. This morning, he stood before all his friends, our extended family, and the temple's entire congregation, flawlessly chanting the Hebrew blessings, then sailed through his haftorah portion, no problemo. And though he's usually into freakishly proportioned cyberchicks he controls with his thumb, I see he's already making headway in the love department, teaming up with Sarah Sternlicht, the cutest girl in his seventh-grade class, as the Coke to his Pepsi.

For me personally, "becoming a woman" didn't change a thing. I'm still flat as a flapjack, with no Curve Ahead in sight. There's been no discernible transformation in my love life. And my parents still treat me like an infant. I'd naively thought things would be different once I hit high school. But my first year at Riverdale High was the same old, same old. Same kids from junior high. Same too-short guys and too-spoiled girls. My parents haven't helped, with their ridiculous rules to monitor my every movement. I may live in one of the five boroughs of New York City, the capital of cool, but honestly, my life is so sheltered, I may as well be in Hicksville, U.S.A. My parents don't let me ride the subway after dark, which pretty much limits my nightlife options to hanging out aimlessly in front of the neighborhood ice-cream shop or newsstand.

For the reception, I've resigned myself to nursing my (virgin, like me) banana daiquiri and avoiding getting cornered by any extended family, who will undoubtedly ask whether I enjoyed my summer at camp, and am I psyched to begin my sophomore year in a few weeks. The answer is: not so much.

Too late. Shattering my tranquility, my Aunt Merle swoops in for the kill.

I barely need to turn my head to know she's coming. I

3

catch a strong whiff of her Chanel No. 5 long before she drapes her blinged-out hand on my shoulder. "Darling," she rasps in her hoarse voice, battered by decades of Virginia Slim Ultra Lights. "Why aren't you up there dancing?"

"I don't feel like it." I shrug.

The truth is, who would I dance with? Aunt Merle doesn't realize I scoped the guest list weeks ago, hoping for a potential love connection, and came up with a big fat zero. Aside from Howard, my annoying next-door neighbor, there's no one remotely my own age here. Sure, thanks to my mathematical brain, I've easily pegged the crowd's average age at about thirty, but statistics can be highly misleading. In reality, there are two very different subgroups: the over-fifty set: geriatric relatives and friends of my parents. And, on the other end of the spectrum, the under-thirteen set: Ben and his seventh-grade buddies, who look like they're playing dress up in their fathers' Brooks Brothers suits and ties. Impossible to fathom, I was once interested in boys this age. Now they just look so . . . short.

Aunt Merle's face lights up.

Please, please, I chant in my head, *don't let her suggest I dance with her son, Ira.*

"I bet Ira would dance with you," suggests Aunt Merle, a master of the Vulcan Mind Meld. My cousin Ira is an investment banker living in Hoboken, who used to torment me as a child by locking me in a closet. But he's practically thirty, making him closer to my dad's age than mine.

4

She scans the crowd, looking for his already-balding head. All I can see is a sea of bobbing white yarmulkes. Inside of each one, my parents had printed "Stolen from Ben's Bar Mitzvah"—just one example of their screwy sense of humor they'd like to tell you is "Jewish wit."

"That's all right," I say weakly. Getting asked to dance doesn't really count when your aunt has to play matchmaker.

Sadly, come to think of it, the last time I officially slow danced with *any* guy was at my own bat mitzvah two years ago, when Marc Goodman asked me out a week beforehand and pursued me for the rest of the year. The rest of the year lasted all of two weeks until summer vacation, when I never heard from him again.

And if you want the honest truth, the only reason I think he asked me was because that last month of seventh grade, I was the momentary It girl, the Paris Hilton of J.H.S. 141, for having the last big blowout bat mitzvah of the season. My social standing slipped back to neutral by the fall and hasn't recovered since. Sometimes I wonder: is it possible to peak at thirteen?

Just then, my mother strides over to make sure no fun is being unhad. "So, what do you think?" she asks my aunt, nudging for a compliment.

But my aunt will not be thrown off course.

"I'm trying to find a nice boy for Rachel to dance with," she says, as if I weren't sitting right there.

I begin to tell them that there's no one even remotely interesting to dance with, when my mother brightly chimes in, "Oh, well, what about Howard?"

I'd been praying she'd forgotten about Howard. I've been trying to forget him my whole life, without much luck.

Howard Goldstein's been hanging around since forever. Literally. His family moved in next door to us before I was even born, and our parents still go gaga over this picture of us holding hands in the sandbox, when I was three and he was four. Naturally, they'd love to see us hit it, ". . . Baby One More Time." My parents are sure it could happen, given enough not-so-subtle nudgings. But he's soooo not my type. He's got kinky brown hair, thin wire-rimmed glasses, and a total obsession with Yu-Gi-Oh! graphic novels. Plus, he always has a perpetual put-down when he sees me. We haven't really been on good terms since I picked him to be my square-dancing partner in fourth grade and he threw up all over me during the dosie-do. His mother tried to blame it on the stomach flu, but I knew he did it on purpose. Even worse was in sixth grade at his bar mitzvah when I heard him and his friends sniggering at my flat chest while I was doing the limbo. Things between us have never been the same. I guess you could say that, today, we have a relationship based on mutual disrespect. Dancing with him would be unimaginably, incestuously gross—like having to French kiss my little brother, Ben.

Now my mom begins scanning the crowd for good ol'

Howard. Any second now, she'll march up to the band and have him paged over the loudspeaker. *Howard Goldstein, please report to the dance floor.*

"Mom, really," I say, nervously chewing my thumbnail. "It's okay. I don't want to dance with Howard."

"Don't be silly," she says, pulling my fingernail away from my lips with one practiced swipe. "I know he's dying to dance with you. I'll go find him." She stalks off into the crowd as if she hadn't heard a word I'd said. As usual.

Hoping Howard has gone AWOL, I return to picking at my limp lettuce. A busboy circles our table, refilling our water glasses.

"More water?" a voice asks from above.

When I look up, a blond Adonis is standing before me. I try not to choke on my radicchio.

I nod and sneak another peek as he fills my glass. He looks about sixteen, his sun-streaked hair flapping over his soulful eyes, the bluest I've ever seen. His lips are plump and hint at light-years of experience beyond my own virgin lips.

A most bussable busboy.

He is simply an angel, dropped down from the heavens above—if we believed in cherubs and the Pearly Gates and all that heavenly bliss stuff. Which, in my religion, we don't. But maybe, just maybe, I'll have to reconsider.

He catches me staring and gives me a little smile. Or am I imagining that?

In the background, I can vaguely hear my aunt lamenting

Ira's latest travails in online dating at J-Date, a Web site for lonely-heart Jewish singles. But by the time I can steal another glance, he has moved on to the next table.

Why, I fume, can't a guy like that show up as a guest, instead of Howard? The son of one of my parent's friends, maybe, or a long-lost cousin, several times removed enough to be incest-free? I toy with the fantasy of pulling him out onto the dance floor, certain of the instant whispering that would erupt among the gossip-starved yentas. *Oy gevalt! Sylvia and Herb's daughter is dancing with the hired help!*

The band launches into the festive Jewish tune, "Hava Nagila." The bandleader clears his throat and leans into the microphone. "Can I get everyone up on their feet?"

"Oooohhhh," squeals my aunt. "Come on, bubbulah, you don't need a partner for this." She grabs my wrist and practically pulls me out of my chair toward the dance floor.

I groan at her choice of words. Did the bussable busboy hear them? Perfect. Now he's going to think I was sitting there alone because I couldn't get anyone to dance with me. My aunt clasps my hand firmly, and we are sucked into the vortex of the beast.

I hate to admit it—and if anyone ever mentioned it I'd deny it to my grave—but I actually don't mind dancing the hora. It's like a combination of ring-around-the-rosy and a country-western hoedown. Only geekier. You link hands and form a chain, and circle around until you're dizzy. Every so often, you rush forward, giving the guest of honor in the center a giant group grope. To an outsider, it probably looks like some weird African tribal ritual. But it always gives me the warm fuzzies.

I try to sneak a peek at where the busboy has gone to, but the music is whipping everyone into a frenzy, and I keep getting yanked around too quickly. Now I am in the center, spinning around with my mom and dad, as my brother Ben gets his turn to be lifted in the air, followed briefly by each of us.

That's my favorite part of all time—getting lifted in a chair while everyone dances around below. You know how when A-Rod makes a game-winning home run and all the Yankees sweep him onto their shoulders and carry him around the entire stadium? It's just like that, except—as my dad says—as Jews, we figure, why should we be uncomfortable? So we use a chair. Of course, when it's my turn, I have to rely on my scrawny cousins Ira and Zachary instead of studs like Johnny Damon and Derek Jeter to do the heavy lifting, so I nearly slide right off the seat and onto the floor. But still, I figure, given my athletic ineptitude, it's the closest to a We-Are-The-Champions experience I'll ever get.

Flushed, I catch my breath as the song ends and the band launches into a painful rendition of Usher's latest ballad. Thank God no one from Riverdale High is here to witness this musical travesty. I had campaigned heavily for Degenerate Pumpkinheads, this amazing local rock band whose members graduated from my high school a few years ago. But what do you expect when your 'rents have final say on the choice of tunes? Elevator Muzak Live!, that's what.

Suddenly I notice Howard across the room, lumbering toward me with that unmistakable glint of interest reflecting off his thin-lens glasses. My mother's mission must have been a success. Oh, no. Get me out of here.

I step backward, inching against the wall. Without warning, it gives way to a swinging door, and I practically stumble on top of someone lurking on the other side.

It's my blue-eyed, bussable busboy.

chapter 2

"*SORRY*," *I STAMMER*, as my eyes adjust to the dimly lit waitstaff break room, which smells of stale cigarettes and sour milk. I feel a puddle of water at my feet, and when I look down, I realize our collision has splashed the contents of his pitcher onto the floor and all over his arms. "Oh, God!" I cry.

"No problem." He smiles ruefully and rubs his hands dry on his pants, as a damp stain quickly spreads up the white sleeves of his uniform.

"I should go," I say, regretting the offer almost as soon as it leaves my lips, as I hear the band break out into the Electric Slide on the other side of the door.

"On the lam?" he asks teasingly.

"No, I just needed a break. You can only hora so much."

He looks at me blankly. *Why, oh why, do I make such lame jokes in the presence of hot guys?*

"I'm Luke," he offers, hand outstretched. "Luke

Christiansen." Hmmm. Definitely a New Testament name, if you know what I mean.

"Rachel," I say.

His palm is still damp and clammy from the spill, but his grasp is firm.

"So, whose party?" he asks casually, as if making conversation in the back room of a catering hall is the most natural thing in the world.

"My brother's bar mitzvah. He's a man now, apparently."

Luke looks at me uncomprehendingly for the second time in two minutes, a personal world record.

"It's a Jewish tradition," I explain. "His thirteenth birthday. It marks the start of adulthood—theoretically."

What I don't mention is that the whole coming-of-age premise is a bait and switch. Maybe Ben still buys into the party line, but I'm wise to the scam. Sure, we're adults—who can't legally vote, drink, drive, or make our own decisions. Maybe thirteen-year-olds were truly treated like adults back in ancient times, when our ancestors wandered the desert and kicked it at thirty, but today it's just an excuse for a kick-ass party.

"I get it," Luke says, slowly nodding. "Must be great ammo with the 'rents."

"Huh?"

"If you're an adult, you can do what you want." He grins. "Have you ever tried it?"

Doing what you want: not a concept I'm familiar with. Clearly, this guy has no such hang-up.

"Yeah, right," I snort. "You've never met my parents." *And hopefully never will—at least, not until our wedding day,* I add silently.

Luke doesn't seem fazed by my comment, but gestures to the world behind the swinging door. "Well, it must be a big deal to them. They went for the Champagne Package. Top-of-the-line spread. Sushi. Martini bar. And mini-hot dogs."

"They do like to go all out," I confess, thinking shamefully of the video recording booth I insisted I had to have at my own reception so my friends and I could lay down Britney Spears tracks. "You should have seen mine two years ago. They've actually shown some rare restraint this time. They didn't go for the rock climbing wall." I fail to mention that, instead, they just went for Ben's equally outrageous runner-up requests: an Xbox game station, karaoke machine, and a basketball hoop.

Luke chuckles again. God, his teeth are Crest stripy–white. I pray he's mentally doing the math—two years plus thirteen—in his head, and likes what he comes up with.

I try to dig for some deets. "So is this your summer job?" Brilliant.

"Yeah, it's my uncle's place. Good for making some quick cash over the summer. Two more weeks and it's back to the grind at St. Joseph's," he says with a mock shudder. "Those nuns know how to crack the whip, you know?"

"Mmmm," I murmur neutrally, although I don't. My associations with nuns are clearly more benign than Luke's, shaped primarily from *The Sound of Music*, where the Mother Superior helps the von Trapps escape the Nazis.

"How about you?" he asks, refilling the pitcher with tap water and transferring it onto his serving tray.

How about me *what*? I freeze like a deer in headlights. My best friend Jen says it's one of my worst traits: total lack of grace under pressure.

Before I can figure out a reply, I hear my name being called as the band launches into "We Are Family." Oh my God. They must have started the candle-lighting ceremony, where friends and family each light one of the thirteen candles on my brother's birthday cake (Death by Chocolate, with his face airbrushed on top, at his request). As Ben's sister, I'm the next-to-last family member to be called up, right before my parents. If I'm not there, my mom will kill me, despite the hundreds of witnesses.

"That's me. I gotta go," I say, jumping up guiltily, not looking behind me to see his reaction. I rush back through the swinging doors just in time to slip into the crowd and step forward for my cue. I light my candle, taking care not to drip wax on Ben's nose, and slide in next to my mom and dad.

My mother gives me a semi-annoyed glance. "Where were you?" she whispers, draping her arm around me and squeezing my neck, hard.

"Outside," I reply, hoping the red flickering flames will hide the flush in my cheeks from my mad dash inside—and the thrill of my illicit rendezvous.

She opens her mouth to question me further, but I am saved as she and Dad are called up to light the final candle, and we all launch into singing "Happy Birthday" to Ben.

Only halfway though the verse, as I replay my conversation with Luke in my head, do I finally realize that he was simply asking what school I went to. Obviously! And I didn't get a chance to tell him. What an idiot! I should just throw myself on the cake and impale myself on one of the long slender candles. Death by Chocolate, most literally.

As soon as the ceremony ends and the cake is whisked away to be cut, the mustachioed bandleader mouths deep into the mike, "Can I have all you lovers out there," and launches right into an earsplitting rendition of some 1970s Burt Bacharach song. It's like we're caught in a bad-music time warp. All the adults around me begin coupling up with ease. My parents. My Aunt Merle and Uncle Milt. Aunt Adelle and Uncle Dave. My cousin Zach, the med student, and his girlfriend. My brother, Ben, and Sarah. Two by two, like animals boarding Noah's Ark. I see my first cousin Julia, Aunt Merle's daughter, and her fiancé, Brad, their bodies crushed together for dear life right there on the dance floor, Brad's hand scandalously creeping down her lower back. I guess no one cares, now that they are making it legit in a few weeks in a formal wedding at the Essex

House. Even Ira has found a willing partner: my sixteen-year-old cousin, Naomi.

Except me, of course. Partnerless, as usual.

The only other female all by herself is my eighty-three-year-old grandmother, Bubbe, as we call her, who looks like she's nodding off at a table in the corner.

I begin edging off the dance floor, hoping to slink back to my seat unnoticed. Maybe wait for a piece of cake to cheer myself up. Instead, when I turn, I somehow end up two feet from Howard, also still standing awkwardly on the dance floor, while his parents sway next to him. We eye each other warily. There's no escape now.

Out of the corner of my eye, I finally see Luke, who has emerged from the back room and is replenishing water glasses with gusto. I'm sure a guy like him wouldn't have any problem coming up with a partner. Any second now, he'll turn and see me standing all alone on the dance floor like a total loser.

What the heck. Even dancing with a dork is better than standing here looking like a dork. And maybe, just maybe, Luke will see me dancing with another guy and mistakenly believe I'm wildly desirable.

"Hey, Howard." I turn to him, trying to mask my reluctance with a note of irony. "Wanna boogie?" I can be the bigger person, call a truce, just for a minute. And he probably won't puke on me this time.

For a second, his eyes flicker with interest, before they

narrow in disgust. "Me? Dance with you?" he says suspiciously. "Lowenstein, I think you've had one too many nada coladas."

He stomps off toward his table, leaving me standing alone on the dance floor, speechless, floored. Only I could let myself be rejected by someone I didn't even want.

chapter 3

SEVEN THINGS THAT ARE guaranteed to put the sophomoric in sophomore year:

1. The only upperclassman I know totally hates my guts. Every time I see Howard in the hallway the first week back in school, I try to give him a conciliatory smile, but he ducks his head and totally blows me off.

"What did you say to Howard at Ben's bar mitzvah?" I finally demand of my mother.

"What?" she says, all faux innocence. "Nothing . . . I just told him that I knew you really wanted to dance with him, no matter what you said."

No matter what I said??? No wonder he was so offended! Who knew her mastery of the backhanded compliment extended to non–family members?

2. First-period gym class. What this means is I get to wake up at an ungodly hour dictated by the school district, whip my body into some outfit deemed acceptable by the sadistic thirtysomething editors at *Teen Vogue*, only to have

that ensemble disassembled a half hour later, crumpled into a smelly locker, and then put back on my sweaty body for the rest of the day. Worse, because our gym class is so over-crowded, we've been exiled outside the building, banished to jogging around the muddy track while it's still practically dark out. Mr. Gee insists our merry band of twenty will run two miles each crisp autumn morn. *Brrrr.* I want to ask why the youth of America has to suffer just because some district bureaucrat can't balance a financial budget, but I don't want to put my foot in my mouth when I'll so be needing it to hobble around the field.

3. At least first-period gym means I get to work up an appetite for fourth-period lunch—at the equally ungodly hour of 11:15 A.M. Who is ready to scarf down Sloppy Joes this early in the morning? The saving grace is that all sopho-mores are stuck in culinary exile together, so neither Jen nor I has to do the tray-trembling Walk of Shame, slowly scop-ing the cafeteria for a safe haven. We end up claiming a respectable spot in the master-planned seating community, not loserdom by the cashier booths, but not Master of the Universe status by the windows, where goddesses like Tara Silver and Alissa Feiner sit—members of what Jen and I call the So Very crowd.

4. Speaking of seating arrangements: instead of letting us choose our own seats, my new geometry teacher, Mr. Diamenties, insists on seating us up and down the rows in alphabetical order, which somehow lands me in the dead last

row, behind Aidan Levine—a total player in the So Very crowd whose summertime growth spurt shows no signs of slowing—and next to Wayne Liu, who's this big-time underground computer hacker and is *allegedly*—as my former-journalist mom would say—on the Department of Homeland Security's watch list. I can't even see the board over Aidan's broad shoulders, and I'm scared to look over at Wayne, whose cousin, people say, is a member of one of those Chinatown gangs. I swear he spent the entire first lesson hunched over in his black leather jacket, MP3 headphones quietly thumping in his ears, cleaning his fingers with a switchblade beneath his desk.

5. Even scarier, the first thing my new English teacher, Ms. Jensen, does is hand out this long cautionary article on the evils of plagiarism, outlining the lengths the school will go to to detect and punish abusers, by using some new word-scanning software called PlagerStop. Nice to know our teachers trust us and won't get all Big Brotherish on us. Then she hands out a list of about a bazillion vocabulary words we'll need to know for the PSAT by next month, and encourages us to start *deploying* them in everyday use.

6. So. Then. I never noticed before that my best friend Jen is turning into such a *sycophant*. That means a fake, flattering suck-up, in case your vocab list is already crumpled up at the bottom of your book bag, like mine. Well, let me clarify that description. The "best friend" part. Back in junior high, Jen, Leeza, and I had been a cozy threesome. Then,

for high school, Leeza ditched us for a prep school on the Upper East Side, and we lost touch. Jen and I originally got tight by default. At first I thought she was kooky, but her courageousness grew on me. The girl has no fear—she's constantly dragging me to raves, or to talk to strange boys in the park, or to join some crazy after-school club like Rockclimbers or Shutterbugs to meet upperclassmen.

None of it ever works. She's had some random hookups, but like me, she's never really, truly, had a boyfriend—I think most guys are scared off by her boldness. But at least there's been comfort in our mutual rejection. The two of us constantly fantasize what it would be like if we actually snagged guys. My dream date is to rent rowboats in Central Park and make the boys paddle us around the lake, like in some Jane Austen novel, only without the bonnets and parasols. Jen's is to swap spit while riding the Kingda Ka roller coaster at Six Flags.

But lately she's been giving me hives. It's not that all of a sudden, guys have been checking her out everywhere we go. It's more that ever since her alleged fling with some counselor at her camp this summer, she's become a different person—possessed—when any member of the male species comes within a ten-foot radius. Giggling. Flirting. Twirling a lock of her short golden brown hair, which somehow has utterly no frizz issues. Plus, so far this year, she's been totally sucking up to Alissa Feiner, captain of the girls' swim team and one of the most popular (i.e., psychotically evil)

21

girls in our school. I admit, I've been holding a one-sided grudge against Alissa ever since she signed my fifth-grade yearbook this way:

Roses are red
Violets are blue
You look like a monkey
And you smell like one too.

Childish? Yes. But it is exactly the kind of passive-aggressive bitchiness that passes for her sense of humor. The kind of thing that, when you call people on it, they always respond, "Can't you take a *joke?*" And then everyone thinks *you're* the one being a baby. I hate that.

But Jen doesn't see any of this. She's been doing anything and everything to get on Alissa's good side before tryouts, bribing her with Luna bars during French class and listening to endless stories about Alissa's first conquest of the year, Robbie Luskoff, a *senior*, did she happen to mention?

7. Which is how Jen got the inside scoop when Alissa came back from summer vacation with the mother of all show-and-tell items: breast implants for her sixteenth birthday. The entire student body can't stop buzzing about her bodacious bod. According to Jen, who eagerly related the sickening story over fourth-period brunch, as we call it, Alissa's mother didn't want her to go through adolescence with 32 Bs, God forbid, like she was forced to. Oh, the

inhumanity! She figured she's giving her daughter an early start on being a winner in the Game of Life, in a manner that Milton Bradley never intended.

Personally, I'd have a boob job in a New York nanosecond if it didn't involve major surgery, major cashola, and majorly selling out my gender for the approval of the male pubescent population. Still, I can't decide which is worse— the small daily indignities of going through high school with a flat chest, or the huge insta-mortification of having everyone know I cared badly enough about my invisi-boobs to actually do something about it. After careful deliberation, I've concluded I'd take tiny indignities over mega-mortification any day.

But clearly, Alissa Feiner is taking the Road More Traveled, and I bet it makes all the difference. The latest joke already making the rounds among the guys in our class: Alissa is now fine and finer.

chapter 4

DID YOU KNOW THAT, according to this article I read in the *New York Times*, forty percent of Americans attend church every Sunday? Actually, maybe it wasn't the *Times*. It might have been *USA Today*, come to think of it. And maybe I didn't exactly *read* it, but more like scanned it, since it was one of those snapshot statistic boxes they run on the front page. But still, it's true. In my mind, that amount of dedication is staggering, since my family is known in the industry as twice-a-year Jews. Meaning, we can only manage to get off our butts and go to temple two times a year, on the High Holidays: Rosh Hashanah and Yom Kippur, the Day of Atonement. Pretty pathetic, huh? And even that can be too much of a commitment for my dad, who will stay home from work for appearance's sake, but would rather sit around in his underwear all day than put on a suit and go to temple.

"Do you know how much we paid for these tickets?" My mom nagged him all morning before finally giving up.

"Why doesn't he have to go?" I griped later, as we were getting dressed.

"You just worry about yourself," she snapped, slowly unrolling her panty hose from the toe on up, trying to avoid getting a run. Clearly she's pissed he's not coming, too.

On the bright side, because the High Holidays signify the start of a New Year, tradition says you get to buy new outfits for the occasion. Is this a great religion, or what? So my mom and I had been shopping for new clothes the week before school started, kicking off the first clothing battle of the year. As usual, she tried to get me to buy something garishly red or purple ("It would look *soooo* good with your dark coloring," she wheedled), while I held out for something more neutral, settling on a conservative knee-length fitted gray skirt and matching black sweater. At least she's finally realized I've outgrown tweenybopper outfits from Limited Too. There is hope in the world.

But not to sound totally shallow: shopping excursions aren't the *only* things I love about my religion. I also like the way the Jewish New Year, a time of fresh starts, falls pretty much around the beginning of the school year, which makes total sense, much more than the traditional New Year, which falls right in the middle of everything and generally signifies nothing.

I also love how we don't make a habit of trying to pressure others to join us. Other religions even have missionaries—loyal followers on the prowl to sign up new recruits, like our music teacher, Mr. Isaacs, who's always pressuring kids to sign up for Band Squad. Being one of the "chosen people" is more like being in the So Very clique in school: we're not out looking for new converts, and to get in, you've got to go through all sorts of intense hazing rituals. In other words, you've got to want it really, really bad.

But there are some things about my religion that tick me off. Like last year, I was sitting in synagogue, aimlessly flipping through the prayer books—reading ahead like I've been doing since second grade—and I came across this morning prayer for men. It went something like: "Thank you, God, for not making me a woman." Hello?! I mean, with all the strain between the sexes, I don't think men and women need to go around dissing each other in our prayers. This seems no different than girls who wear those "Girls Rule, Boys Drool" T-shirts. You'd expect more righteous behavior from a deity.

Ding-dong.

"Rachel? Bubbe's here. Let's go!" my mother calls, breaking into my thoughts. When I come downstairs, all three of them are at the front door, waiting for me. My bubbe, who pinches my cheeks like I'm two; perfect Ben, in his pinstriped bar mitzvah suit; and my mother. Like me, my mom is wearing a modest ensemble, a skirt and a jacket, although she does get to wear a neat little white hat on top of her head. I think it's to signify she is a married woman—and thus off-limits for any High Holidays hanky-panky.

She keeps it pretty low-key, while the rest of the women at Congregation Beth Shalom seem to be entered in a Hatstravaganza—some kind of twisted competition for the most flamboyant head covering. I'm talking garish gold spangles and the occasional peacock feather. Creepy. Although, I guess if I did get married someday (like that'll ever happen!), I'd probably want to show off, too. I'd get one of those extremely wide-brimmed hats with lots of trim, like in that old movie musical my mom loves, *Easter Parade*, with Judy Garland.

In the meantime, it's not like my uncovered head is the signal for a High Holiday hookup. If you can believe it, my parents actually met each other at some temple in Manhattan, at an event for swinging Jewish singles back in the go-go eighties. They listened to the sermon, then had coffee and cake in the basement. For years, this fostered a fantasy that temple is a perfectly legit spot to scope for guys.

Sad but true.

But I've long since learned that, even though I get new clothes, I might as well go to temple looking like a fashion victim. There's no one to impress. Just the same few guys from Hebrew School I lump in with Howard in the known-forever, practically-incest category, Ari Levy, with his big ears and shockingly bright orange hair, and his sidekick Ravi Lefkowitz, who is still a whole head shorter than me. Trust me, the pickings are slim.

Along the way, we all stop to pick up Leah and her

parents, our temple buddies. Leah has long, dark, thick, braided hair that hangs like a horsetail down her back, and serious, droopy brown eyes. She and I were forced to sacrifice countless hours of our carefree youth slaving away after school at Hebrew School lessons to get ready for our bat mitzvahs. Then, as if three full years of extracurricular religious indoctrination weren't enough, her parents insisted she enroll in the local Hebrew High, for the "superior" private education. Even though I barely see her in real time, we still IM and call each other a lot. Sitting with her in temple makes all the chanting and self-flagellation much more bearable.

I guess that makes it sound bad, but to be honest, I don't mind going to services so much, because I really don't pay all that much attention to what's going on. Mainly, because I figured out long ago that ninety percent of the prayers essentially just praise God over and over for being mighty and glorious, all-knowing and majestic, benevolent and just, and yadda yadda yadda. I swear, if I turned in an essay like that to Ms. Jensen, she'd slash it with her red pen and write "repetitive" all over the margins.

But even when my mind wanders from the text, I do find something relaxing, yes, even spiritual, about sitting there, for once, pondering more weighty issues than Jen's newfound sex appeal or Alissa Feiner's misguided use of plastic surgery or Mr. Diamenties's refusal to call on me so far in geometry. Like the meaning of it all, and why we're here, and why bad things happen to good people, and why nothing ever happens to me at all.

The real point of the holidays, though, the reason we come these two days, is to repent before the New Year, asking those you have wronged to forgive your sins and vowing to do better in the coming year. It's a worthy goal, I guess. If you do repent, God won't put you down for a horrible death by stoning or being trampled by wild beasts, but he will write your name in the Book of Life. And on the final, most solemn day, you have to fast from sunset to sunset, to show you really mean it. Of course, for rail-thin girls in my school, like Alissa Feiner and Tara Silver, who are practically pro-ana, this isn't much of a punishment since they live on a starvation diet. But I like to eat, so it's serious torture.

"On Rosh Hashanah, your fate is determined, and on Yom Kippur, it is sealed," intones Rabbi Wasserman. "But repentance, prayer, and just acts, will avert the severity of the decree."

I rack my brain, trying to think up misdeeds, but to be honest, I haven't sinned much this year. Nothing really juicy. Nothing repent-worthy. I know it sounds like I'm whitewashing the truth, but that's the pathetic story of my life. Honestly, if I'd had the opportunity, I would have sinned much, much more.

I know I have no right to complain. I'm not a problem child from a broken home. My dad hasn't had a midlife crisis and run off with his longtime secretary, Phyllis. My mom's not a welfare crack addict who keeps popping out kids. They don't beat me, berate me, abuse me, or shut me up in the attic with my siblings, like in this spooky book I stayed up reading until dawn at summer camp. At ten o'clock, my parents *always* know where their children are.

Maybe that's what's wrong with me. Maybe if they had screwed me up a little more, I'd have lived a more troubled life; I'd have gotten wasted, wrecked the car, had an intervention and ended up in a Lifetime made-for-TV movie—but at least I'd have plenty to repent over during my time in rehab.

I sneak a peek over at Leah, who has lowered her head and seems deep in thought, her lips silently reading along in her prayer book. Wisps of her dark hair escape from her braid and frame her face, preventing me from seeing her expression. I wonder what secret sins Leah could possibly be repenting over. Honestly, she's an even bigger priss than I am.

On the other hand, maybe I have committed tons of sinnage, but I'm repressing it. Trying to jog my memory, I mentally flip through the Ten Commandments to see if there's something I'm missing. Adultery? Clearly not an issue, as you'd need a willing participant. Coveting Thy Neighbor's Wife? That would be Howard's mom, Mrs. Goldstein. Gross.

The problem is, so many of these commandments are *soooo* two millennia ago. Someone ought to come up with a

more relevant set of guidelines, something my generation could relate to.

Instead of the Ten Commandments, how about the *Teen* Commandments?

THE TEEN COMMANDMENTS

1. Your parents may think they are your Lord, but your peers are your God. Thou shalt follow their will.
2. Thou shalt not worship false idols, like cheesy boy bands with no innate musical talent or those manufactured by FOX reality shows.
3. Thou shalt not swear goddammit when in the presence of a teacher, or risk detention.
4. Thou shalt observe the Sabbath, unless you've got a "hot date," as my dad calls it, which is unlikely in the foreseeable future, i.e., ever.
5. Thou shalt respect thy parental units, and not roll thine eyes in front of them, or use "that tone of voice."
6. Thou shalt not kill thy little brother, no matter how much he deserves it for sailing through puberty angst-free.
7. Thou shalt not mess around with your

best friend's boyfriend, her ex-boyfriend, your boyfriend's best friend, or any other possible romantic configuration.

8. Thou shalt not shoplift lip gloss from Sephora, even if you know girls (who shall remain nameless) who do and get away with it.

9. Thou shalt not lie while playing Truth or Dare, or it becomes a totally pointless exercise, now, doesn't it?

10. Thou shalt not covet your best friend's Neutrogena-model clear skin, frizz-free hair, genuine C cups, alleged summertime fling, and social success.

After I check down the list, I sadly conclude that my conscience is pathetically clear. I wonder if God thinks I'm shirking on my atonement duties and is punishing me with such a boring existence. Maybe it's better to sin and repent than never to sin at all. I bet if I started racking up some serious pointage on the Sin-O-Meter, my life would grow far more interesting.

And why not? For the first time, it occurs to me that God has granted us a loophole: since I'm guaranteed to be forgiven as long as I repent next year, nothing is stopping me from sinning as much as I want this year. Just considering breaking the Teen Commandments gets my heart racing.

Could I really get away with it? Or will I always be doomed to my good-girl ways? I glance at Leah, wanting to share my brainstorm, but her head is still bowed.

As we all rise for the bleating wail of the shofar, I push the idea to the back of my mind. Right now I have to come up with *something* to repent for this year. Okay, I'd been a little cruel to my brother, Ben, like the time I told Mom the movie he wanted to see was rated PG-13, so he couldn't tag along with me and Jen to the multiplex.

And I definitely shouldn't have called my mother a witch when she wouldn't let me go to that concert out at Jones Beach last summer. And yes, she was creepily clairvoyant, as everyone with infinitely more lenient parents was either trampled or groped. But I'm still bitter I missed out. At least I kept my tongue in check at the last possible second, calling her a witch instead of a bitch. So that doesn't really count.

Really, if anything, it's others who have wronged me. Like Howard. How dare he turn me down to dance, when I only asked him because I thought he was going to ask me? Yeah, maybe I shouldn't have insisted I didn't want to dance with him, but I didn't say it to his face or anything. He should be over here on one knee, begging my forgiveness for leaving me hanging.

According to Jewish law, you have to ask forgiveness three times, and I'd make him go through every last one.

"Sorry, Rachel. I'll never turn you down again."

Nope.

"*Please forgive me, Rachel. I don't know what I was thinking. I was a complete idiot.*"

Getting warmer . . . But no.

"*I'm human waste, Rachel. I must have been delusional to say no to a goddess like you.*"

Well . . . Fine, Howard, I'll forgive you—this time.

Oh, and by the way? I didn't really want to dance with you, either.

chapter 5

AFTER SERVICES, we all have to walk clear across town to get home because you're not allowed to drive on the High Holidays. Leah and I deliberately dawdle until everyone has gotten a few blocks ahead of us, so we can debrief each other on the school year so far.

Leah fills me in on her schedule—which sounds like the normal state-mandated curriculum in the morning, but then a whole afternoon spent learning to read and speak Hebrew. And I thought taking Latin all throughout junior high was pretty useless. More important, she moans about the lack of anything brewing on the romantic front. Leah usually acts like she knows everything, so I'm surprised she could be so naive. I mean, what does she expect? As bad as I have it, she has it much worse. She now goes to a school made up entirely of dorky, vertically challenged über-Jewish guys. She may as well be in a convent.

I'm totally sympathetic—until she confides that she's doing BBYO. "My parents made me sign up," she says, tugging on the six-point star hanging from her eighteen-karat gold necklace, a present every bat mitzvah girl receives as a gift from our temple. Mine is buried somewhere at the bottom of my jewelry box. I think.

I look at her in horror.

"It's . . . not so bad," she insists, as if she's trying to convince herself more than me. "Really."

I'm not buying it. B'Nai B'rith Youth Organization is this national Jewish youth group that holds Teen Nights after school at the Jewish Community Center. It's for Jewish teens to get together and play wholesome games of Ping-Pong, or make fudge, or whatever. It's the kind of thing your parents are always encouraging you to go to, with the same fake jolly tone of voice they used when you were a trusting toddler, the voice that told you that beets are delicious and that the shot won't hurt a bit. And it is exactly the kind of thing that no self-respecting teenager would be caught dead at: the ultimate social suicide. It's hard to say why BBYO isn't cool. There's just something inherently embarrassing about embracing your heritage with that much enthusiasm.

"Are you kidding?" I ask, not bothering to mask the withering tone in my voice.

"Some of the guys in the group are kind of nice," she says. "You should come sometime."

"Hmph," I mumble neutrally.

"What about you?"

I consider telling her about Luke, not sure what there is

to tell, when suddenly, my stomach practically cartwheels into my throat. Am I hallucinating? As if I'd mentally materialized him, there he is, hopping off the #7 city bus across the street. He is flanked by a group of guys, all wearing carefully pressed khaki pants and gold-crested blue blazers, clearly the St. Joseph's uniform. Unlike the snowboarding thrasher guys at our school, who swagger around in ripped jeans practically around their ankles with their boxers peeping out, Luke looks just like Prince William during his Eton days: royally cute. Better still, in contrast to the military precision of his uniform, his hair has that rumpled, just woke-up, bed-head look. Super sexy.

My heart skips a beat. Should I wave? Cross the street and say hi?

Then I remember what I look like. *Ack!* I can't, repeat, can't, have him see me looking like such a dork in my frumpy temple garb. Especially considering what I was wearing when I first met him at Ben's bar mitzvah, that not super-flattering suit my mom insisted I wear. Why can't this guy ever see me when I'm wearing something sexy-casual, like a pair of Seven jeans and a tight Miss Sixty top?

Leah notices my total panic attack.

"What?" she demands, following my non-gaze to the group of guys, now roughhousing across the street.

"Is he looking?" I gasp as I slouch and try to hide behind her body. "Is he looking this way??"

"Whaaa? Who?"

37

"The tall guy in the blue blazer," I mouth, although they're pretty much *all* tall guys in blue blazers. "The blond one."

"No. Wait!"

My heart seizures.

"No. They're not looking."

If I were with Jen, she'd toss her hair, stick out her chest, and insist we cross the street to talk to them. But Leah is even more mousy than my dearly departed pet hamster, Shamu, who I got right after a trip to SeaWorld when I was ten. We scuttle by, concentrating on looking invisible, until they are well behind us, heading in the opposite direction.

Thank God he didn't notice me.

Why didn't he notice me?

I mean, when I like someone I become hyperaware as soon as they enter the room, like I've planted a GPS tracking device on them that bleeps when they breech security. Don't guys have the same auto-detection system?

Clearly, Luke doesn't. Or worse, he just doesn't have it set to detect *me*.

After dropping Leah off, I head for home, deep in thought. The cold hard truth is, I'll never get a guy like Luke. Even if I could somehow get his attention, even if he liked talking to me at the party, there's no way he'd really go for someone like me.

As I once overheard the saleslady at Saks tell my mom,

I've got "a lovely pear-shaped figure," which you know is code for childbearing hips and no chest. I'm constantly breaking out, but my mom's dermatologist refuses to put me on Accutane, saying that it's too extreme for a mild case like mine. Even without the braces that tortured me in junior high, it's all for naught: there is still the matter of my hair.

I inherited it from my dad: thick, wild, and kinky. At least it's not sprouting out all over my back, like his, but it's totally resistant to any taming whatsoever. Why can't I have the kind of hair that girls like Alissa Feiner have, shiny jet-black hair you can swish and flip from side to side, like in those Herbal Essences commercials? The kind that a guy wants to run his fingers through? My hair texture is more like the kink of the Jackson Five. A guy could run his fingers through my hair and not find his way out for three days.

And every time I go to the hairdresser, it's the same story. They always coo and swoon over my alleged curls, trying to convince me to let it go "natural." Which would be fine if I had adorable ringlets like Andie McDowell or Nicole Kidman. Instead, "natural" tends to end up resembling a Brillo pad. Of course the stylists can't admit defeat, so they cheerfully say, "Gorgeous," and send me on my way, looking like a freshly shorn poodle. At which point, I rush home, wash it out in the sink, spend an hour brushing it into sub-mission, and end up with it back in the ponytail I started with.

I'm not exaggerating: my hair has ruined practically

every social occasion involving water, for fear it would kink up: Karen Wilkinson's seventh-grade pool party; day camp trips to the Six Flags Hurricane Harbor water park in New Jersey. Thank God I wasn't born somewhere rainy like Seattle, where I'd be a total year-round frizzhead. I've begged Mom to let me do the Japanese hair-straightening process, which *CosmoGIRL!* insists can permanently straighten your hair for an entire year, but it costs something like five hundred bucks.

A small price to pay for beauty, I say.

She says, "Start saving."

Even if I had gone over and talked to Luke today, there's no way anything would have come of it. I mean, everyone knows tall, dark, and handsome guys lust after petite, blond cheerleaders. But the inverse? Does the tall, blond, sexy Nordic guy ever pick the short, frizzy-haired brunette? Don't think so.

As I turn onto my block, I see my mom, Ben, and Bubbe in the distance, still in their temple garb, standing outside our house talking to the Goldsteins. Howard and his family, like most of the kids from my school, get to go to the reform temple, where most of the service is in English, and the cantor plays an acoustic guitar. Meanwhile, we have to go to the ultraconservative temple to please my bubbe.

"*L'Shana Tovah*, Rachel," Mrs. Goldstein says, wishing me a Happy New Year and leaning in to peck the air on each of my cheeks. Mrs. Goldstein is one of the city's top ob-gyns; she's constantly being featured on the cover of *New York* magazine or being interviewed on the news. In junior high, the mere mention of his mom's occupation made Howard blush uncontrollably. I guess we all have our own cross to bear.

"Rachel, my love," Mr. Goldstein exhales, pumping my hand. Howard just sort of nods in cool recognition. Clearly, he's still mad about what my mom said to him at Ben's bar mitzvah. The conversation turns to the upcoming Day of Atonement.

"So, Rachel, are you going to fast?" Mr. Goldstein asks me in a hearty voice.

"I guess so," I reply. I hear Howard suppress a chuckle. "What?" I demand. "Aren't you?" *After all, he's the one with something to repent for.*

"Yeah, I am." He shrugs. Then he announces to everyone, "It's just the idea of Rachel not eating for an *entire day*. I've never seen a girl that skinny pack it away like she can."

Being told you're thin should be a good thing, right? But the way Howard says it, it's hardly a compliment.

"Maybe you have a tapeworm!" Ben chimes in, and now even the grown-ups are laughing at me. I punch Ben on the arm while I try to think of a fitting reply, unsure if I'm more mad that Howard called me "that skinny" or for suggesting I'm a pig.

Before I can think what to say, my mom puts her arm around me. "I wish I still had a metabolism like Rachel," she sighs. "Right, Linda?"

"God, yes," Howard's mother chirps in agreement.

As we say good-bye and head inside, my bubbe pokes me in the rib cage. "See, Rachel, you should eat more," she declares. "Boys don't like skinny girls."

Like I care what kind of girls *Howard* likes!

Still, his digs burn me up. It's bad enough having to put up with a bratty younger brother, but being tormented by someone who's not even a blood relative? Honestly.

chapter 6

IT'S CONFIRMED: all the guys are in love with Jen. Besides her summer lovin' with Danny, the counselor-in-training, she's already been asked out by this guy in her gym class, Norman, a junior with questionable breath and a low coolness factor. She turned him down because she said there was "no spark" between them, but the truth is, she's afraid of what people like Alissa would think of her dating such a loser, even if he is an upperclassman.

Back at school today, at lunch, she tells me that during homeroom, she found an anonymous declaration of love carved on her desk. Someone had written J.M.: U R A Q T in black ink.

"JM URAQT? What's Jem Uraqt?" I ask, stumbling over the acronym.

"Jen Mackler. You are a cutie," she sighs. "Clever, huh? I think it's this guy Matt in my English class. . . ."

Personally, it all sounds a bit twisted to me—wooing

someone via secret code, defacing public property—but Jen doesn't seem to mind.

I've mentioned it to Leah, who swears it's pheromones, that Jen must be putting some kind of come-hither scent into the ether, like when her dog, Bela, goes into heat.

Jen denies it. Still, I've been surreptitiously sniffing her all throughout lunch, but beside the general cafeteria stench, I can't detect any aroma, other than the reek of her Glow by J.Lo, liberally applied.

"What?" she demands, catching me mid-sniff.

"Nothing," I say hastily, while I subtly try to determine the source of her newfound popularity.

Cynically, I suspect that the natural (unlike Alissa) progression of her bra size up the alphabet from A to B to C has something to do with it. Which hasn't gone unnoticed since she's been practicing with the swim team, including the male half. Meanwhile, no guys ever look at me, anywhere, anytime, probably because I smell more like Eau de Desperation than hip-hop diva cologne.

Even though she is careful to downplay her conquests, she has this undeniable Glow of triumph. It makes me sick. I try to remind myself of Teen Commandment number 10: Thou shalt not begrudge thy best friend's social success.

Still, why is it that wanting something too much ensures you'll never have it?

Take my dad, for example: ever since he and Mom flew to Vegas to renew their wedding vows by an Elvis impersonator

last year, he's been gripped by the poker bug. Now, all he ever does is read obscure poker magazines like *Card Player* and worship the pros on the World Poker Tour, total miscreants with nicknames like "Jesus" and "Slim." It's not gambling, he tells me, it's all mathematical calculations of odds. He's a financial whiz who crunches numbers all day as a CPA for one of the so-called Big Four accounting firms, and yet, every time he plays poker with his buddies, who care more about the potato chips than their chip count, he gets his butt kicked. He'll come home wailing about how his pal Joe had no business drawing to that inside straight, making it on the river, no less, whatever that means. Mom just looks at him and asks wearily, "How much did you lose this time?" It's not the money that makes the loss so painful, though. It's that he cares so much.

It's the same thing with my mom. All she ever wanted to do was be a famous journalist for the *New York Times* or CNN. She even would have settled on being a reporter for Page Six of the *New York Post*, which runs all sorts of juicy celebrity gossip. But it turns out she never got any further than writing about health care for the *Asbury Park Press*. Today she works part-time for the city's public health department's publications office, which means she produces glossy brochures like "Ten Things to Know About Hypertension!" or "Nine Steps to Having a Healthy Baby." But she's addicted to watching the nightly newsmagazines like *Dateline* and *60 Minutes*, convinced she could have been the next Diane Sawyer or Barbara Walters.

And Ben? Ben's greatest aspiration in life is to be the high scorer on Dance Dance Revolution at the Nathan's arcade in Yonkers, but even though the kid has the moves, someone with the initials SYS (See ya, sucker?) always beats him out.

For me, I could care less about card games, although I do play a mean game of Spit. And even though I do well in English, I've sworn off putting anything in writing ever since Ben found my seventh-grade diary detailing those excruciating two weeks of romantic turmoil with Marc Goodman and threatened to post it on his blog.

What do I want? All I really want is to be good at boys.

So naturally, instead, I'm only good at math, which I have calculated has a direct, inverse correlation to being good at boys. Like, in freshman algebra last year, every time Mr. Fried announced, "The highest grade in the class went to . . ." and handed me my test, with a huge "99%" circled in red ink, I could precisely calculate the dip in my chances of being asked out by any guy in that class, down to the decimal point. The only boy who ever seemed turned on by my math aptitude was class president and front-runner for future valedictorian, Josh Green, the smartest kid in our class, who always walked me out on days we got our tests back. It took me months to figure out he didn't actually like me, or anything, he just wanted to ask what I got.

How can there be justice in this world, when so often, people are just no good at the one thing they desperately want to be good at? Except for Jen, of course. Jen wants to be popular, and *voilà!* Jen's Q rating has reached the Tipping Point.

"I can't believe you're eating that." Jen breaks into my thoughts with a cry of disgust.

"What?"

"That burger!" She points at my cardboard tray as if it were holding human excrement.

"What's my alternative?" I shrug, taking a bite of my soggy, foil-wrapped hamburger. Our cafeteria isn't known for its haute cuisine, and we're not allowed off campus for lunch until senior year.

"From now on, I'm swearing off all meat," she says with a sniff of disdain. This from the girl who practically has Platinum frequent flyer status at Taco Hell. Only then do I notice her lunch tray has departed from the ordinary. It now holds Yoplait, French fries, and a low-fat muffin.

What's the deal? Did I miss another mad cow scare? Is the Atkins craze finally over? "Why?" I finally ask.

"Do you know what they do to the baby calves before they kill them?"

I stay silent, hoping that it's a purely rhetorical question, and she isn't about to actually describe the blood and guts of a slaughterhouse while I'm eating.

"The next great civil rights struggle is going to be over animal equal rights," Jen says dramatically. I can see it coming: another crazy after-school activity I'm about to be dragged to, this time to meet tofu-eating, Birkenstock-wearing college guys. But then she adds, "Alissa says there's a Harvard professor trying to bring a case to the Supreme Court as we speak," and starts talking excitedly about their private plans to attend PETA sit-ins and picket fur coat stores and bust up research labs, never once stopping to invite me. All I can think about is the irony of Alissa supporting animal rights. Her Highness treats half the student body like we're dirt beneath her French manicured fingernails— but thinks cows, pigs, and goats are her equals. I wonder if they would be So Very worthy of a seat at her royal lunch table by the window?

"Who knew she was such the humanitarian?" I muse. "Or, should that be, animalitarian?"

But Jen totally misses my sarcasm. "Good question," she says thoughtfully, stirring her yogurt as if it'll morph into a chocolate malt if she only stirs hard enough.

Personally, I'd take a juicy steak over a friendship with Alissa Feiner any day. But I keep that thought to myself.

Instead, I take a final chomp on my burger. With relish.

chapter 7

THIS EVENING, the minute her parents declare the two-day holiday officially over, my cell rings; it's Leah, calling to further dissect my crush. On the way home after the botched close encounter with Luke, I filled her in on our epic meeting, but we still have to rehash it a hundred times over, looking for any significant detail we might have missed.

"I think he was maybe going to ask for my number," I exaggerate, just a teensy bit, with dramatic license, "but then I had to bail for the candle lighting."

"So will your parents let you go out with him?" Leah asks incredulously. Both of us know how insanely overprotective my parents are.

I know it sounds like I'm exaggerating, but if there were an Olympic event for overprotectiveness, my parents would be the Dream Team. Only, in my case, because I'm so socially retarded, it would have to be the Special Olympics. They don't let me go anywhere without practically running a background check on the who, what, where, when, and how, courtesy of my mother, the ex-reporter. She's even equipped me with a beeper *and* a cell phone with a real-life GPS system, so I have no excuse not to stay connected. Then there are the rules restricting my whereabouts: I'm not allowed at parties with no adults. I'm not allowed to be alone in the house with a boy, or have a boy up in my room at all. Is it any wonder I've never hooked up with anyone?

"Sure," I say bitterly. "Once they've fingerprinted him, taken a blood sample, a polygraph exam, and fitted me for a chastity belt." Even then, I bet they'd insist on chaperoning.

She tsks sympathetically.

"They have to let me date sometime," I wail. "Don't they? I mean, I'm fifteen and a half. Almost sixteen."

"I know. But I actually meant, would they let you date him . . . since he's not . . . Jewish?" Leah blurts out.

Her words stop me short. Honestly, the thought hadn't entered my mind. My parents not letting me date Luke— because of his faith? I'd assumed my biggest challenge was getting Luke to notice me. And then getting my parents to call off the dogs and let me go on a date. It never occurred to me they might veto my selection based on his religion. I didn't even know exactly what Luke was, anyway. Catholic, Episcopalian, Protestant, Baptist? The distinctions were all kind of lost on me, blurring together in some Christian stew.

"Are you kidding?" I ask, thinking Leah is clearly out of her mind.

"Mine are pretty strict about that. They wouldn't let my older sister go out with anyone who wasn't Yeshiva-bound."

"Really?" I can't believe she's never shared that juicy tidbit before.

"Uh-huh," she says matter-of-factly. "Why do you think I'm stuck at Hebrew High?"

"Because your parents want you to have a quote-unquote quality education with an emphasis on traditional Jewish values?" I say, mocking what I imagined to be Hebrew High's mission statement.

"Because my parents want me to associate mainly with other Jews," she says. "Especially guys. And I bet yours do, too."

My mind flashes to *Fiddler on the Roof*, this musical my mom dragged us to last summer in the city. In the show, which takes place in a shtetl in the "Old Country"—a small village somewhere in Europe, but, trust me, nowhere you'd want to spend junior year abroad—three of the sisters defy their father and pick spouses for themselves, rather than have the local matchmaker pick their husbands. One husband is a poor tailor, which is pardonable; one is a political outlaw, which is forgivable; and the last one is a Gentile, which, apparently, is inexcusable. At the end of the show, the girl's father disowns her, acting as if she is dead even though she is standing right in front of him begging for his acceptance. But that was a million years ago in a foreign country—and in a Broadway musical. Not exactly reality.

"That is so nineteenth century," I tell Leah. "Tons of people are in mixed marriages these days."

"It still happens more than you'd think," she says, in her most annoying know-it-all tone of voice. "My great-aunt Harriet supposedly cut off Simon, my second cousin, for marrying out, to this Italian girl. And it's not just our religion. The Catholic Church has even issued a warning against marrying Muslims. People take this really seriously. Die for it, even."

I think of my dad, who won't even get up off the La-Z-Boy for his religion. "Not my parents," I reassure Leah, trying to sound certain, although I'm not so very.

In fact, the more I think about it, the more worried I get. In our entire family tree, everyone from Mom and Dad, Aunt Merle and Uncle Milt, even my cousin Julia and her fiancé, Brad, are Jewish.

Suddenly my whole life clicks into a new perspective. Although they'd never specifically said I couldn't date someone of another religion, hadn't my parents practically engineered it so that every guy I'd met, from summer camp at Camp Kinder Ring to weekends at Kutsher's in the Catskills, had been just like me? They'd raised me in a neighborhood so homogenized that we used to tease the token Protestant at my elementary school for bringing ham-and-mayo sandwiches. Sure, they'd sent me to a high school a little more ethnically diverse, but it was still so predominantly Jewish that the So Very clique is mostly made up of JAPs like Alissa Feiner and Tara Silver—Jewish American Princesses with perfect shiny hair, doctored noses, and thin hips, defying five-thousand years of ethnic destiny.

All their weird behavior makes sense now. It's a plot. A plot to predetermine my love life before it even begins. No wonder I'd been enrolled in all those YWHA after-school programs, the equivalent of the Junior League for Jews. No wonder we work out at the local J.C.C., instead of Gold's Gym. No wonder my parents always make sure to ask the *last* name of any friends I spend time with. I always thought they were just being nosy, but obviously, they've been checking whether my friends are members of the tribe.

Clearly, neither of them will be happy unless I stay a true-blue Jew. And now they're doing the exact same thing to Ben. Ever since he refused to return to post–bar mitzvah Hebrew lessons, they've been trying to guilt him into participating in some other kind of Jewish activity: my dad suggesting he write a book report on *The Diary of Anne Frank;* my mom encouraging him to volunteer to cheer up octogenarians at the Hebrew Home for the Aged.

Leah's warning plunges me into a whole new level of despair. I get off the phone, mumbling some excuse. What if my parents do limit my dating life to nice Jewish boys? Math geek that I am, I make some quick calculations. I start with the worldwide population of a scant 0.2 percent, cut that in half for the male species, and factor in the ratio of guys who have liked me that I have liked in return. My final answer: the likelihood of finding a boyfriend my parents will approve of? Approximately negative infinity.

chapter 8

GYM CLASS IS BECOMING the bane of my exis-
tence. Now that it's getting chilly, it's impossible to dress
properly for such an outing. It's cool in the mornings, which
means I come to school bundled up in gloves, a scarf, and a
thick woolen coat. But have you ever tried running with a
scarf? Inevitably, it gets unraveled and snags on a tree as you
go by. You could end up involuntarily strangling yourself.
Anyway, it doesn't matter, because by the end of the first lap,
you're not cold anymore, you're panting and dripping with
sweat. But there's no place to hang up your coat at that
point. So most of us have resigned ourselves to wearing
sweatpants and a thin T-shirt, shivering as we exit the locker
room and begin the Bataan Death March across campus until
our lungs feel like they're going to explode.

"People, people. You might want to cut back on those cigarettes," Mr. Gee calls out as he clicks his stopwatch for the
last few stragglers, myself included. As I limp back toward
the locker room, I don't bother replying, but I think his

assumption is ill-advised. How does he know I don't have asthma or a club foot, or something?

Have I mentioned that I'm not exactly brimming with athletic ability? Forget about achieving jock status like All-American Darren Wald, this guy in our class whose bulging letterman's jacket has already run out of room for all of his state championship emblems. Or even Jen, who found out this morning she officially made the cut for the girls swim team. I'd just be grateful not to flunk gym class.

In addition to being a mousy pushover who avoids confrontation like the plague, I'm a physical wimp, too. I'm a total klutz at anything involving hand-eye contact, have no stamina, and don't have an athletic build. I'm kind of scrawny, but short, without the long limbs required of Amazonian status. I think I got my ineptitude from my mom, whose only form of exertion is lazing by the Skyview pool all summer, occasionally jumping in to cool off, on the principle that she doesn't care to sweat.

Athletically speaking, I wish I'd grown up during my mom's era. You can tell that thirty years ago, nothing much was expected of women on the sporting field. Bowing out gracefully was a woman's prerogative. Then along came Billie Jean King and the WNBA and Mia Hamm, and all these incredibly over-achieving role models, making all of us non-Olympians look like we're wimping out if we're not striving to be uberjocks. Plus, thanks to Anna Kournikova, now we have to look hot doing it, too.

Shut up! I want to scream every time I see a Tampax commercial with some girl bragging that she can ride a horse, finish a triathalon, whatever, even during her (ahem) heaviest days. Nowadays, no gym teacher will excuse you if you vaguely allude to menstrual cramps. You've got to be practically hemorrhaging blood to get a pass.

Thanks a lot, Title IX.

Plus, all this forced jockitude is having unintended effects on my academic achievement. I've been late to geometry almost every day this week. I've tried telling Mr. Diamenties that it's not my fault. Ten minutes is just not enough time to clean up, change, repair frizz damage done to hair, and make it from the ground-floor locker room to Room 401 before the last bell. But he doesn't want to hear it. As a result, I've been designated a delinquent in his eyes.

Still sweaty, I slink into class five minutes after the late bell and collapse into my seat in the back row.

"Late again, Miss Lowenstein?" He picks up his giant red Sharpie and jots down a note in his attendance book. I nod and slump down further so he can't see me behind Aidan's big head. Already Mr. Diamenties has launched into his lecture on polygons. I consider asking Wayne for his notes for what I've missed so far, but he doesn't deign to acknowledge my existence much.

I started off the year confident in my mathlete status—overconfident, you could say. For the first few days, I shot my hand in the air whenever Mr. Diamenties posed a question, to the amusement of Wayne, who'd either roll his eyes or snort as I waved my hand—pointlessly, as Mr. Diamenties continually called on kids like Josh Green, who happened to be seated at the front of the room and whose hands were in his face.

I'd never been a victim of back-row discrimination before. I felt like Rosa Parks, ushered to the back of the bus. It burned my pride. Eventually I took a lesson from Wayne instead of Diamenties, and stopped raising my hand. Why bother? At this point, I figure, I'll just wow him on the first test; he'll realize the error of his ways and begin treating me like the math prodigy I am.

"So, what do we call a triangle with an angle greater than ninety degrees?" asks Mr. Diamenties, who I've started calling Mr. Demented in my head.

At the front of the room, Josh Green waves his hand frantically. Josh is so clean-pressed, I've heard he irons his own T-shirts—or more likely, has his mother do it for him. In front of me, Aidan nudges his seatmate, a curly-haired guy named Rick. He coughs a word—"loser"—into his hand, and they both silently snicker. From my newfound vantage point, I can see how pathetically eager Josh comes across.

For once, Diamenties ignores him and stalks down the aisle like a mountain lion looking for a victim. He pauses right in front of my desk, picking up the scent of weakened, bloodied prey.

"Miss Lowenstein?" he purrs. He's one of those jerky teachers who insists on using your last name to make it seem like he respects you as an equal. So how come it always comes out dripping with contempt?

I can tell that now, because he thinks I'm a little befuddled, he can't wait to pounce on me. Little does he know that I actually get the difference between isosceles, equilateral, and all things triangle. This is my moment of vindication, when he finally realizes I'm front-row material, a true math goddess. When I take my rightful place as math pet alongside Josh Green.

Obtuse, of course, I am about to say, and open my mouth to answer. But for no reason, I hesitate. I am suddenly hyperaware of the rest of the class, watching me, judging me, labeling me. From the back of his big head, I can practically see the sneer on Aidan's face, the icy indifference on Wayne's. I can visualize what will happen the rest of the year when I give the right answer, how I will get dubbed the math brain again, the female equivalent of Josh Green, the girl no one wants to be with.

"I . . . don't know . . . acute?" I hear myself saying uncertainly, hating myself the whole time. I expect some immediate reaction; some giggle or gasp of disbelief. But there is nothing. Most of the class probably doesn't know the answer, either. And there aren't any kids here from freshman algebra, who know me to be a brain. Except for one. From across the room, Josh Green shoots me a confused look, one

59

part superiority that he knew the answer and one part disbelief that I didn't.

But Diamenties, who tried and convicted me after the first week of school, doesn't look surprised at all. "Obtuse, Miss Lowenstein. Obtuse. What you should be striving not to be."

I flush with embarrassment. Even though my answer was totally, completely mangled, I still can't believe a teacher— a math teacher, no less—has just called me an idiot in front of the whole class. Granted, most of my classmates probably don't know the definition of obtuse, unless they've been reviewing their PSAT vocab list. But still.

"Cretin." I hear the words murmured in my ear. Who said that? Mr. Diamenties didn't seem to hear it, already back at the board scribbling *obtuse* in yellow chalk and underlining it three squealing times for emphasis. Next to me, Wayne seems engrossed, carving something with his pen onto his hand, probably a Linux computer code or something. Aidan and Rick are hunched over their notebooks, concentrating intently on not being picked next.

I feel a tap on my thigh.

Wayne is holding his hand beneath our desks, revealing to me what he has written in black ink across his palm.

"Diamenties = Demented."

I can't help but sputter out in laughter. Maybe there is no such thing as an original thought, but there's always the comfort of knowing I'm not alone.

Mr. Demented whirls around. "Miss Lowenstein? Mr. Liu? Something you'd care to share?"

Wayne and I both stare stonily back at Mr. Demented. The spikes of Wayne's jet-black gelled hair tremble defiantly.

"Ummm . . . no," I mutter, blushing with shame.

"Nope," Wayne says coolly, crumpling his fist so the words disappear from sight.

Diamenties gives us a bone-chilling look, then resumes lecturing about the square of a hypotenuse. Wayne and I don't dare look at each other, but I feel a definite wave of newfound respect from him. Incredible. Had Wayne Liu and I just shared a moment of fellowship?

The bell rings. "Don't forget," Diamenties calls over the shuffling of feet and desks as we are released, "since you're all off Monday, your homework for Tuesday is to finish the questions from chapters four *and* five." Groans fill the air.

But I just smile, realizing that Monday is Yom Kippur, another mandatory holiday that excuses me from the nightmare that has become my life. Even a somber day of self-recrimination and starvation is preferable to the daily grind of sophomore year.

LEAH AND I TRUDGE home from Yom Kippur services famished, our stomachs growling so loudly we can barely hear ourselves talk, but our souls are presumably saved for another year. I haven't eaten a bite since sundown last night, when I crammed an entire refrigerator down my throat before today's fast. Tonight, once sunset has officially arrived, according to the official timetable listed in the *Times*, Leah's family will hold a traditional Break Fast with bagels, lox, cream cheese, pickled herring—the works. My family will just chow down on Chinese takeout from Golden Gate the nanosecond it grows hazy.

While we walk, Leah and I torture each other with our fantasy meal of what we would eat first—sort of the opposite of the Last Supper.

"My grandma's chicken matzo ball soup, my mom's pot roast—" I say dreamily.

"And . . . sweet potato fries."

"Yes. Or the Bloomin' Onion from Outback."

"And chicken parmesan."

"Pad Thai noodles."

"Dessert," Leah commands, moving us on to the final course with military precision.

"A plate of Krispy Kremes, fresh off the conveyer belt."

"The original ones," she clarifies. "Frozen hot chocolate at Serendipity." She groans in delicious agony of her own making.

Good one. "Chocolate-chip pancakes from IHop, with boysenberry syrup," I counter.

"Oh, gross." She clutches her stomach and sticks out her tongue. "What time is it?"

I glance at my watch. "Four forty-five."

This time we both groan. Sunset isn't until 5:49 P.M. Still a whole painful gut-wrenching hour to go.

But in the meantime, we have a plan.

We told our moms we were going to take a long walk, but instead we are going to stand at the same bus stop that Luke and his friends used, pretending to wait for the next bus. Of course, we can't actually get on, since you're not allowed to carry money on this holy day, and I'm not sure if bus passes count or not.

When Luke gets off the bus and sees me standing there waiting, I just know he'll come over and pick up where we left off. And then we'll talk more about, I dunno, the evilness of nuns, and summer jobs, and doing what you want. That's about as far as the plan goes. But this time, I foxily got my mom to approve a better temple outfit: a sweater, a pair of black velvet lo-rise pants, and my flip-flops. It wasn't easy. Unfortunately, temple fashion and religious dogma dictate that most women show up on Yom Kippur looking like a *Glamour* Don't: a skirt, panty hose and a pair of WHITE SNEAKERS! This fashion travesty, which I would never commit voluntarily, is mandated by an arcane rule against wearing shoes made from leather on the Day of Repentance. Who knew God was a charter member of PETA?

But there was no way I was wearing sneakers with a skirt, in case I saw Luke. So this morning, I slipped my feet into my flip-flops. My mom took one look at me and said, "Flip-flops in shul? Absolutely not." But I wheedled, pointing out that they are technically made entirely of rubber, until she grudgingly approved.

Of course, flip-flops aren't made for hiking half a mile across town, so my feet are killing me. I have to admit, there might have been a higher plan for those white sneakers, as Leah stuck with her Pumas and is feeling no pain.

Once we reach the bus stop, we linger under the shelter, letting at least half a dozen buses roll on by.

"Girl Scout Thin Mints or Samoas?" I try to continue the fantasy meal.

"Thin Mints, obviously." She rolls her eyes. But she has lost her appetite for the game. I can't blame her. She is being a total trouper, willing to simultaneously stalk and starve for the sake of a friend. But it's beginning to feel like we've been waiting forever, with no St. Joseph's contingent in sight.

"Maybe we should just go," I finally say. Lying to our moms, stalking Catholic schoolboys—probably not a good idea an hour before our fate is sealed. I'm beginning to think Luke's absence is a sure sign we're angering the gods. Er, *the* God, that is.

"I guess," Leah agrees. "Wait!"

I follow her gaze.

"Is that him?" The #7 bus has rolled up to the bus stop, and sure enough, a group of boys is tumbling out. A dark-haired boy first, followed by a gangly redheaded boy. Then finally, him.

I freeze.

They are coming right at us.

My inner *Teen Magazine* voice begins screaming instructions at me. *Look at him! Make eye contact! Smile!*

Simultaneously, my central nervous system begins firing axons down my spine and shooting rounds of adrenaline through my veins, as though a giant game of laser tag is going on in my body. *Run away. Avoid eye contact. Don't say anything stupid.*

I can hear the boys laughing about something as the bus wheezes out some toxic fumes and rumbles its doors closed. At the last possible second, I look up. Luke is about to brush by me.

"Dude, you are so pathetic," says the dark-haired boy, glancing briefly at me and Leah, and then breezing on by.

"Isn't he, Mick?" I miss hearing what Mick thinks because Leah is jabbing me in the ribs, urging me to act. But what should I do? Act surprised to see him and ask *What are you doing here?* Shout *Hey there!* and punch him on the shoulder?

In the end, I smile tentatively and seek eye contact. "Hi," I exhale softly.

"Whatever, Sully," Luke tosses back at his friend.

Then he looks directly at me for a split second. And looks away.

He wasn't saying "whatever" to me.

I know that rationally. He was saying "whatever" to his friend, Sully.

Still, I just lose it. The instant Luke is out of sight, I promptly dissolve onto the curb.

It is just like in one of those exorcism movies where someone is possessed, and when the spirit leaves their body, they just lose control of their muscles and flop helplessly to the floor.

"Come on, get up," Leah begs, standing over me, unsure what to do as I lie, thrashing on the sidewalk like a piece of human roadkill. "He wasn't talking to *you.*"

But back at home, sinking into my Tempur-Pedic bed, it seems like that's exactly what he thinks of me. *Whatever. I could take it or leave it.* He looked right at me and registered nothing at all. It's ten times worse than not noticing me from across the street. It's like being dissed and dismissed.

Well, that's that, then. The thing to do is forget all about Luke Christiansen. Maybe Leah was right. It's probably better this way. Easier all around. My parents will win this battle without even knowing we'd been at war.

I pull out a piece of loose-leaf paper to distract myself. It is the New Year, isn't it? Time for a clean slate. Everyone says that writing your intentions down is the first step to keeping them. So every year, in January, the whole world writes the same tired old New Year's Resolutions. But they never stick. Why? Obviously, because they don't have a higher force behind them. But what if they did? This year, in honor of the High Holidays, I'm going to try writing my *Jewish* New Year's Resolutions. And the first one is going to be finding a boyfriend from my own tribe, one that my parents won't hassle me over. One they might actually approve of. Like Howard. Except, obviously, not Howard.

MY NEW YEAR'S RESOLUTIONS
1. Forget heathens like Luke Christiansen
2. Flirt madly with appropriate So Very boys like Aidan Levine
3. Wash face every day with Proactive Solution
4. Stop biting nails (This year I really mean it)
5. Get to geometry on time

"Rachel," my mother calls, interrupting my concentration. "Food's here."

"One minute, Mom," I call back.

"Rachel! Now!" she calls.

6. And, oh yeah, STOP LETTING MY PARENTS CONTROL MY LIFE

I quickly scan the list, but my eyes keep getting stuck at the very first entry: *Forget Luke*. Forget him!

Forget him?

Then I remember my insight from temple last week: what if I really did start committing a few sins here and there? My life could only improve. And, according to Leah, pursuing Luke would definitely be a huge no-no. Anyway, everyone knows New Year's Resolutions are meant to be broken, right? So I revise my list, crossing out parts of resolution number one, changing it to read:

1. ~~Forget heathens like~~ Luke Christiansen

"Rach—"

"Cominnnnng!" I yell, finally satisfied, as I add one last resolution to the bottom of the list:

7. Break the Teen Commandments

APPARENTLY, THE GREATEST dilemmas of a bride's life are: dress—white or ivory? Honeymoon—Tahiti or Fiji? And finally, hair—up or down? It is this final decision my cousin Julia has been grappling with for months. Now, with a week before the wedding, it is crunch time. There is only one way to make the call: a hair tryout. So Julia and Aunt Merle are heading downtown to get her hair done both ways in preparation for the Big Day next weekend. And since I'm her junior bridesmaid, she had said I should come along and have a hair trial run, too—but I think it's only because she thinks my current 'do will ruin her pictures.

Naturally I'm not too thrilled by the idea, usually hating that "just stepped out of a salon" look. But Julia insisted, and I've quickly learned not to cross a bride on the rampage.

So instead of getting my hair done by Kimberly at the same neighborhood salon where my mother covers her gray every six weeks, we're sipping herbal chai in a tres chic "hair boutique" in Soho called Fresh, one of those beauty salons staffed with gorgeous people who make you feel hideously ugly the minute you walk through the door.

After Remy, Julia's stylist, spends an hour teasing her chestnut hair into the perfect French twist with curly tendrils framing her cheeks, and spends another hour disassembling the whole thing until it hangs in curls down her back, Julia stares at herself in the mirror, still torn. "What do you think, Ma?" she asks uncertainly, like a child bride, her white veil quivering as she turns her head. My Aunt Merle doesn't hesitate. "I told you what I think. You can never go wrong with an updo. What if it's humid in Manhattan that day, God forbid?" She turns to me for support. "Am I right?"

"I guess so." Satisfied, Julia slowly nods her head.

Then, before I know it, it is my turn. I am ushered to the shampooing area, where a girl vigorously scrubs my scalp as if I have lice, then plops me down in a swivel chair in front of a large mirror.

Pedro, my Peruvian-born stylist, has slicked-back black hair, tight black jeans, and a flair for the dramatic. He squints down at the bird's nest sitting on top of my head and makes little clucking sounds with his tongue. I pray Pedro is up for a challenge.

"We will do a blow-out, yesssss?" he asks me, although I know a rhetorical question when I hear one. I'm not sure what a blow-out is, so I nod mutely and let him work his magic.

A full hour later, Pedro has attacked every inch of my

head with an industrial-size hair dryer, globs of wax, and a huge boar's-head brush. For most of the process, he's twisted my chair to face away from the mirror, so I have no idea what is going on. To be honest, we are both a bit worn from the ordeal, with him grunting and sweating, while I try not to wince in pain as he tugs at my head. It's like we're two survivors stumbling out of some besieged building at the end of some disaster flick, bonded for life after our shared ordeal.

"Okay, *Mamacita*."

He swivels me around to greet my reflection, and I almost don't recognize the girl looking back at me. Those are my dark eyes, my nose and lips. But my hair is sleek, sexy, swishable! I reach up to touch it in disbelief, amazed at its softness. I never knew I had it in me.

"Fabulous, eh?"

Julia, who has been hovering behind a copy of *Modern Bride* the whole time, shrieks her seal of approval. "You look great!"

I want to keep tenderly stroking my hair, but Pedro is already playing with it, sweeping it up in a bun, then pulling out the tendrils.

"Up?" he asks Julia and Aunt Merle. "Like the bride?"

My face falls. After fifteen years of severe hair angst, I have finally achieved swishable hair, and now they're going to wind it up in a bun like a librarian and hide it away?

Julia gives the question as much scrutiny as if it were

Final Jeopardy. I hold my breath. Knowing Julia, if she says my hair should be up, up it will be. But she notices my tense frown.

"Why don't we leave it down." She winks at me. "It's more appropriate for a junior bridesmaid. Right, Ma?"

"Absolutely," agrees Aunt Merle, apparently unconcerned about the possibility of *my* hair frizzing up on Julia's big day.

Victory.

"You like?" Pedro asks, eager for approval.

"I wish I could have my hair like this every day," I say in all honesty.

At that, Pedro perks up. He hustles over to the counter and comes back with several bottles and vials of waxy goop and a rounded brush. "*Mira*, sweetie," he says, piling them into my arms.

Pedro shows me how to straighten my hair by rolling each section under the hot air. I should be happy that I am finally going to have the hair of my dreams. But instead I am fuming. All those unnecessary years of hair trauma and water avoidance. All those years of hairdressers who only wanted to leave it natural—because it was easier on them. How come no one had ever *mentioned* that it was possible to straighten out my hair? How come no one had shown me how to do it? All it took was a little sweat equity, twenty-nine dollars of waxy goop, and a spare hour. If I'd had better hair that day at the bus stop, I just *know* Luke would have noticed me.

Even though the final charge comes to a whopping one hundred twenty-nine dollars, plus tax and tip, which Aunt Merle slaps on her AmEx, I figure it is still much cheaper than Japanese hair straightening. Plus, I rationalize, we are actually getting a bargain. Like the old adage says: straighten a girl's hair and it will last a day. Teach a girl how to swish, and she can swish for a lifetime.

chapter 11

ALL I CAN SAY IS, this top better stay up.

This entire morning, I've been staring in the full-length mirror at myself, wearing the strapless, shimmery, lemon bridesmaid dress Julia picked out. It seemed like an okay idea at the time.

To me, at least.

Little did Julia suspect it would cause an uproar behind closed doors.

"Strapless?" my father roared when my mom and I, exhausted, lugged the dress all the way home from Kleinfeld's in Brooklyn after the third fitting. "Isn't that a little sophisticated for a girl her age?"

"Dad!" I wailed. "What's the big deal?" He didn't understand. Julia might just boot me out of the wedding party if I failed to conform with her three other bridesmaids, all best friends from high school and Vassar. She is big on uniformity. Plus, I wanted to look sophisticated. I didn't want to be the only one stuck in a sweetheart neckline like a six-year-old flower girl.

He had turned to my mother for support. "Sylvia?"

"Herb, it's what Julia wants. . . ." She had thrown up her hands as if to show the futility of it all. "Anyway, it's too late now. Kleinfeld's doesn't do refunds after alterations." Somehow, this last point had convinced him that the lack of strappage was apropos.

But now, the morning of the wedding, I am wondering whether my dad just may have been right all along. Although, if anyone tells him I said that, I'll have to kill them.

I inspect my chest dubiously. Do I have the Right Stuff to keep it up? Yes, Zelda, the Russian alterations lady has made it awfully tight. Rib-busting, suffocatingly, bustier-wearing tight. But what if I leap into the air to snag the bridal bouquet and my top fails to come along, like what once happened to poor Jenna Bush? Why, oh why, did I have to inherit my mom's boyish body, rather than both of my aunts', who have been generously blessed by the mammary fairy? I resolve to keep my arms squeezed tightly against my sides and hide in the bathroom during the bouquet toss.

I am so loving this wedding.

To me, a wedding is basically a modern-day miracle, offering undeniable proof for us doubters that true love can exist—even if we've never personally experienced it. And probably never will.

Plus, there's always the prospect of the open bar, where you can try to snatch a drink of some sort without your parents noticing.

Somehow, I make it down the aisle without starting on the wrong foot, tripping over my hem (thanks, Zelda!), ending up in the wrong place, or any other of the items on my long list of irrational nuptial fears. Now I am standing on the platform, lined up with the other bridesmaids, feet aching, but smiling for the cameras.

I'm close enough to see Julia and Brad giving each other huge smiles of relief. Brad is sorta short and squat, and to be honest, I was never sure what Julia saw in him before today. But during the ceremony, he's so nervous he's practically crying, and his trembling hands can barely hold the note cards with the vows he wrote himself. It's pretty cute.

Julia and Brad chose a female rabbi—another cool thing I love about my religion, although not a career option I'd ever pursue, considering my limited grasp of the language died about two minutes after my bat mitzvah.

The she-rabbi, who has short curly hair and wears a long black robe, launches into some long speech about marriage not being easy, and respecting each other's differences, and other thoughtful truisms that no one will remember an hour from now because they'll be too busy descending upon the table of hors d'oeuvres.

But I'm paying close attention as the rabbi begins to

review the symbolic aspects of the wedding: the chuppah, the white linen canopy Julia and Brad stand beneath, representing the home they'll make together; the shared glass of wine, signifying hopes for happiness; and a glass wrapped in a handkerchief, which Brad will step on at the end of the ceremony, symbolizing the shattering of the Temple and the reminder that hard times go with good.

I try to imagine myself, someday, standing up under the chuppah, too . . . with Luke. Maybe Leah was right: a mixed marriage *was* pretty complicated. He'd probably want to get married by the Pope downtown in St. Patrick's Cathedral with a gigantic organ and the Vienna Boys Choir singing, while I'd be tripping all over myself, struggling to kneel down while wearing a white gown with a long train. How do brides do that? I'd have to make the sign of the cross, which I'm not entirely sure how to do, and the priest would probably get ticked off if I did it backward or upside down. My parents wouldn't get to print something clever inside the yarmulkes. And what about the absolute best part of the wedding ceremony, where the groom stomps on the glass, and everyone shouts *Mazel Tov!* We'd probably have to skip that, too.

Then again, who says we have to get married in a temple or a church? Jen wants to get married by a Justice of the Peace on a black-sand beach in Hawaii, wearing just a lei and a grass skirt, inspired no doubt by the weddings of the entire cast of *Friends*. But I'd rather get married by an Elvis impersonator at the Graceland Chapel in Las Vegas. My parents wouldn't even be able to object, since they renewed their vows in Vegas for their tenth anniversary, dumping me and Ben at Bubbe's for the weekend and coming back way too giggly and with pictures of them singing with Elvis. But in my version, we'd be wed by a young, cute, postage stamp Elvis in the pink Cadillac—not their Elvis: the fat, bloated, white-sequined jumpsuit Elvis who OD'd on jelly donuts and prescription drugs. I could imagine it: Luke, me, and Elvis, cruising down the Strip, a "Just Married" sign on the back of our white limo, my veil flapping in the dry desert wind. The best part of my plan? Everyone in my family would be so scandalized that we'd eloped in Sin City, they'd completely forget all about our petty religious differences.

I am so hating this wedding.

I thought that, by virtue of being a full-fledged member of the wedding party, I had an automatic in at the main table, sort of like getting to sit at the table by the window in the school cafeteria where all the So Verys hang out.

But no, according to my place card, I am *not* sitting up on the dais with the other members of the bridal party and their beaus, messing up the cozy coupledom. Instead I'm stuck sitting next to my brother at the "young persons" table, which everyone knows is a euphemism for pubescent and desperate. Then again, it could be worse. At least I'm not sitting with my parents.

The young persons' table is located just where I expected it to be, stuck right next to the jumbo loudspeakers, on the assumption that, because we're teenagers, we like deafeningly loud music and our eardrums are ripe for abuse. As I slide into my seat, my seatmate, a weasely-looking boy with dark hair and buckteeth, whose white linen place card reads Jared Schulman, demands, "Aren't you one of the bridesmaids? Why aren't you sitting up there?" He points to the head table, where the rest of the wedding party is settling into their seats.

So I can have the pleasure of sitting beside you all night long, is the obvious reply, delivered in a husky breath. But I restrain myself and simply shrug, as if to say, *Tell me about it.*

Jared tells me he is a cousin on Brad's side, that he and his parents flew in from St. Louis, home of Budweiser. Before I can tell him I'm not into long-distance relationships, he turns away and starts flirting with my second cousin Naomi from Florida, who's always deeply tanned and has blond streaks in her hair. The seat on the other side, reserved for Ben, is still empty. If I know my brother, he's probably hiding out in the crapper playing his Game Boy. The first course hasn't even been served, and I'm ready to go home.

As the bandleader asks us to welcome, for the first time, Mr. and Mrs. Brad Jacobs, I head over to my parents' table to escape watching Jared and Naomi flirt. I slip behind my mother and Aunt Merle, who are leaning conspiratorially against the back of their seats, watching as Julia and Brad make their entrance and trip through their first dance to some old Sinatra number.

"You must be *kvelling*," my mother clucks, lapsing into one of her Yiddish expressions, as she and my aunts always do when they're together.

"When I think of all the *schmucks* Julia brought home over the years," Aunt Merle confides in a whisper. "Brad is such a sweet boy."

"A *mensch*," agrees my mother.

"For a while, we thought for sure she'd end up with that *shegetz* from Vassar."

"The WASP from Connecticut?"

I remember Finley. Julia brought him home during Thanksgiving break one year. He had dark hair and green eyes, and looked like he had stepped out of a Ralph Lauren catalog. Plus, he was a riot. I remember we had a lively battle over the wishbone. I never did ask Julia what happened to him.

"He wasn't for Julia. A mother knows. Brad is much better for her."

"Her *bashert*." My mother nods, saying that Brad is Julia's meant-to-be. Her fate. Her destiny.

"Thank God she finally saw it our way." Merle smiles smugly. "Now, if we could just find a nice girl for Ira. . . ."

I couldn't believe it. Leah was right. Clearly, Aunt Merle had somehow put the kibosh on Julia's old boyfriend to make sure she would end up with someone like Brad. What had they done to Finley? Gotten the Jewish mafia to put out a hit on him? And would they do the same thing to poor Luke, if I dared to bring him home for the holidays?

I must have sent out some sign of distress, because suddenly my mother turns and spots me. "Hi, sweetie, having fun?" She casually leans over and picks a piece of lint out of my hair.

"Ma," I protest, jerking away with disgust. I swear, she has this compulsion to constantly be poking at some part of my body, like the gorillas at the Bronx Zoo who constantly pick nits off each other. I'll be standing, unsuspecting, and she'll come along and stick a finger into my ear, scooping out some ear wax or something, right in front of everybody. Does giving birth to someone give you the right to manhandle them for the rest of their life?

I icily nod hello to Aunt Merle.

"Didn't Rachel look beautiful during the ceremony?" Aunt Merle asks no one in particular, stroking my hair, which Pedro had blown out again early this morning and now fell smoothly around my shoulders.

"Yes, if she'd stop hunching over," my mother says, wrenching back my shoulder blades with a sharp twist of her thumb. I'd spent all day clenching my arms to my side and leaning forward, out of fear that my strapless top would slip if I didn't. But I'm not going to give her the satisfaction of telling her that.

As Julia and Brad finish their first dance, Brad dips her deeply, and the crowd sighs in appreciation. They practically waltz over to our table, hand in hand, for their coronation. Everyone in my family rushes to congratulate them.

"So are you having fun talking to Jared?" Julia whispers in my ear when she comes around to hug me. "We sat you right next to him." Julia is firmly convinced that because she is in love, the rest of the world has to be, too.

"He's okay," I say flatly.

Out of the corner of my eye, I can see him and my cousin Naomi slow dancing, practically doing the nasty right there on the dance floor. Since I'd seen her last, Naomi has become such the village bicycle. Clearly her family is completely clueless.

"Who's okay?" asks my mother, butting into our personal convo.

"Brad's cousin, Jared." I gesture to him on the dance floor.

My mother, as usual, takes the guilty party's side. "Why didn't *you* ask him to dance?"

"He's not my type," I snap.

They all seem to find this hilarious.

"Oh, so you have a type?" My mother laughs, the traitor. "What's your type?"

Luke! I scream silently. Tall. Blond. Charming. Unattainable.

My bubbe, who had been sitting quietly at the table and

didn't even seem to be following the conversation, leans forward and wags her finger at me. "Rachel," she says in a voice tremulous with concern and with the distant quality of a soothsayer, "find a nice Jewish boy to marry. Don't go vith the *goyim*."

My jaw drops. Can she read my mind? Or had she seen me lusting for Luke at Ben's bar mitzvah?

"Bubbe," I start to protest, thinking that I've never even had a boyfriend, let alone a fiancé. Marriage seems light-years away, a concept as foreign to me as the small Czechoslovakian town she was born in.

"Leesten to me," she insists, raising her age-spotted hand into the air. "Look at how happy Julia has made me, findink a good boy like Brad."

She beams and slips a gift envelope into Brad's tuxedo pocket. "Thanks, Bubbe," Julia practically sobs, wrapping her arms around Bubbe's crinkly neck.

"Don't cry," Aunt Merle says, alarmed. "You'll smear your mascara."

Just then the hora starts up. This time, my Aunt Adelle and Uncle Dave grab my hands and pull me onto the dance floor. Like déjù vu, again we are twirling, faster and faster around the dance floor. This time, it is Julia and Brad who are being lifted onto chairs, linked only by a handkerchief pulled from Brad's breast pocket. This time, I am happy to escape the conversation, and lose myself in the excitement of the dance. This time, I'm rushing toward the center of the circle, arms up in the air, when suddenly, I feel it. A snap.

In the immortal words of Homer Simpson: *D'oh!*

Panic floods my body as I sense what has gone wrong: one of the stays in my strappy top has burst free. I can feel it beginning to slip and try to grab it, but my hands are clenched tightly by my aunt and uncle, and neither will let go. I feel it slip sliding away and, Ohmygod, the wedding photographer is circling closer, snapping pictures, like a paparazzi on the prowl, and I think I'm about to make Page Six of the family newsletter.

Finally, my Aunt Adelle notices the panicked look on my face. "My top," I gasp. "Slipping." With a swift move, she spins me out of the circle and grabs it just in the nick of time. "Hold on," she says, leading me back to her table, where she flips open and begins rummaging through her oversized sequined purse. Ever since Uncle Dave had a sudden heart attack five years ago at the Met during the third act of *Aïda*, she carries around practically an entire first-aid kit in her purse. She may even have a defibrillator in there, for all I know.

"Ha!" she cries, holding up a safety pin. "Never go to an affair without a sewing kit." She holds the material of my dress tightly behind my back and pins it together.

I am flushed with gratitude.

Saved by Adelle.

"Thanks," I stammer.

She snaps the sewing kit back into her clutch bag, looks up, and frankly assesses my bosom. "You know, *bubbulah*, you really should fill out a bit before wearing this kind of top."

My gratitude deflates like a burst silicone implant.

I vow never to hora again.

chapter 12

IT'S HARD TO ADMIT Leah was right, but really, what other choice do I have?

"You won't believe this," I blurt out as soon as I get home from school Monday and can speed dial her cell. "They got rid of Finley so she could be with Brad."

"What are you talking about?" she says. "Who's Finley?"

I quickly relay what I'd overheard between Aunt Merle and my mom at the wedding. "So you were right. About everything."

"Of course I was," she says, just a little too happily, in my opinion.

This morning in homeroom I conducted an unofficial poll on the interfaith-dating issue, asking everyone sitting around me if there were people their parents wouldn't let them date. Apparently, the whole world is full of forbidden love. Ariya, this Indian girl in our class, told me her parents wanted her to marry someone Hindu, and would introduce her to the right boys when she got a little older. Instead of being pissed off, she seemed calmly resigned to it, but I think it's because her faith emphasizes serenity, while mine encourages agitation. And Julie Chou, one of the most Americanized Chinese girls in our class, told me her parents still call her Wei-Lin at home and send her to an all-Chinese camp every summer, and wouldn't hear of her dating a white boy.

My sad conclusion: our parents and teachers are just paying lip service to this multiculturalism crap.

"Deep down," I tell Leah, "they're all just bigots."

"It's not bigotry," Leah protests. "Most people just prefer their own kind. There's nothing wrong with that. It makes things . . . easier."

"So you're saying you wouldn't date a guy you really liked who wasn't your own religion?" I demand.

"I just think it's better not to go down that path, where you might be tempted," she says thoughtfully. "What's the point of dating someone when there's no future in it?"

I don't want to hear that Luke and I have no future. "But you can't control who you like," I argue. "What if the perfect guy for you . . . just isn't?"

"I don't believe God would make my perfect guy not Jewish," she shoots back.

I'm stumped. It's tough to debate someone when they claim God is on their side.

"You can do what you want," she says, "but what if everyone thought that way? My parents say if everybody married outside the faith, our people would just die out."

For a minute I feel a twinge of guilt, imagining a world with no one like me. No Kyle on *South Park*. No Seth Cohen on *The OC*. No Ross and Rachel on *Friends* reruns. The idea gives me the creeps, like a late-night episode of *The Twilight Zone*.

But why does our future have to rest entirely on my bony shoulders? Why do I have to change my life course for something that doesn't seem that relevant anyway? Why do my own parents expect me to prioritize something they personally blow off 363 days of the year? At least Leah's parents get points for consistency: they are truly devout. I can respect that. Mine want me to upend my life for something they don't value themselves. It's so hypocritical.

Besides, I've given my own kind a chance, and look what has happened. Every guy I've crushed on since fifth grade was a member of "the tribe," and all it's gotten me was a steady drumbeat of sorrow. Maybe it is time to seek out fresher pastures.

"I don't care what they think," I say hotly. "I'm dating who I want." So what if some people would consider it wrong to be with Luke? I know if I just repent hard enough next year, God will forgive me.

The only question is, will my parents?

chapter 13

NOW I KNOW THAT the end of the world is nigh: Howard Goldstein has a girlfriend.

Worse, Howard Goldstein is dating Tara Silver. This is simply indescribable in my native human tongue. You need a whole other language to define the improbability of this combination. It's like we're learning in chemistry, some compounds simply don't mix. They repel. Strongly.

At our school, Tara Silver is 1. best friends with Alissa Feiner, 2. head of the dance squad, and 3. the undisputed Queen of the So Verys. You can't miss her in the halls; she has this riveting shock of bright red hair she is always tossing around. Red hair on a girl can go only one of two ways: it can be all freakishly freckly Pippi Longstocking, or it can be magnetically sexy, like Lindsay Lohan in her natural hair-color days. On Tara, it is definitely the latter. Normally, her below-average I.Q. and above-average pedigree mean she should be terrorizing teenage girls at Spence, an elite private girls school down in Manhattan, but her father was elected to Congress last year, and had to walk the walk by sending his precious offspring to a public high school, to mollify the liberal Riverdale masses. Tara is the kind of girl who flaunts her wealth by putting others down. I am still smarting over her snide comment hissed at me during junior-high drama class, back when my mother was still picking out my clothes and her taste veered toward denim overalls and frilly collared shirts. "OshKosh B'Gosh, Rachel?" she sneered at the childish label on my pants. You never forget a slight like that.

Howard Goldstein and Tara Silver.

Mr. Hapless and Her Highness.

How could this have happened?

The thought of them together made me sick to my stomach. Or maybe that was just the daily special: Chicken Enchiladas Con Queso. Which Jen refused to eat, after giving me another lecture about industrialized chicken farms.

According to Jen, who got the scoop from Alissa during swim practice, it happened in physics class, where Tara, naturally, was on the brink of failing, and Howard magnanimously offered to tutor her. I have yet to take physics, but it seems that even the thrust of a supercollider couldn't meld their respective atoms into the same room, let alone the same dating orbit. Clearly the threat of flunking Mr. Collins's physics class has more force than previously imagined.

"Wait!" I stop Jen, holding out my hand like a school crossing guard. What is Tara, a not-so-bright sophomore, doing taking physics this year? Everyone knows the natural order of the universe is bio freshman year, chem sophomore year, and physics, the most challenging subject, junior year.

Jen nods solemnly. "I heard she flip-flopped the order to meet junior guys." She lowered her voice to a whisper. "It's . . . genius, actually. Why didn't we think of it?"

Maybe, I think, because we're not skanky dumbwits who base major academic decisions on mate-worthy opportunities? Still, it's annoying to get outmaneuvered by a ditz to the nth degree.

"But still, out of a class of junior guys, why would she pick Howard?" I ask. What am I missing? Howard isn't exactly the biggest nerd of all time, but he is definitely not a member of the So Very Society.

"He's looking *fine* lately," Jen points out. "Since he got contacts and made the track team. And doesn't he have a car? How did you not notice this?"

Generally, I try to pay as little attention to Howard as possible, but I guess she's right. Since he got his learner's permit, he has commandeered his parents' beat-up green Volvo. And I vaguely registered his new letterman's jacket and contact lenses. Worst of all, jogging maniacally all summer long has paid off—Howard has somehow gone beef-cake.

Still, it just seems wrong wrong wrong. People don't just change social status willy-nilly in high school, even with summertime growth spurts and contact lens prescriptions.

It's practically the law, codified by every teensploitation movie ever made.

But Jen begins rattling off a whole list of guys who had gotten buff over the summer, while I kind of neutrally murmur my agreement. To be honest, before Luke, I never got into lusting over a guy's physique. I mean, most adolescent male bodies are an assortment of throbbing Adam's apples, hairy armpits, and big smelly feet. And man nipples? Eww. So not hot. The whole concept always made me more nervous than anything else. But I have to admit, now, I kind of get the point.

Jen also has news of her own. This guy in her English class, Matt Wallen, has finally asked her out. "He *was* the one who wrote that note on my desk!" she says happily, giving me the blow-by-blow of their latest conversation. As she goes on and on, I can't help but tune out. Jen getting asked out was probably inevitable, but now Howard? Clearly, something is amiss in the universe if even Howard Goldstein can bag a significant other during physics class. Pretty soon Howard will be demonstrating the Big Bang theory to Tara, while my own love life is being slowly sucked down a giant black hole.

chapter 14

JEN AND MATT ARE all over each other: in the hallway, before class, at Halley Goldbaum's Halloween party, where they came dressed as Romeo and Juliet, oblivious to the fact that those particular lovebirds were *doomed*.

It's disgusting.

I'm totally jealous.

Instead of channeling Alissa, now, every other word out of her mouth is *Matt does this* and *Matt says that* and *Matt and I think*. Even though he's barely spoken to me, I feel I know him intimately just from hearing Jen yak about him ad infinitum.

For a sophomore at Riverdale High, Matt isn't totally horrendous. He is every Jewish mother's dream: good-looking, smart, polished. Jen, of course, is so blinded by lust she'd be better off taking Braille than French. But he's a little too slimy for me. He's the kind of guy who always tries to get the edge, who sets his margins at 1.2 inches instead of the standard inch so he can write a shorter term paper without Ms. Jensen knowing the difference. He's supposedly this star debater who has perfected arguing as an art form, the type you know will someday end up a corporate attorney defending Big Tobacco against lung cancer victims.

Still, I'm insanely depressed that Jen gets to be with the guy she likes every single day, while I pine away, reliving a five-minute conversation between me and a guy who clearly doesn't know I exist—let alone what school I go to. If I tripped and fell in a forest, would Luke hear me fall?

Anyway, all the time Jen is spending with Matt leaves me in the lurch. You'd think the way she gets on my nerves, I wouldn't miss her that much. But I do. At least when neither of us had boyfriends we had each other. And I always had Leah as a backup, before she was constantly booked with BBYO. But now I don't think I can stand another minute of singletude. I don't even care how unenlightened that sounds. If you read *Cosmo* or *Glamour*, you know that they're always preaching how you must relish the time on your own and grow as a person, that guys are only attracted to girls who love themselves. But that is so untrue. It's the least secure, most shallow girls who get snapped up like iPods for Christmas. It seems like every girl in my school has an invisible stamp upon her forehead: date-worthy or not. Guys don't want to ask a girl out until some other guy has pronounced her datable first, so the same girls get asked out over and over again. My stamp must read "Untouchable."

This afternoon, Matt has debate practice, so Jen and I

head over to her house to hang out, for the first time in weeks. I've always loved Jen's room. She painted it deep purple, and has these dramatic posters on the wall of people hang gliding and parasailing, and all the X-treme things she swears she'll do someday once she doesn't need a signature from her legal guardians, i.e., her parents. From Jen's perspective, their refusal to let her go bungee jumping for her fifteenth birthday shows that her parents are every bit as neurotically overprotective as mine.

The whole way over, I'd rehashed the futility of my crush on Luke. "My parents would freak. And my grandmother would disown me."

"Thank God Matt and I don't have this problem," Jen says, typically self-absorbed. Jen's parents joke they are atheists descended from communists, which is why she never has to go to temple and didn't even have a bat mitzvah. They could care less who she dates. In fact, they've already met Matt at one of her swim meets, while I'm scared to even say Luke's name out loud in my house. Who knows what techno spy gear my dad has rigged inside my Vermont Teddy Bear?

"It doesn't matter anyway," I say, mentally reliving the horrible encounter with Luke at the bus stop. "He didn't even remember me that time I ran into him." I had been too embarrassed to tell Jen that our casual "run-in" was actually something Leah and I had carefully planned. I bounce down onto her bed. "He's just not that into me, right?"

"When a guy is into you—you know," Jen says, sitting

95

across from me, yoga style, on her bed. "Like with Matt. I knew he liked me from the moment he . . ." Sometimes I think Jen and I don't talk to each other, we just talk *at* each other. I don't think she hears a word I say, and I know I tune out half of her monologues. But that's okay. Sometimes friendship is just partnered venting.

Still, it was obviously pointless to keep talking about my own lackluster love life in light of Jen's real one. "So where do you see Matt on The Scale?" I ask.

Last year we devised this primitive system of ranking the boys we liked, a shorthand to describe our latest obsession, like for those couple of weeks when I actually thought I liked Josh Green because I thought he liked me, until I finally realized he just liked comparing test grades, and I just liked beating him in algebra.

The first number, on a scale of 1 to 10, ranked how much we were attracted to him, and the second number represented our mental connection. So a studly dud would get an 81, while an average Joe with wit could score a 79. The idea, naturally, was to score a straight A, in the high 90's. You could argue that there were flaws in the system, like how looks mattered more than character. And I'm sure given time, I could have come up with something more sophisticated, with several variables that assigned different weights to each quality. But Jen is seriously mathematically challenged, so we kept it simple. Besides, we were only freshmen.

"Matt?" Jen pursed her lips thoughtfully. "Oh, he's like, an 88."

"Solid."

"What about Luke?"

"Maybe a 95? Only because I don't know him that well yet."

Jen frowns, clearly ticked that I would give the theoretical Luke a higher score than her real-time boyfriend. "You can't really score him until you're actually dating," she scolds, changing the rules of the game midstream.

"Since when?"

"Since, you don't even know what your mental connection is when he's just a crush. And I think we should really add a third number: for physical connection. Looks and personality don't matter if there's no chemistry."

"I guess . . ." I say slowly, trying not to get mad. She knows I have no way to rank Luke on her new-and-improved three-digit scale. She knows I have no way to rank *anyone* on her new-and-improved physical scale.

"So what would Matt be?"

"889999!!" she shrieks, burying her head into her pillow in mock shame.

"That's not how the scale works," I grumble.

"Don't get all numerical on me, please," she says, flinging the pillow aside. She bounces over to the radio, changing the station simultaneously with the subject. "I'm positive I bombed the math section of the PSAT. My parents are making me sign up for Princeton Review, which will totally cut into my time with Matt. . . ."

By the time I get home from Jen's house, the sun is practically setting, depressingly early as we march farther into the fall. I can barely make out a dark figure sitting out on the front steps, slowly lacing up his Nikes. It is Howard. I've barely spoken to him since he'd turned too cool for school, when he started dating Tara Silver. But I figure I may as well be cordial.

"Hi," I volunteer.

"Huh," he grunts. Could he *still* be pissed about what I said at Ben's bar mitzvah? Well, I can't let this feud drag on forever. What are we, turning into some Northern version of the Hatfields and the McCoys: the Lowensteins versus the Goldsteins?

"Hey, Howard. About what happened at the bar mitzvah . . ."

He looks up at me expectantly.

Remember how I said I'd make Howard beg for forgiveness three times for dissing me when I asked him to dance? Well, instead, I break down and ask *him* for forgiveness.

"Don't take what my mom said seriously. It wasn't you— I didn't want to dance with anyone. Honest. No offense."

"What?" Now he doesn't look mad, he looks totally confused. "What are you babbling about, Lowenstein?"

"Oh," I say flatly. "Nothing." Here I'd been stressing that he was still mad at me, but the reality is, with his new big-man-on-campus status, not dancing with me comes in so low on his radar screen, he doesn't even know what I'm talking about. It is almost more infuriating.

"So what have you been up to?" I ask, trying to change the subject.

His mood visibly changes with the turn of the conversation. "Track," he says, springing to his feet and flexing his calves against the curb. "Did you hear I made the team?"

"Oh. Yeah." That's an understatement. The whole school knows that he already broke some long-standing record at their last meet, and the coach is seriously considering him for captain next year. Which, to me, finally explains what Tara sees in him. "I guess miracles do happen," I tease.

"I know," he gushes, so jubilant he doesn't even acknowledge my dig. "I grew something like three inches this summer. All in my legs. And I ran every day. And suddenly I'm fast."

I nod, sick to death of hearing about Howard's summertime growth spurts.

He looks at me earnestly. "I totally get off on it," he says, switching to stretch his other leg. "The endorphin highs. It's . . . like . . . spiritual."

Clearly, Howard has found God. On Riverdale High's muddy running track. Now he is arching his back, gripping his hands together over his head. I can't help but notice his chest muscles rippling below his thin T-shirt. If running is Howard's newfound god, his body must be his temple.

One of those well-endowed ones on the Upper East Side.

"Mr. Gee's making us run laps in first-period gym," I volunteer. "But all I get are leg cramps and athlete's foot."

He chuckles. Incredible. For once we are actually making pleasant conversation. Suddenly he bends over to touch his toes, giving me a bull's-eyes view of his bright red nylon running shorts. Gross. I try to avoid looking, but his butt is practically wiggling right in my face.

I don't know what fineness Jen had been rhapsodizing over. Howard's tight butt? His lanky limbs? All right, maybe his once-scrawny legs are looking more muscular. And they aren't hairless like a plucked chicken, or overgrown like a forest, but covered with just the right amount of light brown hair, like a well-manicured lawn in the dead of winter. But I don't feel a need to slobber or anything.

I grasp for something to say, keeping my gaze firmly fixed on the horizon. "So, I heard you're running the marathon this weekend." I swear, we are such complete opposites. I can barely schlep my bod two miles around a track for gym class, and he's voluntarily sprinting across all five boroughs.

"Yup."

I sneak a peek to see if it is safe to look. Thankfully, the coast is clear. I quickly push the image of Howard's rear end out of my mind.

"That's, what, twenty-six miles? Impressive." I feel like I should whistle, if I knew how.

He looks abashed. "Actually, you can't do the whole thing until you're eighteen. It's just the High School Invitational. We only run the last two miles of the course."

"Still. I can barely make it that far in gym class," I confess in return.

"I'm not surprised." He looks me up and down with a smirk in his eye. "I bet you could use the workout, Lowenstein. Get some muscle on those chicken legs."

This is the old Howard I know and hate. The wiseass who, just when I let my guard down, always finds a way to put me down. Plus, all his rapture and, well, his chest rippling, is starting to piss me off. I guess that must be what possesses me to ask about Tara.

"Speaking of workouts—I hear you're getting one, too. From something other than running." I trail off my innuendo, hoping to see him squirm for a change.

But Howard has no shame. "Tara? She's spectacular," he says. "Really fun, athletic, sweet."

I can't help but look skeptical at that last one.

"Sweet?" I snort. His syrup goggles don't blind me. Tara is more like Sweet'n Low—completely artificial.

Me-ow.

"You just don't know her that well," he says condescendingly. In other words, I interpret, *You're not exactly hanging with her So Very crowd.*

"I haven't really noticed her chairing the welcoming committee."

"You shouldn't judge her like that. I mean, she has her group of friends—"

"Who have never spoken to me once," I interrupt. "Did she ever talk to you before this year? Before you made track?"

"No . . . But so what? We only met when Mr. Collins asked me to tutor her."

So Jen had it wrong: Howard hadn't leaped at the chance to tutor Tara; Mr. Collins had asked him to. Still, it was so typical of him to defend her. Guys like Howard just can't see past the sunny exterior of a girl like Tara to the heart of darkness lurking within.

My scoff turns into a full-blown sneer. "How come she's even taking physics this year? That's pretty accelerated for a sophomore. Why'd they let her take it if she needs a tutor?"

I can't believe these harsh words are coming out of my mouth. I'm usually not so confrontational, but it's like I'm possessed, intent on tearing the blinders from his eyes.

"At least she's not sarcastic and rude, like some girls I know," he shoots back. "She just likes to have a good time, not tear everyone down."

Who is he referring to? *Me?* I'm not like that, I think indignantly. Not at all.

"Well, have a nice run," I say frostily. But inside I am steaming mad.

This feud is so on.

chapter 15

A 75. I can't believe it. I've never scored so low on a math test before. A 75 is, technically, three-quarters correct. A passing grade. So why does it feel like complete and total failure?

I'd been a little nervous after I handed in the first test of the year. I guess I've missed a few key points lately, blown off some homework assignments, and was spending most of class nodding at Wayne's whispered wisecracks. During the test, I even had to guess wildly at a couple of answers. But I hadn't expected the news to be *this* bad.

When Mr. Diamenties sets the paper facedown on my desk, I know I'm in trouble. I've never had a math test returned facedown. Even from the backside, I can see the grade, circled in red ink, bleeding through the paper. When I flip it over, the page is covered with red X marks, and little sarcastic notes, like "Wrong proof!" and "Try again!"

"Whoof." Next to me, Wayne exhales some kind of snort of defeat. Out of the corner of my eye, I can see his score.

A 67. He shrugs, crumples it up into a ball, and pulls out his sunglasses. "Complete exercise in futility," he mutters to no one in particular from behind his shades.

What I really want to do is cry. But I force myself to look indifferent. "Exactly," I mimic, slumping down in my seat.

Aidan whirls around, eyeing my score. "Too bad. I didn't do much better." He flashes his grade: a 77.

"I just don't get this stuff," I complain, as I hear Mr. Diamenties from across the room purring, "Verrrry nice, Josh," and putting *his* exam faceup on his desk, just as the bell rings.

"This class is bogus," Aidan continues to rail as we head toward the door. "They should teach us stuff we need to know. Tax returns. Mortgages. Stock investments. Geometry's useless in the real world. When I'm down on Wall Street, like my dad, no one's going to ask me to calculate the circumference of a hexagon. . . ."

I'd never thought of it that way before. I'd always considered striving to get good grades just something you did, like brushing your teeth or drinking milk, for a valid reason that didn't need to be questioned, even if the payoff was decades away. But Aidan almost totally convinced me. Why should I care about a grade in math, since I definitely didn't want to plan my life around it? And I couldn't help but notice that he'd walked me out of class—a first.

At the doorway, Future Valedictorian of America Josh Green intercepts us. Even though it obviously drove him nuts when I cleaned his clock in algebra last year, I figure he wants to continue the tradition. For sentimental reasons.

"Whatdidyaget?" he says by way of salutation.

I hesitate. Should I tell Josh it was none of his business? Lie and inflate my grade? Or—God help me—ask him to tutor me?

Out of the corner of my eye, I can see Aidan giving me a disdainful look—*Do you actually know this loser?*—while he just stands there, pointedly ignoring Josh, a gnat to his windshield.

"Would you believe . . ." I confide, as Josh eagerly leans in.

". . . I've got better things to do than rehash my test grade?"

Aidan's guffaw, and the stunned look on Josh's pale face, make me feel a little better. Almost.

Still, as I wander down the hall, I sink back into a Prozac-popping depression. I can't believe that the subject I used to kick ass in keeps busting my butt. How did I become one of those real-life Barbies who giggle and say "math is hard"? It's such a lame cliché.

With the way my love life is going (not), I should at least have my academic career under control, since I'm clearly on a one-way track to spinsterhood. If I can't support myself, I'll end up a bag lady hauling a Waldbaum's shopping cart around the city.

But the more I think about it, so what if I don't ace

105

geometry? I'll kill myself if I end up becoming an accountant or something boring like my dad. Maybe Wayne and Aidan are right, calling it a pointless exercise. Besides, what have good grades in math ever gotten me? Nothing. Not even with a nerd like Josh Green. But one C–, and a So Very guy like Aidan is walking me out of class.

I think back to my New Year's Resolutions. It might be time for a revision. Maybe the answer to my boring existence isn't to do better in geometry. Maybe the answer is to do worse.

chapter 16

A WEEK LATER, at the end of class, Wayne leans over to me. "Tomorrow's the Junior-Senior football game," he whispers. "First and second period. A bunch of us are ditching to go watch. You should come." It isn't a request.

Still, I am flattered for the invite. The underground game, typically attended by upperclassmen and only premium sophomores, traditionally takes place the Wednesday before Thanksgiving weekend. The actual time is a closely guarded secret decided only at the last minute, to control who is in the know. This year, it will be first and second period. In other words, right during first-period gym and Diamenties's math class.

I've never cut class before, but I know there must be a way to do it so my parents won't find out. I know I can miss gym easily enough—I'll just check in for attendance and slip away while we're supposed to be running laps. I finally figured out that Mr. Gee doesn't check whether or not we actually come around each time, so lately, I've been hiding out at the far end of the track, and sailing in for the final lap like I had run the whole course.

As for math class, Diamenties was supposed to be reviewing chapter nine. And he always took attendance. But in the spirit of breaking the Teen Commandments, skipping class seemed like the wisest thing to do.

When Jen and I confer at lunch, she already knows all about the game, killing my pride in getting the invite. "I already heard from Alissa," she says importantly, her official source of all things unofficial. "Who told you?"

"Some guys in my math class," I say vaguely.

Matt can't ditch, she groans, because he has debate that period, so Jen and I agree to meet ten minutes after first bell and head over to the field.

The morning of the game, a crisp autumn day, we wander out behind the school, onto the usually-deserted field, where the stoners get high. As we pick our way awkwardly through throngs of upperclassmen, most of whom we barely know and are probably wondering who invited us, a whistle blows, releasing a collision of crunching flesh out onto the makeshift football field. It's like watching a game of testosterone Twister. And this is only the warm-up.

"Men," Jen says disdainfully. "They're such . . . animals." I guess Ms. PETA USA only loves animals when they're cute and fuzzy, not when they're a pack of rutting male *homo sapiens*.

Farther down the field, it's hard to miss Tara Silver with

her bouncing red mane, Alissa Feiner, and some other girls, standing on the sidelines, giggling and waving pom-poms they'd borrowed from the dance squad at one of the players. I follow their gaze. They are cheering loudly for Howard, who shyly nods at them before he goes into the pregame huddle.

"There's Alissa," Jen says. "Let's go say hi."

I hesitate. The last thing I want is to hear Tara start bragging about Howard's tight end and scoring ability. Besides, I'm nervous about barging into the So Very group uninvited, even with Jen's bravado.

Luckily, I hear someone calling my name. "Lowenstein!" It's Wayne, summoning me over to his posse.

Jen squints at him disdainfully. "Wayne Liu? Do you know him?"

"I'll catch up with you," I say, grateful for the excuse. "I'd better see what he wants." I stroll over to Wayne, who is surrounded by a throng of sophomore guys and is holding a tiny spiral notebook.

When I make my way into the circle, a familiar supersize head swivels toward me. "Rachel Lowenstein!" Aidan says in mock disbelief. "You delinquent."

"Whatever," I say, all casual bluster.

He turns back to Wayne and thumps him on the back. "So I got ten on the juniors, right?"

"Yeah," Wayne grunts in response and jots it down at the bottom of his list.

Then he turns to me. "How much you in for?"

"Huh?" I look at Wayne inquisitively until I realize what is going on. Besides being a mastermind hacker, Wayne is apparently Riverdale High's resident bookie.

"Look." Wayne pulls out a Palm Pilot and quickly explains he's written a program that models the outcomes of the past seven years of games and predicts this year's winner. "According to this"—he taps the screen—"the spread is, seniors win by five." It's the most enthused I've ever seen him.

I try to look intrigued, but inside I'm disappointed. Clearly, Wayne only invited me to rack up another bet. But what choice do I have? "Give me five on the seniors," I say. There's no way I'd endorse a win by Howard and his team. Even though gambling isn't really a sin, it still feels deliciously illicit as I hand over a five dollar bill to Wayne and he pockets it smoothly like we're concluding a drug deal.

The whistle blows again, this time signifying the official start of the game. At the far end of the field, I see Jen waving frantically at me to come join Alissa and Tara and their crew, but I just cheerily wave back, deliberately misunderstanding her message. Shaking a pom-pom isn't my style. "Stick around," Wayne says unexpectedly, his head buried in his notebook, scribbling calculations. "I may need you."

I end up helping Wayne take bets, make change, and calculate payoffs until the end of the game. Before I notice, the seniors are up by six and there are only a few minutes to go until the final bell. I stand on my tippy toes, counting down the seconds. If I followed Wayne correctly, I'm about to be in the money. I suddenly get the thrill my dad finds in poker and why my bubbe is a bingo nut.

Aidan wanders back over to me and Wayne. "Man, juniors suck this year. When we play next year, we're gonna kick some ass!"

Wayne and I just nod, concentrating on the final seconds of the game.

"Did you hear?" Aidan turns to me. "Diamenties sprung a quiz on his first-period class."

"What??" My casual cool cracks before I can help myself. I hope Wayne and Aidan don't notice my inward freak-out.

"Rick Diamond just told me." He cackles and thumps me on the back. "Better enjoy the game. There'll be hell to pay next week."

Suddenly there is a rustling among the crowd. When I turn back, I can see Howard, sprinting alone down toward the end zone, frantically waving for Todd Tannenbaum, a junior who'd been designated quarterback by virtue of his good looks, to go for the Hail Mary attempt. As if anyone in their right minds would throw to Howard, I think.

But defying logic, Todd hurls the pigskin into the air, and lo and behold, there is Howard standing, stunned, in the end zone, cradling the ball in his hands awkwardly, like someone had just stuck a colicky newborn in his arms. *Touchdown!* Half the crowd moans in despair, while the other half roars

111

with approval. Tara races onto the field, hanging her arms and legs around Howard's body like an orangutan, leaving Jen and Alissa and the rest of the dance squad doing high kicks in their best Laker Girls imitation. From opposite ends of the field, Howard and I stand there, seemingly the only two people in the universe, frozen in disbelief at the unlikely catch.

The juniors begin chanting: "Jun-iors! Jun-iors!" And then Howard's teammates pick him up like *he* is A-Rod getting bar mitzvahed, and they begin chanting: "Marathon Man! Marathon Man!" After Howard broke some record at the marathon a few weeks ago, the school paper, *The Riverdalian*, wrote up this nauseatingly glowing profile of him headlined "Marathon Man." Ever since, the nickname has stuck.

Pretty soon Howard is pumping his fist in the air. The pom-pom girls look like they're having epileptic seizures of joy. In my left ear, I can hear Aidan celebrating his newfound wealth. "Yesssssss!"

I want to scream as well. Can't my classmates see it's just the same old, lame old Howard Goldstein hidden behind his new letterman's exterior and soft-lensed brown eyes? I feel like the proverbial truthful child from *The Emperor's New Clothes*—the only one who can see reality behind the pomp and circumstance. Worse, did I just refer to a *fairy tale*? I really am losing it.

"Check it out." Wayne grins, impartial to the outcome

since he comes out cash positive either way. "Your Marathon Man just beat the spread."

"He's not *my* anything," I say.

Wayne looks confused. "I thought you two were tight."

"We're just neighbors," I snap. "That's it. I barely know him."

And I really don't, anymore.

Chapter 17

OVER THE RIVER AND through the woods, to Grandmother's house we go. Or in this case, down by the Henry Hudson River and past the Spuyten Duyvil park, to swing by my grandmother's apartment, so we can bring her back to our house for dinner. Bubbe flat out refuses to relinquish the rent-controlled apartment she has been living in for the past fifty years and move to an "assisted living" home. My grandmother has, however, been willing to hang up her proverbial apron, passing the golden baster of honor to her three daughters. This year it's my mom's turn to fuss over a twenty-five pound Empire kosher turkey all day. By the time we get home, the entire clan has arrived; Julia and Brad, with fading tans from their honeymoon; Aunt Merle and Uncle Milt, broke from the wedding; balding cousin Ira, single as ever; Uncle Dave and Aunt Adelle, with her trademark noodle kugel; and cousin Zachary, pale and sleep-deprived from med school. My mom parades out the slaughtered poultry so everyone can *oooh* and *ahhhh* and praise her oven-tending skills, while my dad begins sharpening his knives like a Samurai warrior. Good thing Jen's not here to see this. I think she actually convinced her mom to do a Tofurkey this year.

"Before we begin . . ." My dad brings the table chatter to a standstill. I know what's coming. Every year, like the biggest cheeseball in existence, he insists we go around and recite what we're thankful for. Easy for him. He's got his stock answer: my beautiful wife and family. That's my mom's cue to squeeze his hand and simper "Likewise." *Likewise?* Ben recites how happy he is with all his earthly possessions. My bubbe says she's grateful to be here but *who knows* whether she'll live to see next Thanksgiving, while my mom and aunts try to hush her up.

This year is no different. While Ben goes over his especially long list of thanks for all the gifts he raked in at his bar mitzvah—his new Game Boy, copies of Halo 3, Tomb Raider 9, Mortal Kombat 17—I try to figure out what I am grateful for in my sad excuse for a life.

Not something shallow, like Ben's litany of material things. Not my friends, who are too busy lately to make time for me; Jen with her boyfriend and Leah with her BBYO. Not my ongoing lack of a love life. Honestly, about the only thing I have to give thanks for is that my parents don't realize how badly I'm bombing geometry.

I am still mentally calculating what to say, when I feel all the faces around the table swivel expectantly toward me.

Ben must have finished up his Thanksgiving dinner product placement.

"Rachel?" my dad prompts.

"Do I have to . . ."

His stern expression answers my question. There is no way out.

"Fine. I'm grateful that the Native Americans are finally getting revenge on the white man for destroying their culture, by building megacasinos."

My dad nearly lets out a pip of laughter before my mom shoots him a look.

"Is that all?" she demands.

My mind is blank.

"Since the Pilgrims came here for freedom of expression, then I'm glad I'm free to express myself by not expressing any thanks."

There. The table is stone-cold silent.

"The Pilgrims came here to escape religious persecution," Ben chimes in. "We learned that in Mrs. Gruber's history class."

He's right, of course.

But the more I think about it, the less sense it makes. In addition to turkey gravy, this holiday is just dripping in historical irony. If the Pilgrims came to America to escape religious persecution, why did they establish a country completely obsessed with religion? We have it everywhere: on our money, which says "In God We Trust"; in homeroom, where we stand, one nation, under God, chanting the Pledge of Allegiance; at the ballpark, where we sing "God Bless America." Even in our sexless sex-ed class, where we are told to rely on abstinence-only. It doesn't make sense. How come no one notices the discrepancy but me?

"Well, then I would appreciate not being *persecuted* today," I snap, knowing that if I tried to express these unorthodox thoughts they would come out all garbled. "I don't have any-thing to give thanks for."

My mom's mouth forms a small O of shock, and my dad presses his hand against her arm, as if stopping her from speaking. For a second, I feel really good. But they both look so crestfallen that, if I weren't in such a pissy mood, I might have felt bad. What's gotten into me?

Julia jumps in. "Weeeell . . . if Rachel is finished, I have tons I'm thankful for. . . ." And she rattles on about how thankful she is for her dreamy wedding and romantic honey-moon in Tahiti, and the charming write-up in the *Times* and her new copper cookware from Williams-Sonoma, until everyone has forgotten all about me.

Or so I think.

"I'll vash," Bubbe announces, as we all push back from the table an hour later.

"Don't be silly," my mom says, with as little enthusiasm as she can muster.

"Go, relax, you cooked all morning," Bubbe says, practi-cally shoving my mother behind the rest of the family, who lumbers into the family room to sprawl and digest. I tag along behind Julia, hoping to hear more about exotic Bora Bora, when I hear a piercing voice from the kitchen.

"Rachel, darlink, vill you come help me?"

I'm being wrangled into domestic service, while my brother gets off the hook. Talk about gender discrimination.

"What about Ben?" I whine to my mom. "Boys can do housework, too." I know this will get to her. My mom was a charter member of the Free to Be You and Me generation.

"Ben will help me put away the china later tonight," she says, adjudicating like a Supreme Court justice.

"Fine." I stomp back into the dining room, carefully stacking the remaining Wedgwood dishes and lugging them into the kitchen, where my bubbe is already scrubbing each one and placing them out on a towel to dry.

"Can't we just stick them in the dishwasher?" I grumble.

She ignores me. "Vhat does zees mean, you have no thanks to give?" Clearly, she has a deeper agenda than grooming my domestic goddess skills.

"It was nothing, Bubbe."

"It's not nuthink."

"I couldn't think of anything to say."

"So, you say you are persecuted. Bubbulah, you don't know vat being persecuted really ees." She turns and rests the plate in her hand on the dish towel. "Your grandpa, may he rest in peace, vhen he escaped from Europe, he hid three days in a rucksack, a filthy tugboat, until finally Canada let him in. And zees country made him vait seven years more."

I know the story, vaguely. It is one of those family legends that gets repeated at every reunion, but if you were ever quizzed on the details, you'd realize you had never really been paying attention.

"And I vas only fifteen vhen my parents came here from Czechoslovakia," she continues. "My father vas a smart man, he knew vhat vas coming. He had to get papers for zee whole family, changink our names."

I never realized she had been exactly my age when she'd had to move with her family across the world. I tried to imagine what I would do in her place. What if my dad came home tomorrow and said we had to move to some random Eastern European country, just because, say, a Republican had been reelected President and the country was headed in the wrong direction? (Not so far-fetched a scenario, considering my left-wing dad, come to think of it.) I'm ashamed to say, I think I might tell him I'd rather stay.

"Did you want to leave?" I inquire curiously.

"Leave? No. Zhere vas a boy in my village . . . My father and I fought for veeks. But he vas right."

I try to imagine my grandmother arguing with her father to stay in some Czech town to marry the village idiot. My mom, Ben, me—none of us would ever have been born.

"Never mind zee Indians"—my bubbe is totally un-PC; she still calls Native Americans "Indians" and Asians "Orientals"—"ve are also zee persecuted people. And only

119

by zee grace of Gott are ve all here today. You, bubbulah, must never forget zat."

Jewish grandmother guilt. It is like normal Jewish mother guilt—squared. I instantly feel ashamed. She's right. I've been acting like a brat, so wrapped up in my own misery, I'm unable to appreciate true suffering.

"I'm sorry, Bubbe," I whimper. "I'm glad you listened to your father."

"Zat's vhy you must be a gutt girl," she says, smothering me in her mammoth chest so I can barely make out the rest of her words. "Respect your parents. And carry on our faith."

By now, I know what that means. It is code for "Don't go vith the *goyim*." What I still don't understand is, if *we* were the persecuted people, why is it okay for us to look down on everyone else? But that is one question I don't dare ask.

chapter 18

MY MOTHER IS INCREDULOUS that I'd want to go to a Christmas party on the first night of Chanukah. Of course I had been careful not to call it a "Christmas" party. Instead, I'd vaguely mumbled something about a holiday party, the more PC-conscious, all-inclusive term, which technically encompasses celebrants of Saint Nick, Judah Maccabee, and Kwanzaa, to boot. She can draw her own conclusions.

Still, she is pouting as she is standing up to her elbows in soaking, peeled potatoes and a sizzling skillet of grease, preparing to make her annual ode to joy, potato latkes.

"Who plans a party on the first night of Chanukah?" she complains, as if it were my fault Chanukah falls on a prime Saturday night in the middle of the holiday party season.

"I dunno," I mutter. Jen will be at the door any sec.

"And you don't want us to drive you?"

My parents have designated themselves my personal chauffer, always at the ready to pick us up or drop us off. It's yet another way for them to keep tabs on me. But the sad truth is this: it also gives them something to do. They have no life.

If this is their idea of parental supervision, the joke is actually on them. If they only knew how little they have to worry about. Thanks to their meddling ways, my inner party animal has been kept caged and heavily sedated. And the few times I've tried to break free have been a disaster.

Exhibit A: Seventh grade. The first time—also the last time—I tried to smoke a cigarette. Todd Tannenbaum—at the time, a So Very *eighth* grader, handed me a cigarette at a junior-high party. Trying to shed the ashes, I gave the cigarette a strong flick—and broke it in two, sending the lit butt flying onto his arm and scorching a hole in his new cashmere sweater. Mortifying.

Exhibit B: Ninth grade. Last year after Passover, Jen came up with the idea of making Jell-O shots with a leftover bottle of grape Manischewitz we swiped from our fridge. Grape Jell-O and grape wine. It sounded good in principle. Nas-tee. We both puked, and our tongues turned purple for a week.

I know it sounds impossible that I've lived such a sheltered life, but thanks to my parents' ridiculous rules, most of the parties I went to freshman year were of the pajama variety. Or were heavily supervised by roaming packs of parents. Jen and I weren't on the invite A-list for the NC-17 fests thrown by the So Very crowd. Even if we did try to get away with anything, my parents are practically Human

Breathalyzers, able to detect the whiff of alcohol from well across a room.

I realize my mom is still waiting for my answer about the ride. Even though this party will likely be tame, it is always better to travel parent-free if possible. "No, he lives literally a few blocks from here."

"And whose party is this again?"

"I told you. It's a friend of Matt Wallen's, Jen's boy-friend."

"And his parents will be there?"

"Hm-mmm," I murmur neutrally, although, honestly, I have no idea.

What I do know is this: Jen, to her credit, has totally redeemed herself. Last week, the first day back after Thanksgiving, she bragged that she had gotten us invited to a kick-ass party. I had braced myself for the worst, sure she had gotten us on the guest list for a party thrown by her new best friend, Alissa.

Instead, she revealed that Matt happened to be buds dating back to elementary school with a bunch of guys from St. Joseph's. And he'd gotten us invited to a Christmas party at one of their houses. And—drumroll, please—there was a good chance that Luke would be there.

I knew I was friends with her for a reason.

For this party, there was no way I could let my parents ruin my best chance to see Luke again. So Jen and I had spent some prep time carefully strategizing how to play it. We'd even role-played this exact moment, where my mom would press for party deets, and how I'd respond. Too little information and she'd demand to know more. Too much and we'd be unable to shake her. We had to release just enough information to satisfy her.

And now, the moment of truth had finally arrived.

As I hold my breath, I can actually see my mom's mind digitally processing the information I have given her, like a Pentium chip had been implanted in her brain. *Proximity: nearby. Surname: acceptable. Parental supervision: present.*

Approved.

"Fine." She nods. "Just leave me the address of where you'll be."

"I wrote it on the fridge," I say, with just the right level of teenage irritation. The address is a barely legible scrawl. With any luck, she'll never be able to pinpoint our exact destination.

"And call us as soon as you get there, so we know you arrived safely."

I'm the only one of my friends who always has to call when I get there. Which I forget to do half the time, causing them to call me right in the middle of a party's high point.

"Okay," I say, not wanting to pick a fight now.

"And be back by ten."

"Ten??" I say in disbelief. "Most people don't even show up until ten. Can't we stay until midnight?"

"Eleven," she amends. "But no later."

"Fine."

The doorbell rings. Jen. "I'm outta here." I pull open the door, but my mother is too fast for me. She hovers behind me and invites Jen to enter.

"Now, if you girls just wait a minute, you can have latkes before you go." Tempting. Latkes were once my fave annual treat, until I realized the combination of fat and potato was like, Death by Carbohydrates. Thanks a lot, Dr. Atkins.

I shake my head no.

She frowns. "You used to love my latkes."

"Carb city, Mom."

"Jennifer?"

"Thanks, Mrs. Lowenstein, but I ate already." I can't tell if Jen is thinking fast on her feet or is actually telling the truth.

My mother squints at my flip-flops. "Shouldn't you put on socks? It's cold out." I swear, she has some sort of obsession with footwear. Socks, stockings, slippers. She's always trying to force them on me, as if bare feet were sacrilegious.

"Jeez!" I shake my head vehemently, heading for the door before she can pull out her sandalwood control-top panty hose and force me into a slip and girdle.

"Well, at least take a jacket!"

"Ma, we're going to be late!"

"Girls!"

We freeze. What now?

"I know! How about I save you some latkes for later!"

chapter 19

THE FIRST THING I realize when Jen and I reach the brick apartment building is that my feet are practically numb after walking twelve blocks in the cold. The second thing is that we don't recognize a soul. The third is that, except for a few skanky-looking girls, some wearing skimpy Santa's helper outfits, the party is a total sausage fest.

"So, whose place is this again?" I whisper nervously as we push past the huge wreath hanging on the front door and inside the apartment.

"I told you," she says impatiently. "It's this guy, Mick, that Matt knows from elementary school." Jen has no fear, striding confidently through the small entry and into the dimly lit living room, while I follow. A huge Christmas tree looms in the corner, but instead of traditional ornaments, this one is decorated with tiny bottles of liquor, the kind people buy on airplane flights because they're scared witless of flying. From behind a swinging door that must lead to the kitchen, I can hear kids chanting *"CHUG CHUG CHUG!"* while traditional holiday music tinkles the air. A lively game of quarters is underway around the coffee table.

Secretly, I'm almost glad that Leah begged off from my invitation, stammering something about a Chanukah BBYO party. Who wants her here, anyway, Nostradaming dire predictions about interfaith romance and the death of our race?

Thankfully, just as we step into the living room, Matt spots us, or should I say, spots Jen, and barrels across the room toward us, practically causing an international incident.

"You made it," he yelps, ten decibels louder than is really necessary. "Come on, let me grab you a drink."

We follow him into the kitchen, where he heads straight for a silver keg in the corner. "Brewski?" he offers. Even though I know for a fact she thinks beer tastes like wet sewage, Jen giggles and accepts the red plastic cup, ignoring my pointed look.

"Rachel?" Matt turns to me, cup outstretched.

My dad gave me a sip of his beer once at a Yankees game, and in my humble opinion it tastes marginally worse than cheap Jewish wine. "Sure," I say casually, planning to take a sip, and if it tastes gross, dump it as soon as possible. We head out to the living room, where within minutes, Jen and Matt are making smooching baby talk on a lumpy brown couch and I am trying not to gag on my beer. Sure enough, it is as vile as I remember. "Be right back," I say to no one in particular, and make my way back to the kitchen, where I find a punch bowl, and swap my drink for a ladleful of eggnog. It is so delectable I have another on the spot.

When I return to the living room, I find Matt and Jen shamelessly hooking up in a corner. I sit back on the couch and sip my drink, feeling like the proverbial third wheel.

Across the room, I watch as a blond chats up some guy over by the fireplace. She is dressed as a Santa's helper, with a Santa cap set saucily atop her head and high heels unsuitable for tromping through the Arctic snow. Her skirt barely covers her bare butt, while a big gold cross dangles between her breasts, undulating for attention. Can you say, *Ho-ho-ho*?

When she bends down to fix her stockings, I freeze.

The object of her affection, standing there with a dumb grin on his face, is Luke. What is he doing talking to her? Worse, how can I compete? Dress up as a giant dreidel and spin by?

I have to talk to someone, and Jen is officially Do Not Disturb. I step out into the deserted entryway and pull out my cell phone, dialing Leah in a panic. But all I get is her voice mail. I whisper frantically, "Luke is here, talking to some skank, and Jen's getting busy with Matt. What should I do? Call me!"

As I end the call, I glance at the screen. Three missed calls, the glow screen scolds. I check my call log and hit redial. My dad answers on the first ring, his anxiety apparent by the speed of the pickup and the tone of his voice. "Rachel! Are you okay?"

"I'm fine!" I shout over the music.

"You said you'd call as soon as you got there. Your mother was worried."

It's only eight thirty, and she's worried already?

"I'm sorry, I . . . forgot." I always forget. Don't they understand? When you step into a party, you're worrying about a million things: making an entrance, sizing up who is there, whether you're dressed right, where to stand, whether to drink, if there's something stuck in your teeth. Calling your parents doesn't exactly top your Must Do list.

By the time I return to the main room, Matt and Jen have finally stopped sucking face. "Where were you?" Jen says, grabbing my arm. "This is Matt's friend Mick, our amazing host."

Mick is gangly tall, with strawberry-red hair and freckles. I vaguely recognize him as one of the guys Luke got off the bus with that September day. On the off chance that Luke should stop flirting with the girl and glance my way, I smile encouragingly at him. Mick seems shy, until he starts telling me how he and his friends redecorated the Christmas tree, swapping out the family's traditional ornaments as soon as his parents left the house. I'm pretending to be totally engrossed in the conversation, even though in reality I'm distracted, knowing that Luke is coexisting somewhere in the same room. But where?

Then I hear a familiar voice from behind me.

"Need a refill?" I turn. It's Luke standing right in front of me. "Gotta keep my busboy skills sharp," he says, with a grin of recognition. "Rachel, right?"

"Right," I repeat in disbelief. He actually remembers me! And my name!

"You guys know each other?" Mick asks curiously.

"We had an illicit rendezvous." Luke grins. "This summer, in the break room—"

"He couldn't say no," I finish, amazed at my own bravado. "I was the boss, and Luke was my love slave." Even though I barely know him, I feel like we have this connection when we talk, like we've known each other forever.

Now Mick looks totally confused. Just then, someone grabs his arm, shouting something about needing more ice, and he is pulled away into the crowd. For all I care, he could have melted into a puddle at my feet.

Luke takes my empty cup, then taps it. "So . . ." he says mock-seriously. "Am I going to get a tip this time?"

"That depends on how well you do," I reply, trying to keep my cool.

He smiles the sexiest smile I've ever seen. "I've always gotten great reviews on my performance."

Oh. My. God. I try not to blush. Am I imagining it? Or has this conversation just taken an X-rated hairpin turn. I don't know how to respond.

"Come on," he says, grabbing my hand and pulling me through the dining room to the kitchen, which is jammed with more bodies than the fire code probably allows. He stops me at the doorway. "Wait here."

He maneuvers through the mob toward the punch bowl, his head towering above most of the others. I stand there waiting, trying not to exude loser wallflower standing alone at a party, and instead, girl who's been told to *WAIT HERE* by a cute boy who'll be back with a drink any second now. It's a subtle distinction, one I'm sure is lost on the crowd.

While I wait, something possesses me to look up. A piece of leafy greenery is hanging above my head. *Strange*, I think, until it registers. It must be mistletoe. Not that I've ever seen any before, but what else could it be? I am standing under the mistletoe. Did Luke position me here on purpose? And if so, what then?

I rack my brain to remember exactly what being under the mistletoe means. Is it that if you are spotted standing below it, you *have* to kiss? Or is it an aphrodisiac that makes you *want* to kiss the other person? And does mistletoe mashing follow traditional PDA rules?

By the time Luke returns with another cup of eggnog, I'm so worked up by the tiny sprig of herb hanging over us, I'm almost unable to concentrate on our convo. I sip my drink and will him to be swept away by the forces above.

KISSMEYOUFOOL, I chant over and over in my head, while I hear another, more normal voice explaining how I happened to be at a St. Joseph's party, and tell him, at last, what school I really attend, and where I live, and try to hint at the vital detail that, no, I don't have a boyfriend.

But nothing happens. Luke hasn't so much as glanced upward. I'm getting so frustrated, I'm about to summon up the nerve to kiss him myself. *Just do it,* my mind urges like a Nike ad.

Just then, we're interrupted as a voice booms: "Luke! You can't hog the mistletoe forever, man!" A dark-haired boy appears before us. "Shit or get off the pot."

I blush at the crude image. What will Luke do now?

Luke glances up briefly, but looks nonplussed. "I always thought mistletoe was an archaic ritual," he says airily. "Right, Rachel?"

I try to look nonchalant. *Mistletoe? What mistletoe?* But I'm crushed. Luke had known we were standing under the mistletoe the whole time and didn't even try to use it as a sorry excuse to hook up.

"I guess," I agree reluctantly.

"Sully." Luke waves, by way of introduction. "A real romantic guy."

"I can be romantic," Sully protests, turning to inspect me. "At least, I believe in archaic rituals." Then he puts his hand on my shoulder and runs it down my arm, taking my hand and gallantly plunking his lips on it with a loud smack, like a jester posing as a knight in King Arthur's Court. "And you are?"

Speechless. "Er, Rachel."

"This guy will talk your ear off all night. Let's dance, Rachel."

I hesitate, waiting for Luke's reaction, secretly hoping he'll tell Sully to kiss off, and then kiss me. But he is silent, so I have no choice but to let Sully pull me out onto the makeshift dance floor, where a couple of people are trying to swing dance to "Jingle Bell Rock."

Serves him right, I tell myself. *He had his chance.*

Then I spot the Santa's helper leading Luke onto the dance floor.

I think I'm going to cry.

But I can't, because Sully keeps cracking outrageous jokes I can't follow and twirling me around until I start to get dizzy. Right when I've abandoned all hope, I hear a firm voice behind me. "My turn, Sully," and when I turn, it is Luke. "She's all yours, dude," Sully says, bowing out. Luke grips my hand firmly, and I smile up at him like Cinderella greeting her prince at last.

But just then, the room starts to spin harder, like I've had one too many go-rounds on the Central Park carousel. "Hold on," I say, pulling back.

"What's wrong?" He frowns and follows me off the dance floor.

"I just need to rest," I say. I can feel my stomach beginning to churn, like the time Dad took us on a five-day cruise to Bermuda, and I was so nauseous all I could do was sprawl out on the lido deck and pop Dramamine.

I stagger over to the side of the room looking for a chair, when I see Jen and Matt, Mick and Sully huddled by the Christmas tree. "Jen!" I say brightly, practically falling into her arms I am so happy to see her. I'm trying to simultaneously look like I've been having the time of my life and to not puke on anyone's shoes. It's taking a lot of concentration.

"Rach!" Her eyes brim with concern. "Are you okay?"

"She's a little wasted," Sully says.

"I am not," I say indignantly. "All I've been drinking is eggnog." For some reason, everyone, even Luke, hoots in laughter.

"Spiked with rum, sweetheart!" Sully shouts.

I'm mortified. Why had I assumed a dairy product would be alcohol-free? Come to think of it, my head *was* spinning pretty hard, and I was having trouble making sense. And hadn't I said something about Luke being my *love slave*? How wasted am I?

I see Luke grinning at me, like I'm some dumb child.

"I know that," I say, struggling to reclaim my dignity. "I . . . I just didn't think it was *that* strong."

Jen grabs my arm protectively. "We gotta go, it's almost eleven. You can walk it off."

"You're leaving?" Mick moans. "I didn't even get a chance to dance with you, and you're leaving? Just my luck."

I am woozy from the thick eggnog and the thicker flattery. At my school, none of the guys ever give me a second glance, and here, the St. Joseph guys are literally fighting over the chance to flirt with me, dance with me, bring me spiked drinks.

"Wait," Sully says, looking right at me. "I'm having a New Year's party next Saturday. You'll come, right?"

I glance at Luke. Is he listening for my reply? He is talking to Mick, so I can't quite tell. "Sure." I nod to Sully, disappointed that I can't gauge Luke's reaction to the prospect of seeing me again.

"We'll be there," Jen promises.

Then Luke leans over and cups his hand over my ear. "Gatorade. Ginger drops. And an Excedrin. My sure-fire hangover cure." Through my brain fog, I'm not sure I understand what he's talking about, so I just gape up at him. He smiles kindly. "Trust me, you'll be needing it tomorrow."

"We'll get the deets from Matt," Jen tells Sully, kissing Matt good night and pulling me out the door. We slide out into the night, giddily euphoric.

I want to scream, I am so happy. I'm like a greedy kid in a candy store, wanting to devour as many sweets as I can. Even the air smells like cookies.

"That was awesome," Jen crows. "Matt's definitely The One." Then she remembers me. I am quietly beaming.

"That Luke is pretty cute."

"So cute," I sigh.

"How about Sully? He was so into you. The way he looked at you when he invited us to his party."

"He's kinda obnoxious . . . in an appealing way," I admit. "And . . ."

"And?" Jen presses.

"What about that guy Mick, the quiet one who was like, 'I didn't get to dance with you'?"

Jen starts laughing hysterically.

"What??" I demand.

"Oh my God, Rachel. You've always been boy crazy, but now you're lusting after all these St. Joseph's guys? *You've turned Goy Crazy!*"

"*YOU HAVE TWO CHOICES,*" my mom says, tapping on my door early the following morning. From somewhere under the covers, I manage a groan of recognition.

"You can go watch Ben's basketball game with us, or you can spend some time with Bubbe. I know she'd love to see you. And she wants to give you and Ben your Chanukah presents."

"Ummph," I grunt in agreement and slump back in bed, head pounding.

Every year, Bubbe gives my brother and me essentially the same thing: a package of Chanukah gelt—milk chocolate wrapped in shiny gold foil and a twenty dollar bill to spend as we please. At least it beats those grandmas who are always crocheting wool sweaters decorated with hearts and kittens.

My cell phone rings. It's Leah. It's about time.

"So what happened?" she asks.

"Where were you last night?" I demand. "I left you a message."

"Sorry," she apologizes, giving no reason why she was MIA.

I fill her in on the incredible turn of events, from the mistletoe to the eggnog. Leah gasps and applauds at the appropriate spots.

"So can you hit Bloomies today?" she asks. "You'll need something extra amazing to wear for this New Year's party, right?"

I groan. "I just promised my mom I'd spend the afternoon with my bubbe."

"Bummer. Well, we're leaving for the holidays tomorrow. So I'll see you when I get back."

When we arrive at Bubbe's apartment, she is ready. "Here, *bubbulahs*," she says, pulling out her handbag and, her arthritic hands trembling, slowly, slowly plucking two bills from her wallet.

"Thank you, Bubbe," I say, giving her a hug. I know that twenty dollars isn't insignificant from her fixed income.

"Thanks," says Ben, preoccupied with getting to his game on time. "Dad?"

"Right, we've got to get going," my dad says in response to Ben's pointed stare.

"You two have a good time," my mom says. "We should be home by four." And they are gone.

Bubbe thinks I am scrawny because she thinks I don't eat enough, so she force-feeds me a greasy lunch of matzo ball soup, broiled chicken, and rye bread slathered with margarine. Then we flip through the channels on the TV, but it is Sunday afternoon, and nothing is on but preachers screeching from the heartland. We stare at each other for a moment, not sure what else to do.

"So . . . I'm off to my three o'clock bingo. Vhy don't you valk over vith me?" she finally suggests.

"Okay," I agree, not pointing out that it is only one-thirty.

It takes about twenty minutes to help her assemble everything she needs—purse, keys, snacks, medication, glasses—but finally we head down the elevator and out the door. "Here we are," my bubbe sings as she stops and turns a few blocks later—onto the doorstep of St. Joseph's Church.

"I thought bingo was at Temple Israel?" I say, confused.

"The girls and I made a svitch. The payouts are much better here," she confides. "But the food? Feh, not so good. Ve bring our own noshes."

So now I know what my Jewish grandmother does every Sunday: goes to church.

"You should come in and say hello to the girls," Bubbe orders. "You remember Mrs. Klein and Mrs. Grubman?"

As we reach the entryway, my bubbe seems to lose twenty years. With a spring in her step, she bounds up the stone stairs and ushers me down into the church basement, which is bursting with bubbes, as though there had been a mass exodus from the Hebrew Home for the Aged.

"Rose," calls out one of the elderly women seated at a distant table, waving her hand frantically at my bubbe. "We saved you a seat!"

"Now you just let me do the talking," she says, leaning in as though the room were full of spies.

We descend upon them. "Girls, look vhat I've brought vith me, my beautiful granddaughter, Rachel!" My bubbe introduces me to her clique, Mrs. Klein, Mrs. Grubman, and Mrs. Sklansky, women whose hair tones—shades of canary yellow and orange taffy—are seldom seen in nature. They fawn over me like I am a newborn baby.

"What a treat!" says Mrs. Klein, removing her jacket from the empty folding chair and gesturing for us to sit down. "We haven't seen you since you were this big," she says, pointing her hand at the level of my chest.

"Your grandmother is always talking about you." Mrs. Grubman beams.

"You should visit more," scolds Mrs. Sklansky. "Your bubbe is all alone, you know."

As we settle into our seats, Mrs. Klein leans over and confides in my bubbe's ear. "Harriet Horowitz tried to sit here, but we told her the seat was saved."

My bubbe rolls her eyes.

I can't believe it. Apparently the high-school cafeteria seat scramble never gets old—even if the players do.

I'm dying to know what poor Harriet Horowitz did to be

on the outs, but Mrs. Klein is already trying to engage me in conversation. "So, Rachel, are you going to bring us some good luck?"

"I'm not staying," I stammer. "I was just saying hello."

"Oh, vhy not stay?" my bubbe says. "I'll buy you a card."

"Yes, stay, play!" the ladies all insist, making it impossible to say no.

"Just don't expect much," Mrs. Sklansky says gloomily. "I haven't won a game in weeks. Our luck was better at Temple Israel."

"Irma, don't be ridiculous." My bubbe frowns. "Let's go get our cards," she says, gesturing for me to come with her. We join a long line of chain-smokers attached to either a walker or an oxygen tank. "I don't know vhy vee put up vith Irma," my bubbe confides. "She's such a *kvetch*."

At the counter she barks, "Let me get an eighteen and a nine," then heads over to another table, where she orders three more packets of games. We head back to the table with reams of paperwork, like we're taking final exams. Then things get even more bizarre. My bubbe methodically lays out the cards in front of her, tapes them down to the table, and systematically marks each free space with a pink marker she calls a dauber. Then she starts unloading her purse, pulling out various good luck trinkets, and finally, five little stands holding snapshots of Julia, Ira, Zachary, Ben—and me.

It is my horrible bat mitzvah picture.

"What's that for?" I frown.

She places them all in front of her. "For good luck," she smacks, satisfied.

"But why that one?" I say, pointing to myself.

"Vhat?" she says innocently. "You look beautiful."

Before I can disagree, the room stirs with anticipation as the caller appears at the podium and begins cranking a metal cage with white balls. My bubbe barks out all the various game configurations: small picture frame, six-pack, block of nine, four corners, postage stamp, cover-all.

My head spins. "I didn't realize it was so . . . complicated." This isn't just amateur night, this is cutthroat, high-stakes, professional bingo.

"Don't vorry," she says, patting my hand protectively. "I'll help you."

Just then an elderly woman with perfect posture and gently graying hair glides by our table. "Oh, Mrs. Coniglio, come meet my granddaughter," my bubbe calls out.

Mrs. Coniglio beams as we are introduced. "Aren't grandchildren such a blessing, Mrs. Ziegler?" she says pleasantly.

"Oh, yes," bubbles my bubbe.

"How nice to come spend the afternoon with your grandmother," she says to me, stroking a long strand of rosary beads. "I couldn't get any of my grandchildren here if I begged."

"Vell, I almost had to trick Rachel to get her to come." Bubbe laughs. "She never has the time to spend vith her old bubbe."

"Bubbe!" I say.

They continue making pleasant chitchat until finally the announcer says, "Please take your seats," and Mrs. Coniglio wishes us luck and sails away. "What a nice woman," my bubbe says.

I don't understand it. After my bubbe's warning, what is she doing fraternizing with the enemy?

At the front of the room, a priest who looks like Harrison Ford but introduces himself as Father O'Malley takes the microphone and welcomes us to St. Joseph's. He clears his throat self-consciously. "Now, next Saturday is our upcoming rummage sale . . ."

Mrs. Klein and Mrs. Grubman lean their heads together. "Such a looker," one of them titters. "What a waste," sighs Mrs. Sklansky.

After Father O'Malley steps down, the announcer takes over. "Our first game will be five-number bingo," she calls. "The first number is B-5."

"So, Rachel, do you have a boyfriend this year?" Mrs. Klein leans in with a smile.

"Not really," I say. It is all I can do to concentrate on the swirl of numbers before me.

"O-68."

"What's the matter?" Mrs. Sklansky frowns. "You don't like the boys at your school?

"N-34."

"No, I . . ."

"You should meet my grandson," Mrs. Klein continues. "David. At Horace Mann. He's, what? A ninth-grader. But very mature for his age."

I just nod noncommittally.

"G-47."

"You should meet zees boy," my bubbe says. "Vhat do you have to lose? Nuthink."

"I-18."

"I . . . er . . ." I stammer, praying for a distraction.

Somehow, my prayers are heard.

"BINGO!" my bubbe shouts, pounding the table and pointing down at my card. "Rachel, pay attention. You made bingo!"

Sure enough, I have won the first game.

Mrs. Sklansky shoots me a dark look. "Beginner's luck!" she grumbles, as the attendant comes over and starts counting out ten dollar bills.

"See!" My bubbe beams. "The payouts here are the best!"

I smile weakly. How do I tell my bubbe that bingo's not the only thing that's better at St. Joseph's?

IF YOU DON'T happen to be Christian, Christmas is the most boring day of the year. I mean, there's absolutely nothing to do. Everything is closed; the mall, the museums, the gym. You can't call anyone else even if you know they're not celebrating either, because it's too weird. Anyway, who would I call? Leah and her family are down in Boca Raton visiting her grandparents until after New Year's, and Jen is off snowboarding with her parents at Killington. My family plans nothing, so we sit and stare at each other the whole day long. The only restaurants open are Chinese, so yet again, another holiday is spent ordering spareribs and fried rice from Golden Gate. The only thing on TV is the Yule Log, an endless loop of Muzak holiday tunes played over the image of a burning log, which I suppose might be fun to watch if you were seriously stoned. I wouldn't know. Other than that, it's either watching that little blond boy beg for a BB gun in *A Christmas Story* or watching Natalie Wood cry, "I do believe in Santa Claus" in *Miracle on 34th Street* for the umpteenth time. In despair, we eventually head over to the multiplex and catch a double feature to make the hours go by faster.

Merry Christmas to us.

The only thing that gives me any holiday cheer is reliving the night of the party. I still can't get over the heady sensation of flirting my head off with three different guys: shy but sweet Mick, scandalous Sully, and Luke, the one who still makes my knees wobble.

I try to envision what's going on at their houses. Last night, for Christmas Eve, they got to hang their stockings by the fireplace and stay up late to go to Midnight Mass, which kind of sounds more like an all-night rave than a religious service. Then, this morning, their families woke up and opened tons of presents under the Christmas tree, which they got to decorate themselves with strings of light and tinsel and fragile heirloom ornaments passed down for generations. Now they're enjoying a giant ham and figgy pudding, just like Tiny Tim in *A Christmas Carol*. Later, they'll get to go sleigh riding and sing carols, and eat fruitcake and gingerbread houses. I don't care what Adam Sandler sings, I still feel shortchanged. Eight Crazy Nights does not match one magical Christmas Day.

When I was little, riding around in the backseat of my parents' Chevy during the holiday season, I used to track how many houses were lit up with decorations. To tell you the truth, I was obsessed with counting them, like I was autistic or something. I told myself it was just that I liked monitoring all the different kinds of decorations, but I think I was secretly tallying up all the millions of people who believed in something we didn't.

And secretly, so secretly, I longed for my very own Christmas tree, red-nosed reindeer, and a lawn decorated with strings of colored lights. If Luke and I were together, could I have that? Would we celebrate both holidays? And how would that work?

Tons of kids I know come from mixed marriages. I always saw it as the best of both worlds: Christmas and Chanukah presents, Easter egg hunts and Passover Seders. But this one girl I knew in junior high, Mia Finkelstein, who had a Jewish father and a Catholic mother, said no, her parents were always arguing over whether to send her to Hebrew School or Sunday School, and whether she should be baptized or bat mitzvahed. She said she was so confused, she wasn't sure what she believed. I heard she's now a practicing Wiccan.

Other kids I know said their parents just picked one faith and went with it. But if Luke and I had to just pick one, how would we pick? Who would give up what? How would we decide?

It all makes my head ache, so I decide to think about happier thoughts: counting down the days until Sully's New Year's Eve party. I want to scrap my old New Year's Resolutions and create my *new*, New Year's Resolutions, so I pull out my list and revise the page for the third time.

MY NEW, NEW YEAR'S RESOLUTIONS

1. ~~For~~ Get ~~heathens like~~ Luke Christiansen
to kiss me on New Year's Eve

2. ~~Flirt madly with appropriate So Very boys~~
~~like Aidan Levine.~~ See above

3. Wash face ~~every~~ twice a day with
Proactive Solution

4. ~~Stop biting nails. (This year I really~~
~~mean it)~~ Don't let my mother catch me
biting my nails

5. ~~Get to geometry on time.~~ Flunk geometry

6. And, oh yeah, **STOP LETTING MY PARENTS**
CONTROL MY LIFE!

7. Break the Teen Commandments

"HAVE FUN, GIRLS," my dad calls out as Jen and I
flee his minivan in front of Sully's house. It took several
hours of high-level negotiations to extend my curfew, but
he's promised to come pick us up no sooner than one hour
after midnight, no excuses. At least this beats last New Year's
Eve, when Jen and I commandeered her parents' basement
and sat around in our pajamas all night long, playing with her
Ouija board, reading Tarot cards, and trying to conjure up
mad passion in our future. "I can't believe I'm stuck celebrating New Year's Eve at my grandma's condominium in
Florida," Leah moaned over the phone earlier today. "You
have to call and tell me everything."

My game plan tonight is simple: position myself in
close proximity to Luke at around 11:45 P.M., just in
case he's inclined to finally consummate our missed mistletoe kiss when the clock strikes twelve. Could it be possible
he doesn't go for stodgy traditions like mistletoe, but
does believe in the even stodgier tradition of New Year's

kisses at the stroke of midnight? I'm hoping so.

Naturally I spot Luke the second I come in the door. But amazingly, this time, he spots me, too. As he walks up to me, I can see he is wearing faded jeans and a white T-shirt that reads, JESUS IS MY HOMEBOY. I am so glad to see him, I excuse his sorry taste in fashion and barely even notice when Jen and Matt wander off, leaving us alone for the first time that night.

Somehow we sink into a nearby couch and begin talking about anything and everything: his season on the JV basketball team, the most embarrassing kind of music we admit we actually like—him, Shania Twain; me, Broadway show tunes—and our most traumatic childhood memories. Somehow we end up on our favorite reality TV shows.

"*Survivor*," Luke says. "I totally could win. I've been in Boy Scouts since I was six."

"Gross." I wrinkle my nose. "I could never eat one of those bugs. Plus, you don't get access to a hair dryer." Thanks to Pedro, now I can't imagine going a month on national TV without my defrizzer.

He laughs. "You wouldn't make it in my family, then. Every summer, my dad takes us upstate for a week of hardcore camping. We don't bring anything. It's like Extreme Outward Bound."

I try to imagine my mom and dad camping, but I'm not sure they would even get the concept. *Why would anyone want to sleep outside, in the cold, on the ground*, I can hear my mother asking. My family's idea of roughing it is staying in a one-star motel.

"Worst show ever?" he asks.

"Who Wants to Marry a Millionaire," I say with confidence. "Totally sexist premise. Best show ever?"

"The Real World. It kick-started the whole genre. Best villain?"

"Hmmm. Omarosa from *The Apprentice?*"

"Fat naked Richard from the first *Survivor.* A classic Machiavellian antihero. And a convicted tax-evader."

While we talk, Luke casually drapes his arm around the sofa, right above my neck. Then he lets it drop down, cradling my shoulders. It's painfully heavy; the weight of his long arm presses hard into my bony shoulders and crimps my neck at an unnatural angle.

Nothing has ever felt better in my entire life.

In the background, someone is shouting: "Fifteen minutes to midnight," and flipping the channel on the jumbo HDTV to *Ryan Seacrest's New Year's Rocking Eve.*

I can't believe it's already 11:45. The evening has swooped by; Luke and I have been talking nonstop for at least two hours about everything and nothing, really.

"So have you made your New Year's resolutions yet?" he asks.

"Have you?" I stall.

"Sure."

151

"What are they?"

"I'll tell you mine if you tell me yours."

Considering he was resolution Number One, I decide to change the subject. Fast.

"So," I say teasingly, "you believe in archaic rituals like New Year's resolutions—"

"I'm all in favor of self-improvement."

11:46.

"—but not others?"

"Like?"

"Ummm . . . mistletoe?"

"I'm not real motivated by hanging shrubbery."

"I like rituals." I shrug.

"Like?"

"Watching the ball drop in Times Square." I gesture at the TV screen. "Singing 'Auld Lang Syne.' Champagne toasts."

He moves closer. "A kiss at midnight?"

11:47.

My heart is beating wildly. "I . . . I . . . sure."

"I don't believe in that."

It falls with a thud.

"But I do believe in kisses at, oh, 11:48," he murmurs, pulling me toward him with his arm, his other hand creeping around my waist. My stomach free-falls into my knees. This is the moment, I just know it. I can feel his breath, hot, closing in on my mouth. I tilt my head, determined to avoid the dreaded nose bump, when . . .

152

When suddenly I hear my name being called out, even over Eminem's latest rant-a-thon blasting through the speakers. "Rachel Lowenstein? Is Rachel Lowenstein here?"

What the %*#^*% ?????????

I twist around and see Sully scanning the crowd. I raise my hand tentatively. Have I won some kind of door prize?

"Your parents are here," he shouts.

Your parents are here?

YOUR PARENTS ARE HERE??

My parents are here.

It can't be. It absolutely positively cannot be. But it is.

I jump up and stumble, shell-shocked, past Sully, toward the front entryway, certain I hear snickers all around me. Luke follows me into the foyer, although part of me is wishing he wouldn't. What does he think of my parents showing up in the middle of a New Year's Eve party? And, just as bad, what will they think, getting a good look at him?

My mom and dad are standing awkwardly in the hallway, looking like confused lambs who just wandered into a Satanic ritual sacrifice. Why are both of them here? It was supposed to be just my dad picking me up.

"What are you doing here?" I say angrily, trying to keep my voice down. "It's not even midnight yet. You said an hour after!! I can't believe—"

"Rach," my dad says slowly. "It's your grandmother."

I know something is horribly wrong by the way he says grandmother instead of bubbe.

"Bubbe?" I croak.

"Come on, let's get in the car," he says, gently taking my elbow.

"What is it? What's wrong?" My chest suddenly feels tight and hot.

"She's suffered a massive heart attack, honey," my mom says softly, looking pale.

It didn't make sense. "But I just saw her," I say, confused.

"She's at Mount Sinai Medical Center. We need to get there now, tonight."

"Is she"—I can't say the word—"Is she going to be all right?"

She pauses, a hesitation that tells me everything I don't want to know. My dad answers instead. "We don't know."

When I turn around, Luke is gone. He must have slipped back into the living room to avoid intruding on our family drama. What a relief. This isn't exactly the best time for a formal introduction.

We're halfway out the door, when I stop short. "Wait, what about Jen? We're supposed to drive her home."

"Go find her, hurry."

I dash back into the living room, frantically looking for her. The room is a blur of confetti and noisemakers.

"TEN!"

All around me, people are counting down, chanting along with the television.

"NINE!"

I race upstairs, quickly checking the bedrooms, but Jen is nowhere to be found. I realize I haven't seen her in hours.

"EIGHT!"

Suddenly, someone grabs my shoulder. Luke!

"SEVEN!"

"Are you okay?" He looks down at me, concerned.

"SIX!"

"Have to go . . . hospital . . . my bubbe," I blubber, indifferent to the mascara-laden tears dripping down my cheeks. "But I can't find Jen!"

"FIVE!"

He looks squirmy, not sure how to handle a hysterical female.

"FOUR!"

"Don't worry," he says, taking my hand and giving it an awkward squeeze and release. "We'll make sure she gets home safe."

"THREE!"

"Thanks," I say, but it comes out a whisper.

"TWO!"

I want to say more. So many things are being left unknown: where we stand, whether I'll see him again. But the time is not right.

"ONE!"

"Go," he says, gently pushing me toward the door, toward my parents.

"HAPPY NEW YEAR!"

Even in this hour of darkness, in the midst of all the celebratory madness, I can see my parents checking him out from a distance, scrutinizing his blond hair, Aryan features— and his JESUS IS MY HOMEBOY T-shirt.

chapter 23

FORTY-EIGHT HOURS LATER, I'm sitting in a pew at my first funeral service, comfortably numb. The last two days have been a blur. First the urgent late-night phone calls and the sterile hospital waiting room, then my mom's face crumpling when the white-coated doctor came out of intensive care, all apologetic, and finally, the selection of the plain pine box.

Even now, none of it seems real. I've been trying to cry all day, but I can't force a single tear to form.

In the distance, I can hear Rabbi Wasserman sermonizing about my bubbe, saying how life is a circle, that she lived well, left the legacy of a loving family with devoted children and grandchildren.

I still can't believe she is gone. Just like that. I know it sounds terrible, but instead of thinking about her death, all that keeps running through my mind is that life is so short. I mean, sure, eighty-three years sounds like forever, but I'm sure for her it went by in the blink of an eye. Her death is making my own life flash before my eyes. And instead of wanting to honor her wishes, it makes those choices seem so wrong. Be a good girl. Do the right thing. Worry about my future. Enroll in the Honor Society because it looks good on the college apps. Yawn. Why bother, when it could all go *kabloooey!* tomorrow? Her lecture at Thanksgiving had almost made me reconsider my plan. But her death is forcing me to realize the greater truth: the only thing to do is live for today, seize the moment, and keep breaking the Teen Commandments as hard and fast as I dare.

After the service, we line up in the back of the mahogany-paneled memorial room as family and friends trickle by, consoling my family. Howard and his parents appear before us. After having a stream of elderly relatives pat me on the head, it's good to see someone my own age. Then I remember our fight outside the house that day. I tense, readying myself for some typically snide comment.

But instead he shocks me, enveloping me in a giant bear hug. His arms feel nice and strong. Sturdy. I try not to sniffle onto his blazer lapel. "I'm sorry," Howard says simply, exactly the right response. What had we bickered about, anyway? It all seems so petty now. "I always liked your grandma. You know, the last time I talked to her, on Rosh Hashanah? I told her I had made the track team and she told me to stay away from steroids. Except she kept pronouncing it steer-oids." He wags his finger imitating her.

We both laugh, while it occurs to me that even Bubbe

had noticed Howard's new muscular physique before I had.

"She was a woman who spoke her mind," he says with admiration.

Funny, I got the sense he didn't like girls like that. Demanding and outspoken. But that was Bubbe to a tee.

"It was so like her to give some crazy warning like that." Talking about her, laughing about her traits, makes me feel a little better for the first time today. "Only, for me, the order was 'stay away from the *goyim*!' Can you believe that?"

He nods. "Sounds just like my grandparents. Although they'd never actually say it that way."

We meander out into the front of the funeral hall, where we sit on the concrete steps. For some reason, I find myself telling him all about Bubbe and Luke. "Well, what would you do?" I ask.

"Tough one," he says pensively. "You get the big guilt trip, and then she's gone. What do you think she would have said?"

"I told you," I say impatiently. "She would have freaked."

"Maybe, maybe not." He shrugs. "Maybe she would have surprised you."

"I doubt it. Bubbe *hated* surprises." The first words out of her mouth when we all threw her a surprise eightieth birthday party a couple years back were "Such a fuss, you didn't need to make."

"What about your parents?"

"They're just as bad," I say, thinking of what my mom said

at the wedding. "Can you believe it? I mean, who exactly do they expect me to date?"

He shoots me a piercing look and then says, "I don't know. I guess . . . you shouldn't be with someone just because your parents like him. They're not the ones who have to be with him—you do."

"You're lucky," I sigh. "Your family's probably all thrilled with Tara."

Howard shrugs sheepishly, almost like he is embarrassed I brought her up. "Yeah, although mostly I think my dad's just relieved I'm not gay," he confesses with a grin. It's a relief to talk to Howard the way we used to when we were younger, when we weren't constantly trying to put one another down.

"Rachel!" Ben pops his head out the door. "Mom says the limos out back are leaving. We have to go."

"All right." I stand up, snapped back into the somber formality of the occasion. "Well, thanks."

"Anytime." He nods.

As I walk away, for the first time in a long time, part of me doesn't want our conversation to end. Who would have guessed that Howard the wiseass would turn out to be so wise?

chapter 24

AFTER THE FUNERAL, we all collapse back into the house for some serious shivah sitting, the weeklong mourning process. It's odd: even though my parents generally aren't all that devout, at times like this they fall back into ultratraditional ways. As is customary, my mother has thrown sheets over all the mirrors, the thinking being, you shouldn't be obsessing over a bad hair day at a time like this. Naturally, this being a Jewish ritual, it involves inhaling massive quantities of chopped liver and borscht to bolster our strength. And we all have to wear tiny black ribbons or rip tiny tears in our outfits. This actually was a breeze for me, as most of my outfits already are black and often worn down to the nub. I go upstairs, wiggle out of my black skirt, and throw on a pair of ripped black jeans and a black T-shirt.

When I come back down, everyone is sitting pensively in our family room, trying not to say the wrong thing. My dad gazes out the window, clearly wishing he were anywhere else. My Aunt Adelle and Aunt Merle are distracting themselves by making sure all the food is set out. Ben stomps up to his room, to escape into the grisly two-dimensional world of death and sorrow, rather than face the all-too-real three-dimensional one. My parents watch him leave without comment, although I get the feeling I wouldn't be allowed off the hook so easily.

"She lived a full life, Syl," my dad says soothingly. "Eighty-three years old. That's something."

"I know." I've never seen my mom looking so melancholy, not even when she used to cover the cop beat and had to write up car crashes and stabbings every night. "She just never fully recovered after that stroke."

Stroke? What is she talking about?

"She was stronger then," my dad points out. "She really faded this year."

"What stroke?" I demand, now glad I had stayed.

My mom shoots him a look even I can read as "You idiot."

"Honey, Bubbe had a serious stroke three years ago, when you were away at Camp Kinder Ring."

I can't believe it. A stroke. How had I never known about this?

"We didn't want to upset you at the time," my dad says. "You were having such a nice summer."

Hmmph. As usual, rumors of my delight were highly exaggerated. Camp Kinder Ring, where I went every summer, was a sleepover camp that pandered to preteen JAPs-In-Training, run by the Workmen's Circle. The only real

162

"work" going on there was campers color-coordinating their socks to their scrunchies.

"I wasn't having such a nice summer," I grumble, although it is long beside the point. Nice to find out years after the fact that, while I was weaving friendship bracelets to curry favor with my bitchy bunk mates, my only living grandmother was lying in some hospital room. And they didn't want to upset me?

All at once I realize how little I actually knew my grandma. My dad's parents died years before I was born. My grandpa, Bubbe's husband, died when I was a little girl. Bubbe was the only grandparent I'd ever really known. I knew she and my grandfather had once run a hat shop and traveled extensively, but lately, the highlight of her week seemed to be bingo at St. Joseph's and her weekly Hadassah meetings.

All this time, if I'd only known she was so frail, I could have been an infinitely better granddaughter. I wouldn't have blown off visits so often. I could have begged her to teach me how to make that matzo ball soup, guaranteed to kill off any cold. I could have listened harder when she talked, maybe videotaped her when she told that story of how her family escaped from Europe for a history project, or something.

The sense of her loss, which seemed so unreal during the memorial service and burial, now hits me with full force. I should have been there. I should have known she was sick. I should have been informed. How could my mother not tell me this? My mother may have worked in the media industry, but she wants me to live in an information-free zone.

"I can't believe you never told me she had a stroke!" I say.

"Honey, what difference does it make now?"

They don't get it. Haven't they learned anything from history? Look at Bill Clinton's hanky-panky, or Nixon and Watergate. The cover-up is always worse than the crime.

Which is exactly what I inform them.

"How could you suppress key evidence after the fact!" I say, like one of the interchangeable female prosecutors on *Law & Order*.

It makes me wonder what other nasty little secrets they might be keeping from me. An imminent divorce? New baby brother? A cross-country move? Why should I be kept in the loop? I'm just a member of this dysfunctional family.

My father springs to her defense. "Don't raise your voice to your mother."

"It wasn't a secret," my mom pleads. "We just didn't want you to worry."

The way my parents are always protecting me from danger—from date rape, child molesters, drunk drivers—I don't like it, but on some level I get it. But sheltering me from my own reality is another thing.

"You can't protect me—from everything—from the world," I sputter.

I'd been feeling guilt-ridden over my geometry bust-up, my drunken escapade, my illicit crush on Luke, but now I feel totally exonerated. They don't want to keep me informed? Fine. But it works both ways. My parents are on a need-to-know basis from here on out. And there's nothing they need to know.

"Honey—"

"Fine." I cross my arms. "You keep your secrets and I'll keep mine."

Then I storm out of the room.

Okay, maybe I got a little carried away by my grief. Normally I'm not such a drama queen. But in retrospect, it's a good thing I did.

Because, on my way upstairs, I hear a soft knock on the front door.

I open the door, and standing there is Luke.

chapter 25

"HEY. I HOPE IT'S COOL I came over. Matt gave me your address. I just wanted to see how you were doing," he says in a rush, the words tumbling out of his mouth. He looks like he came straight from practice. His hair is still slightly damp, and he's wearing a sweat-stained St. Joseph's basketball jersey, gray sweatpants, and a pair of high-tops. Then he pauses. "Is your grandmother . . . okay?"

"No, she—" I gulp down the word. He looks down at my all-black outfit, and I don't need to finish the sentence.

"Oh. Jeez. I'm sorry," he says, thrusting his hands into his pockets; then, realizing that his sweatpants don't have pockets, he just rocks back and forth uncomfortably.

"We're sitting shivah."

"Shivah?" Luke repeats the foreign word carefully, like he's scared of mispronouncing it.

"It's what we call mourning."

"Oh. I guess I should go, then," he says, backing away as

though I just told him I have a highly contagious flesh-eating bacterial disease.

In my head, all I can hear are my bubbe's last words: "Rachel, don't go vith the *goyim*." Part of me still wants to honor her request, really I do. It was her dying wish, practically. Who am I to deny it?

But here is Luke, standing on my doorstep, looking undeniably cute and *concerned*.

"Wait." I stop him. "Do you want to take a walk?" I gesture to the street. "I could use some air." I have to get out of here. Besides, all I need is for my parents to come out and for Luke to be standing here. So far they've been too caught up in funeral arrangements to remember to ask me about the boy they glimpsed on New Year's Eve.

"Are you sure?"

"Mm-hmm."

We begin slowly strolling up the sidewalk. Neither of us knows what to say. Out of nowhere, Luke asks, "Have you ever been to an Irish wake?"

"No," I say.

"Oh. Well, in a traditional Irish wake, there's a band playing live music, and everyone dances. And gets wasted."

I've never heard of such a thing. "Really? Weird."

"Yeah. It's supposed to be a celebration of their life and a send-off to heaven."

"Cool." I smile at Luke—my second smile of the day. In fact, I like the concept of a wake so much, I make a mental note to come up with a playlist for my own funeral. Just in case. If it were left up to my parents, they'd probably play something like "The Wind Beneath My Wings."

"How do you know about that?" I ask.

"Oh, my mom's side is all Irish Catholic. I've got six uncles. But believe me, they don't need someone to kick it as an excuse to party." He stops short, realizing what he just said, and gives me an embarrassed look. "Sorry."

"It's okay," I say.

We stand there awkwardly, but there's nothing left to say, so we both turn and continue walking. That's when I feel his arm brush against mine. This is no time to be feeling a jolt of electricity shoot through my body. But I do.

"I actually came over to ask you a question." He hesitates. "Maybe this isn't a good time."

I know what he is about to say. I can just tell. If he stops now, maybe I'll never have another chance.

"No, it's okay," I say, sneaking a peek at his profile.

"So, is it cool if I call you sometime?" he asks.

I'll admit it, for about half a second that stretches into eternity, I am torn.

My relatives would disapprove. My parents would forbid it. My bubbe would flip over in her grave. Now that she's gone, I realize, she'll never be able to forgive me.

"Definitely." I smile, while fighting back the urge, finally, to cry.

chapter 26

BY THE TIME I SLIP back inside the house, my extended family has already left. After dinner, my parents call me out into the living room for a "talk." I know right away it has to be something serious. Living room is a misnomer: no living ever takes place in there. Every time they usher us in to sit on the stiff embroidered sofas, alongside the fingerprint-free glass coffee table and the breakfront full of my mom's collection of porcelain tchochkes, you know something is wrong. There's only one thing they could possibly want to talk about: they somehow got a whiff of Luke. They must have seen us when he walked me back home after our mid-shivah stroll. Or maybe they recognized him as the Catholic boy from the New Year's Eve party. My parents have practically perfect J-dar—the ability to tell whether or not someone is Jewish—from several hundred feet away. Clearly they are going to ask about him—and I have no idea what to say. Do I come clean, give them the benefit of the doubt, as Howard had suggested? Or hold out and continue to break the Teen Commandments?

"We just want to see what's going on with you," my dad begins.

"I'm fine," I say, tensing myself for the Big Question: *Who was that boy we saw you with?*

"Is there anything you want to share with us?" my mom presses.

I try to think if there's a right way to mention Luke. *Actually, there is something. This boy has asked me out, and I'd really like to . . .*

But my mom takes my hesitation for a no. "We were wondering, honey, if you might like to, you know, talk to someone."

Talk to someone? What is she talking about?

"Aren't we talking now?"

They exchange looks.

"No, we mean a professional," my mom says gently.

"You've been really moody lately." My dad jumps in. "Acting out at Thanksgiving, and now with Bubbe . . ."

I may be a little slow, but I know exactly what they mean. A shrink. My parents officially think I'm crazy. I mean, I am going crazy, but I'm not mentally ill.

"I don't need to talk to anyone," I protest, wondering if my parents intend to ship me off to an insane asylum, like in that Winona Ryder/Angelina Jolie movie about wayward girls, if I refuse.

My mother frowns. "You've been really withdrawn, tired every morning. You haven't gotten involved in any after-school activities."

170

I can tell she is citing one of her latest brochures, maybe even one she wrote: *Eight signs your child may be suffering from clinical depression.*

"I'm sorry if I'm not a joiner." I fold my arms across my chest.

Now it's my dad's turn to frown. "Look, we understand you may not want to tell us things—"

Like you didn't tell me about Bubbe, I think.

"—but it might really help to have someone to talk to."

"It's your first time losing someone you care about," Mom says. "It might be good for you —"

"I don't need to see a shrink!"

"It doesn't have to be a psychologist!" my mom quickly counters. "We were thinking it could be a counselor at your school, or maybe Rabbi Wasserman?" She trails off.

Right, just what I need. *Rabbi Wasserman, can you tell me how to grieve properly for my grandmother's death? Oh, and by the way, would it be all right with you if I defied her dying wish and snuck behind my parents' back to date this Catholic guy, putting an end to future Lowenstein bar mitzvahs you can preside over in perpetuity?*

I'm sure he'd have plenty of relevant counsel.

"Just think about it," my mom pleads.

"Actually," I say coolly. "I'd rather handle this my own way."

I just have no idea what that way would be.

chapter 27

IT'S OUR FIRST DAY back after the holiday break, and already we're off to an unpromising start. "I'd like you two to stop by later today," Mr. Diamenties murmurs to Wayne and me, as he places our second math test facedown on our desks. I know without even flipping it over the news is not good.

That's because I kinda planned it that way.

It was an experiment, you understand, to see whether my Theory of Inverse Math and Popularity Correlation held true. I wanted to see whether the worse I failed a math test, the more Aidan and Wayne would talk to me. Yeah, it was killing my GPA, but I figure, if I can prove my ground-breaking theorem before the end of the semester, I could publish it in the *American Journal of Mathematics*, and Mr. Demented would have to acknowledge my computational cleverness and give me an A.

I don't have much time, though: the inevitable midterm and report card are looming. My parents have been distracted by my stellar PSAT results, which came in right before the holidays. With a solid 180, they haven't pressed to see any of my math tests since, assuming everything is under control.

I take a peek at the test, then place it down, trying to morph the smile on my lips into sorrow. "Come back during your lunch period," Diamentis orders us. "I'll be here."

In front of me, Aidan flips his test over and high-fives his seatmate in relief. Clearly he has squeaked by. He turns and grabs my test, as I knew he would.

"Gimme." I halfheartedly try to grab it back, but he is already taking in the red slashes and whistling at the results.

"Well, well, well," he leers. "I thought you were a brain. Looks like you could use some *private* tutoring." He winks at Wayne, who, to his credit, has already slipped on his MP3 headphones and is ignoring both of us.

"That's okay," I say, swiping back the paper and shoving it in my bag. I view Aidan's growing attention to me purely as a scientific experiment. I'm too into Luke to be flattered by his advances. Still, I can't totally dismiss the social satisfaction of having a So Very guy openly pursuing me.

I slowly get out of my seat to leave, and sure enough, Aidan trails after me.

"So, are you a party girl like your friend Jen?" Aidan bends over, whispering lasciviously in my ear.

I scowl up at him. "What?" God, he is gi-normous. His height is simultaneously appealing and intimidating.

"I heard about your exploits over the holidays."

I'm not sure what he's talking about. Had Matt told him about the Eggnog Incident? "Yeah, we got a little buzzed at this party," I say casually.

He snickers knowingly. "That's not all, I hear."

"What do you mean?"

The first bell rings. I'm going to be late to homeroom, but I need to find out what he's talking about. But he is already slinging the strap of his bag across his chest. "Later." He grins, striding cockily down the hall.

Aidan is undeniably a jerk. A big one. But last year, when I had frizzy hair and sat in front and raised my hand to answer every question and got straight A's in math, he never would have glanced my way, let alone propositioned me. I almost, not really, sorta like it.

I'm sick.

"Rach, over here." Jen waves me down at our usual table in the cafeteria. "How are you?" She looks concerned, scanning my face for signs of depression. Since my grandmother's funeral, Jen and Leah have been tiptoeing around me like I'm an invalid, in some misguided notion of concern. What I really need is for everyone to let me get back to normal.

"I can't stay long," I tell her. "Diamenties wants to see me this period. I failed my math test."

Jen groans in sympathy. "Can't you tell him you were distraught about your grandmother?"

"I took the test before she died, Jen."

She pauses to consider, then brightens. "Details, details. He doesn't have to know that. Tell him she was sick, that you were worried about her."

Since she's been hanging out with the So Verys, Jen's grasp on ethical behavior has been slipping, too.

I change the subject, thinking of Aidan's weird remark. "So, with my grandmother and everything, I never got to say I'm sorry we ditched you New Year's Eve. I looked all over—"

"Don't even worry about it," Jen says quickly. "I totally understand. I got a ride home with Matt. So . . ." She leans in conspiratorially. "Are you all set for this weekend?"

Luke finally called me late last night and asked me out for this Saturday. Naturally, I called Jen immediately afterward to help me craft a plan. With my parents still caught up in their period of mourning, now would definitely not be a good time to come clean.

"I think so," I reply with a sigh. It would be so much easier if Luke weren't . . . well . . . Luke. "So, if my mom calls you for any reason—"

"I'll say you're with me, but that your phone must still be turned off from the movie. And then I'll call you right away so you can call her back."

"What if she calls your house?"

"Alissa and I are going to the Village anyway, so I'll just tell my mom it's the three of us so she won't blow your cover."

I feel a pang of jealousy. Going shopping in the Village was *our* weekly ritual. Is Alissa replacing me in the rotation?

"You're going with Alissa?"

"Well, Matt has a debate on Saturday."

"Yeah, but, *Alissa??*"

"Yeah, she wants to scope out the animal research labs at N.Y.U.—What??" Jen stares at me, then sighs. "Can't you give anyone a chance, ever?"

"What does that mean?"

"I mean, sometimes I think you try to dis the whole world before it gets to dis you first. No offense."

It was so untrue. Sort of. Besides, call me cynical, but there are some things you just know are going to turn out bad in the end. Being friends with one of the So Verys is one of them. Why can't Jen see that?

I notice Jen had changed the subject without ever accounting for her whereabouts on New Year's Eve. "So where were you New Year's Eve? I checked upstairs . . ."

She leans toward me. "Okay, I'll tell you, but you have to promise not to freak out."

I tense, trying to prepare myself for what she is going to say. It could only be one thing. She hooked up with Matt. Seriously hooked up.

"You didn't . . ." I make the international *You Know* nod of my head. Before Matt came along, Jen was as virginal as I was, but these days, you never knew.

She shakes her head. "Matt wants to . . . but we've only been dating for two months."

I nod.

"I'm going to make him wait until we've been together at least *three* months."

"Really?"

"Of course," she says, as if a three-month minimum is a rule everyone in the universe knows but me.

"So what did happen the night of the party?"

She giggles, leans back in her chair, and brags, "A couple of us went down to the basement to play poker. Strip poker."

"Who?" I demand.

"Me, Matt, Mick, Sully, that girl Shannon."

"Oh my God," I say, half in admiration, half in horror.

My mind reels. Strip poker. Jen's bravado has risen to new heights. I'm self-conscious just undressing in the girls' locker room, let alone in front of a bunch of high-school boys. Truthfully, I don't even feel comfortable getting butt naked in my own room, paranoid some perv with a Polaroid might be peeping through the shades. But I guess your perspective changes once you have something to show off in the chestal area, like Jen.

"I know! I thought it would be regular poker, but then somehow, the guys suggested we play strip poker. I don't know how Matt talked me into it."

"So what happened?"

She laughs. "Let's just say I lost pretty badly. I don't remember much, I was pretty wasted."

I'm not sure whether to be jealous, impressed, or sickened. "I'm sorry we didn't include you," she says, misreading the mixture of emotions on my face as hurt. "You were so wrapped up talking to Luke, I didn't want to tear you away."

"What if people find out?"

"Most of them don't even go to school here." She shrugs. "Besides, everyone was sworn to secrecy."

I can't bear to tell her that her little secret might be out.

chapter 28

WHEN I ARRIVE at Room number 401, Diamenties is already leaning in the doorway waiting for me. "Miss Lowenstein, I presume," he drawls. "Here for the meeting of the High Counsel?"

I swear, the man is like Satan. Good thing that, besides heaven, we also don't happen to believe in eternal damnation and the gates of hell. "So," he says, gesturing for me to come in, and perching on top of his desk he says, "I was talking to Mr. Fried in the faculty lunchroom, and he mentioned that you were his star pupil last year in algebra. We can't figure out what happened to you."

Easy. You sat me in the back of the class and yelled at me every time I was late from gym class and never called on me when I did know the answer and only called on me when you thought I didn't and eventually I lost any interest I had to begin with and didn't want to look like a math geek and started talking to Wayne and Aidan—and they started talking back.

"I dunno." I shrug.

"Do you want me to change your seat?" he asks. "Maybe you get distracted in the back of the room. Or . . . if certain people are . . . a bad influence on you."

"No!" I protest. "That's not it."

There's no way I want to give up the newfound respect I've earned from being in the back row. Even if it does cost me academic points, the social value—invites to football games, getting hit on by Aidan—is priceless.

"So what's going on here?"

"I just don't see the point."

"The point?"

"Math is for people who want to be accountants, number crunchers, like my father," I inform him. "Which I don't want to be." *Or a high-school math teacher, like you.*

"Not necessarily." He frowns. "There are many fascinating professions that require a solid grounding in math besides accounting."

"Like what?"

He tries listing a few. "Mechanical engineering. Business strategy consulting. Actuarial for an insurance firm." I give him a death stare. Do I look like someone who would enjoy calculating people's risk of death? Maybe I am wearing too much black.

"Look," he says. "I'll make you a deal. I believe you just got off to a bad start. But you can recover. So if you can pull an A on the midterm, I'll weigh it heavily toward your final grade and throw out the earlier tests."

It's a tempting deal. I know if I want to, I can figure out a way to catch up. And visions of schools like Stanford and Cal Tech dance in my head. But how to maintain my numerically-challenged credibility?

There's only one way. But I'll need an accomplice.

"It's a deal," I say. "On one condition."

"Hit me," he says, like we're playing blackjack.

"Whatever I get on the midterm, you won't announce it to the whole class, and you'll still put it facedown on my desk."

He gives me a puzzled look. "I guess."

Then we see Wayne poke his head in the glass window of the door. "Wayne, one minute." He waves his hand. "We're about done here, right, Rachel?" He turns back to me with a look of growing recognition. "Just remember, in the long run, what your seatmates think of your ability matters less and less—and your ability matters more and more."

Right, Mr. Demented. Thanks for the kung fu fortune cookie wisdom. I saunter out of the room and nod at Wayne as he enters. I mean to head right back to the cafeteria to finish my lunch with Jen. But the first sentence out of Diamenties's mouth as I'm shutting the door stops me short.

"I don't understand, Wayne," Diamenties is saying. "According to our records, you're the only sophomore who scored a perfect eighty on your math PSAT. So clearly, you have an aptitude for the subject."

What is this? Wayne, the back-of-the room slacker

hacker, the rookie bookie, had outscored, well, every-one? Even brain-boy Josh Green? Even me? There was no way.

"And your fifth-grade IQ test placed you at 146 . . ."

Well, well, well. Behind those shades, Wayne was actually the class Brainiac.

Mr. Genius mumbles something unintelligible.

I don't want to eavesdrop or anything, of course, so I just press my ear a teensy bit against the door to better hear his response.

Diamenties begins lecturing him. "I don't understand why you're not living up to that potential. Don't you want to get into a top college?"

Wayne finally says something I can hear clearly. "Hackers don't need a degree," he says flatly.

"But there are several excellent computer science programs: MIT, Stanford, Carnegie Mellon. With your scores . . ."

Wayne grunts something in response I can't catch. Apparently, Diamenties doesn't catch it either.

"What was that?" he demands.

"Bill Gates dropped out of Harvard," Wayne repeats. "He did okay."

"But he got *in* to Harvard," Diamenties parries. "At the rate you're going, you won't have a chance at SUNY Binghamton. Look, I know you think geometry has nothing to do with programming. But computer-assisted designers, video game designers, they all need to understand geometric fundamentals."

Wayne doesn't respond, so I can't tell if he is rolling his eyes or taking Demented's words into consideration. It sounds pretty convincing to me, but I want to be a game designer as little as I want to be an accountant.

"Look, here's some brochures about the computer science program at MIT. Read them. Or do your own research. I think you'll be intrigued. Then let's talk again."

"Fine," Wayne grumbles. I can hear him gathering the papers and stuffing them into his book bag. The sad thing is, Wayne would probably really get off on being at MIT, if he weren't too cool to admit it. My cousin Zach went there, and the students' antiestablishment pranks were legendary, like putting a car on top of the school's Dome. I'm trying to remember how he said they'd done it, when suddenly Wayne throws open the door and steps out of the classroom. His eyes flash when he sees me. What had I heard? Clearly, everything.

I try to look nonchalant, like I always hang out in empty hallways, but it is a lost cause.

"I . . . I . . ." I stammer, straining to think of a legit excuse for why I am still standing here in the hallway, picking my butt. "Math camp," I choke out, pointing at a tattered poster hanging by a lifeline to the pockmarked bulletin board.

But we exchange a glance, and I know he knows I know everything, if that makes sense. It's like one of those

183

annoying exchanges my parents do when they're deciding on whether or not to tell me something when I'm standing right there.

"What did he tell you?" he asks.

"That he'd toss this test if I bring up my grade on the midterm," I say quickly. "You?"

"That I'm MIT material," he snorts. "Right." He eyes me warily, as if daring me to contradict him.

I shrug noncommittally and inspect my toes. "I can see you going there," I say quietly. "If you wanted to. With your scores."

He exhales heavily. "This stays between you and me," he says in a low tone, leaning in almost menacingly.

For once, I know exactly what to do.

"Yeah, sure," I say coolly. "Anyway, the way I heard it, you hacked the test."

He stares at me until his lips eventually crack into an almost imperceptible smile. He salutes me, then lowers his shades and saunters down the hallway.

chapter 29

IT'S ALMOST SCARY HOW easy it is to deceive my parents. I casually mentioned last night that Jen and I were going shopping in Greenwich Village, our standard Saturday ritual of browsing the thrift store castaways for fashion finds. Since I am technically going to the Village, not with Jen but with Luke, even my GPS phone won't give me away.

This morning I come downstairs to the kitchen, hoping to strategically bid them adieu from the doorway so they won't notice my sure-to-arouse-suspicion daytime date ensemble: carefully blown-out hair courtesy of Pedro, eye-lined eyes, best pair of jeans, and stiletto boots.

My mom insists I wear "slacks," as she calls them, whenever I go downtown, because she once saw this report on *Dateline* about "Upskirting," where creepy guys with tiny cameras take pictures up girls' skirts and post the shots on the Internet. Twisted, right? At first I thought it was just some urban legend she made up to get me to keep my legs crossed in public, but then it actually happened to Amanda Feinberg, this senior in my school.

"I'm off," I call from the doorway.

My dad is standing at the stove top, apron around his waist, spatula in his hand. "Rachel!" he booms like he's Emeril, the celebrity chef. "Matzo brei?"

Yuck. Matzo brei is basically a fried egg omelet with pieces of leftover matzo crumbled inside. Every Passover, my dad likes to spring for a couple of five-pound mega-boxes of Manischewitz matzos, bragging he's saving money by buying in bulk. Then he tries to foist stale, tasteless flat-bread on us the rest of the year. I'd hoped by now the supply had dwindled to nothing.

"Er, I'm okay."

My dad looks personally hurt by the rejection. "Are you sure?" He's proud of this culinary creation, the only thing he is capable of cooking. It's kind of sweet.

"Sorry, Dad, we're grabbing something downtown."

"Do you have money?" my mom calls out.

"Yeah."

"Yeah?" my mom mimics pointedly. Sometimes she likes to play linguistics police.

"Yes," I hiss back.

"Is your cell charged?" my dad wants to know.

"Uh-huh." They caught wise to the cell phone out of juice excuse for not checking in several trips ago. To stop the questioning, I try to change the subject. "What are you guys up to today?"

"Ben suggested we visit the Museum of Jewish Heritage," my mom says proudly.

I shoot Ben a suspicious look, but his head is buried in his plate as he inhales his matzo brei.

"It's for a school report, right, Ben?" my dad prompts, and Ben nods. "Sure you don't want to come?"

"No thanks," I say, backing out of the kitchen before anyone notices my outfit. "Well, I'm off."

"Be back by dinner."

"I will."

As planned, Luke meets me at the train station halfway between our houses. He looks adorably preppy, wearing khaki pants and a dark blue St. Joseph's sweatshirt. We smile shyly at each other, sliding our MetroCards through the turnstiles and tumbling out the other side. The whole ride downtown, my jittering nerves are indistinguishable from the rattling of the subway car. When we emerge from underground, I point toward our destination, the Angelika, this alternative movie theater known for its independent films. Luke buys me a large popcorn and Diet Coke, and a candy bar for himself, which strikes me as chivalrously decadent, since my family tends to smuggle in snacks.

The movie I suggested won a prize at the Sundance Film Festival and got rave reviews in *Time Out New York*. Yeah, it was foreign and filmed in black and white, but at least it wasn't the latest comic book superhero rehash.

I was just getting the hang of following the subtitles, when I notice Luke's left leg is bouncing up and down, twitching with nervous energy like he has ADD. I glance over at him, and instead of looking at the screen, his eyes are flickering around the darkened theater, then sneaking a peek at his watch. Clearly, he is bored silly. Luke must be thinking I'm a pretentious twit to have picked this movie. The whole thing has been a mistake. Why hadn't we just gone ice skating instead?

Suddenly Luke's leg gives a particularly robust jerk, and there is a flicker of contact against my own. It's like a JumboTron lights up inside me. *Whooosh!* Did he notice? I can't tell if his move was intentional or accidental. And then the leg is gone.

I suddenly become hyperaware of my own thigh, about three inches from his. I put my supersize soda in the cup holder and carelessly dangle my hand over my knee while I inch my leg millimeter by millimeter closer to his.

And then, wonder of wonder, miracle of miracles, his leg starts pressing firmly up against mine. It sort of stays there. Lingering. Meanwhile, the insane thing is, both of us pretend nothing out of the ordinary is happening. I can barely concentrate on the film. To be honest, I can barely concentrate on breathing. What next? Will he put his arm around me? Grab my hand? Or more?

On screen, the camera can't decide what to focus on,

zooming in and out on its main characters, but all I can focus on is the feeling of Luke's pants and the muscle of his thigh under them. I furiously stare straight ahead at the screen, not wanting to betray I'd even noticed our crash collision. Then Luke nonchalantly puts his hand on his own leg. I can see it resting there, just an inch from my own, but bigger, rougher. How do you give a come-hither look with your hand? Give the thumbs-up? Make a victory sign? An A-OK?

Before I know it, just like with our legs, our fingers brush tentatively, while both of us stare intently at the screen, intensely interested in the characters' dissection of the tragedy that had ripped them apart. Then, just like that, he takes my hand. His hand is nice. Gentle to touch, but a little callused on the fingertips, probably from basketball. Soon, Luke begins expertly stroking his thumb against my palm, slowly, then with this insistent . . . rhythm. It is driving me out of my mind and freaking me out all at the same time, while I pretend not to react. He grips my hand for the rest of the movie, dropping it only when the lights come up.

"That blew," Luke hoots as soon as we exit the theater.

I'm hurt. True, I'd stopped paying close attention to the movie in light of real-time events, but what I saw of the film was amazing. Anyway, in my mind, the movie experience hadn't been a *total* loss.

"It won some prize at Sundance," I protest.

"Give me a Will Ferrell flick any day," he says. "I don't go to movies to *read*."

"So you didn't like any part of it?" I ask, disappointed.

"All that psychobabble? And what happened at the end? I didn't get it." Finally he gets my point. "Some parts were great, though," he says, grabbing my hand and swinging it.

We make our way east across Houston Street, browsing in the retro clothing stores and used CD shops. When I look up, I find we are standing directly in front of a fluorescent sign that reads Katz's Delicatessen. "I know this place," I say without thinking, pointing to the rows of salamis hanging in the window. "My grandpa used to take us here when I was really little. He said they had the best pickles on the Lower East Side."

"I've heard of it. Do you want to go in?" Luke asks enthusiastically, eyeing the wave of customers making their way into the storefront. "I'm starving."

Go in? Is he kidding?

Katz's Deli isn't exactly my idea of a romantic first-date bistro. It's strictly old-school, with fluorescent lighting, cafeteria-style service, communal seating, and a distinct lunchroom meat-and-sauerkraut odor. It would be like eating at your high-school cafeteria on prom night.

"I guess . . ." I say, trying to hide my reluctance. We head inside, and I show Luke how to order our food from the gruff old men behind the counters. I pick out our meal: corned beef on rye, a hot dog loaded with sauerkraut and mustard, two sour pickles, two potato knishes, and two Dr. Brown's Cel Rey sodas. "This place is such a dive, it's cool," he whispers as we settle into a greasy wooden-topped table.

I begin to relax. Maybe he's right. Since my grandpa's day, Katz's Deli has become a retro hip place, where people go to see and be seen. Pictures of celebrities like Sarah Jessica Parker and Ben Stiller hang all over the walls. Maybe I'd stumbled onto a way to impress Luke with my New York know-how.

"Let's eat," he says. "I'm starving." We begin to tear into the tray of deli food.

I lean across the table. "Did you know they filmed that scene from *When Harry Met Sally* here?"

"What's *When Harry Met Sally*?" Luke asks, a puzzled look on his face.

I gasp in exaggerated disbelief at his male cluelessness. "You don't know that movie?" I'm about to berate him for not knowing my favorite romantic comedy of all time, but just then I hear a piercing voice calling my name. "Rachel? Sweetie? Is that you?"

When I turn, I see Mr. and Mrs. Goldstein, Howard's parents, heading toward us on their way out the door. Howard's dad is carrying a large salami in his arms.

I panic. We never should have come in here. But in a city this big, what was the chance of a random encounter with someone I know? I don't have time to calculate it, though, as Mrs. Goldstein is already saying, "Rachel, what are you doing here? What a surprise," and bending to air kiss me on the cheek, still managing to leave a red mark with her lipstick.

Without waiting to hear my response, she turns to Luke. "And who is this?"

Now what? Do I call Luke my friend, my boyfriend? I need to figure out the least incriminating way to introduce him so they'll forget to mention him to my parents if it ever comes up.

"This is Luke," I say simply.

Luke nods. "Nice to meet you." I watch Mrs. Goldstein mentally pulling out her stethoscope, conducting a full-body physical, then glancing back at me. I blush, like I've been caught cheating on Howard, or something. Crazy.

"What are you doing here?" I say quickly, distracting them.

"Oh, we're mailing a hard salami out to Cynthia," Mr. Goldstein says merrily, swinging the massive red protuberance our way. Howard's older sister, Cynthia, is a junior out at Stanford. "In California," he adds, waving his hand, dismissing the entire West Coast with a single gesture. The Goldsteins are lifelong New Yorkers, the kind who firmly believe intelligent life doesn't exist outside the Tri-State area.

"You can't find a really good Jewish salami outside of New York," Mrs. Goldstein agrees, as Luke and I eye the salami sticking between us like some giant phallic symbol and try not to giggle.

"So, Rachel, it was a lovely service for your grandmother," Mr. Goldstein says somberly, a little stiffly.

"Yes, it was." Mrs. Goldstein purses her ruby red lips. "I want to stop by this week. See how your mother is doing. Maybe drop off a fruit basket. What do you think, Sol?"

"Fruit's always good," he says.

She nods. "I'll do that. Come on, Sol, let's go. The meter's almost up."

"I'm sorry," I say as soon as they are gone, feeling embarrassed at the awkward encounter.

Luke doesn't say anything for a second. Then he leans in. "So . . . Cynthia misses her big New York salami," he says, lasciviously waggling his eyebrows. Boys can be so juvenile. But I can't help giggling along.

"Shut up!" I say, playfully whacking him on the arm. I take a pickle, suggestively stick it in my mouth, then laughingly take a giant bite.

"So what do you think?" I ask anxiously as he finishes his last bite of knish. I'm relieved to see he has wolfed everything down, even though knishes and pickles are easy to like— nothing compared to more gastronomically challenging fare, like gefilte fish.

"It's good," he says, leaning back in satisfaction. "I've never been big on ethnic food, but it's great."

"Good," I say, although something about his choice of words strikes me as odd. *Ethnic food?* I'd never thought of it that way. To me, it's just . . . food.

Luke insists on ordering a second corned beef sandwich

to go, but finally we are back outside, heading uptown into Alphabet City. I figure we're heading toward the subway and home, but Luke tugs my hand and drags me to a stop.

"Hey," he drawls. "Wanna go in?"

We're standing in front of a storefront with a pink neon sign: TATTOO.

I just laugh. Wait. Is he serious?

"Just for fun," he says, swinging open the door.

We step inside. A girl with multiple piercings and a tattoo of a snake running around her upper arm sits behind the counter. Counter Girl sizes up our peachy smooth skin in one dismissive glance. Underage. Suburban. Posers.

I'm not sure what Luke is thinking. He doesn't seem the tattooing type. Of course, if he wants to get my initials imprinted on his upper arm and swear his undying devotion, I'm not going to say no.

A large sign on the wall reads NO TATTOOING MINORS. NO EXCEPTIONS.

"Luke," I whisper nervously, hanging back by the door. "I think you have to be eighteen."

"Oh, come on," he says, smiling mysteriously.

I put my hand out toward his arm, as if to say let's go, but he is already marching up to the Alt-Culture chick, and leaning casually on the counter.

"My girlfriend is thinking of getting a tattoo," he announces.

I almost choke in surprise. He called me his girlfriend!

"Here's our book," she says, indifferent to the momentousness of the occasion, handing him a thick battered binder. "Take your time. Or we can do custom."

We haul the book to the other side of the room and huddle together, poring through its glossy pages of flowers, animals, hearts, and Looney Tunes characters. The options are endless. "How about a rose?" he whispers.

"What about a ladybug?" I say, starting to get into it. It was a game of Let's Pretend, like when Jen, Leeza, and I used to go to the Metropolitan Museum of Art on field trips in seventh grade and pick out what objets d'art we would someday use to furnish our dream home. Only this was much more sophisticated, obviously.

The ladybug is kind of cute. I can almost picture it on my ankle.

"No, here's what you should get," he chortles as we flip through the religious section of giant crosses, with Jesus writhing in agony.

"My mother would *kill* me," I say.

"Mine would kill *me*." He laughs in agreement. "And she's got them all over the house." He flips past to the next section, stopping and running his finger down the page.

"A heart would be sexy," he says. "Right here." He places his hand on the small of my back. And I almost die.

chapter 30

"WELL, OBVIOUSLY IT MEANS that he wants to have sex with you."

"What?"

It's Sunday morning, and Jen and I are deconstructing Luke's every move from our date, interpreting every significant moment. We'd just reached the mechanics of the in-movie thumb action.

"Rach, everyone knows that that's the international sign for 'I Want. To Have Sex. With You.'" Jen sighs heavily at the tediousness of having to explain the obvious to such a newbie. It's not worth pointing out that for all her worldly-wise attitude, she actually has only about three months' worth of dating experience on me. But in teen time, three months is like dog years. A lot can happen.

I had been thinking Luke was such a gentleman, barely making a move beyond hand holding. Even though my insides told me it was pretty intense for something seemingly so innocent. "So why did I get the cheek-kiss good-bye?" I demand.

After we left the tattoo parlor, it had grown dark and chilly, so Luke and I had headed back to the subway. Then he walked me to the bus and waited with me until it came, loaning me his sweatshirt for warmth. Then he pecked my cheek, and I hopped aboard, totally disappointed.

"Well, it was a daytime date. What was he gonna do? Jump you on the One-train platform? You've got to get together at night. Alone. In private. You should ask him to the Winter Dance."

"Since when are we going to that?"

"Of course we're going!" she insists. "At least, Matt and I are. I thought I told you?"

Hmm. No, she hadn't mentioned it, at least, not that I'd paid attention. Or, she hadn't brought it up until I had a guy to bring and wouldn't be a third wheel.

"I thought we'd made a blood pact against school dances," I remind Jen. "After last year?"

Last year, when we were pathetically overeager freshmen, Jen had insisted we go. We'd primped for hours, shown up stag, horribly overdressed and over made-up, looking like hookers, and basically spent the night getting jostled and ignored around the faux floral-decorated cafeteria. I'd retreated to the girls' bathroom in defeat, and sworn never, ever again.

"This year it's in the gymnasium, not the cafeteria," she

assures me. As though that made a huge difference. Instead of reeking of cauliflower soup, it'll reek of gym shorts.

"Oh, in that case . . ." I roll my eyes.

"Besides, it'll be totally different with boyfriends," she promises. "Bring Luke, and who knows what will happen. Maybe you can answer something I've always been dying to know."

"What's that?" I ask curiously.

She lowers her voice to a whisper. "What are they like… you know . . . when they're not . . . circumcised?"

"Oh my God!" I can't help but sputter in laughter. My mind flashes back to Luke and me losing it at Katz's Deli, and I'm glad Jen can't see the blush on my face, which I can tell has suddenly grown as red as Cynthia's New York hard salami. "Don't even go there!"

"I can't believe he actually suggested that!" After I hang up with Jen, I call Leah for a more sober second opinion. Jen had glossed over the tattoo escapade, enthusiastically endorsing the concept ("Awesome! Maybe he can get you a fake ID?"), but Leah seems horrified by the idea.

I'm glad I downplayed the fact that the idea was really Luke's, passing it off as both of ours.

"So you're not actually thinking of doing it," she says, concern ringing in her voice, like she can't even say the word tattoo.

"No, we were just kidding around. For fun," I explain,

failing to mention Luke repeatedly egging me on during the subway ride home about getting tattoos and promising us that his friend Sully could hook us up with fake IDs. "Besides, I'm not into the idea of some psychotic guy named Jet stabbing me repeatedly with a needle. I have a pretty low threshold for pain."

"Thank God."

I swear, her negative reaction is getting to me. What's the big deal if I want to get a tattoo? The way I see it, the main concern, other than the pain, is my dubious taste in making such a permanent choice. I mean, my track record isn't exactly reassuring. If I had picked a tattoo three years ago, I probably would have slapped a "Hello Kitty" logo on my ass for all of eternity.

While Leah listens, I babble on about the various issues. First, there's the major issue of image selection: L.C.— Luke's initials. Too much pressure for a commitment this early. Definitely a romance-limiting move. More appropriate, something classic, like a heart or star. There's the crucial question of placement: ankle, hip, or the small of my back? I definitely don't want to draw attention to my child-bearing hips, and the lower back is far too bold a choice.

"I'm definitely not the tramp stamp type, but the ankle can be tasteful and still sexy, don't ya think?"

Leah's silence lasts so long, I begin to wonder if she's taken a vow not to speak, like some Trappist monk.

"Well, you can do what you want, but . . ." She hesitates.

"What?" I demand.

"You know it's totally against our faith?"

"What are you talking about?"

"There's, like, a serious commandment or something against tattoos."

"A commandment?" I say incredulously. How come I'd never heard about this? And how come Leah always knows these things? Sometimes I suspect she must have actually been paying attention in Hebrew School.

"Yes! It's considered desecrating your body."

"Desecration?" Nipple rings and tongue studs, maybe, but I hardly think a little red heart counts. I mean, there are a billion more cringe-worthy things people do to their bodies. Women with their fingernails grown out like claws who put little sparkly stars on the tips. Infant baby girls with pierced ears and little diamond studs. Where are the rules against that?

"I'm sure Luke didn't know," she says kindly. True. If I didn't know, there is no way Luke could be expected to. "But he's asking you to do something totally wrong."

"So what happens if you get one?" I ask warily.

"For one thing, if they're really strict, they won't let you get buried in a Jewish cemetery."

My mind flashes to my dad's family plot in Flushing, where we make an annual pilgrimage to pay our respects. After we arrive, we always wander around the cemetery, looking for smooth stones to put on my grandparents' grave- stone as a mark of remembrance. The cemetery trip is always a downer, leaving my dad gloomy the whole ride home. I wouldn't wish it on anyone, let alone my own offspring.

Besides, who wants to spend all of eternity in Queens?

"Leah, that's like, a hundred years from now. And I'll be dead! What will I care?"

"Your parents will care."

"They'll be dead, too! We'll all be completely dead by then!"

"No, I mean, they'll care now."

"They don't have to know. It'll be our little secret."

She is silent for a moment. I swear, too much religious indoctrination is turning Leah into someone I don't recognize, like a member of a cult. "It's not funny," she huffs. "They put you in the section for criminals and gentiles, you know."

The implication is clear: the two are the same. Now I feel a little huffy myself. "Nice." I snap. "You think just because someone is a different religion, that makes them a criminal?"

"'Course not," she replies, just a little too slowly for my satisfaction.

"No, maybe you're right. Maybe I'd rather spend the eternal hereafter on the wrong side of the cemetery. With Luke and the degenerates."

"Rach, I didn't—" Leah begins to apologize.

But I'm tired of Leah making me feel like a felon for dating Luke. It is bad enough having to hide him from my parents. And having to hide my parents from him. Now I have to justify him to my friends?

"I gotta go," I mumble.

Talking to Jen and Leah has left me totally torn. I want to be the kind of girl Luke seems to think I am, the kind who doesn't worry what her parents say, isn't the school math geek, drinks the eggnog, and gets the sexy tattoo without obsessing over the fallout.

Then again, it's one thing to break the Teen Commandments, but do I really have the *chutzpah*—the nerve—to break one of the real commandments? To disappoint my parents? Leah? Rabbi Wasserman? Trying to please everyone all the time is beginning to make my head throb. If I make the wrong choice, I'll have to live with myself—and potentially my tattoo—forever.

And just like that, I know exactly what I'm going to do.

chapter 31

IS IT POSSIBLE TO suffer withdrawal from a person? If so, I've definitely been suffering serious Luke withdrawal all week. With both of us going through midterm insanity, we haven't seen each other in days. In between brief phone calls and text messages, I've been reassuring myself he's real by putting on his sweatshirt (inside out so the insignia is hidden), wrapping the extra-long sleeves around myself, and getting high on the intoxicating aroma of Lukeness, a heady mixture of his Axe body spray and workout sweat.

With the help of my security sweatshirt, I sailed through my midterms for history, chemistry, and Spanish. I am particularly proud of the midterm paper I handed in for Ms. Jensen's English Lit class, entitled, *"Did Hester Prynne Really Sin?"* which basically argues that what constitutes sinning is purely subjective, based on time and place. Hester's hookup with the minister may have earned her the Scarlet A back in Puritan times, but in my school, it would earn her an A+, where the So Verys applaud any cheating, scamming, and doping. To sin is in, I concluded. I wasn't sure whether Ms. Jensen would agree with my argument, so I didn't mention my own personal strategy to increase my sinnage quotient.

Now I have only one final test to go: my math midterm. Since I'd promised Diamenties I'd bring up my grade, I've been faithfully making my way through the textbook examples, almost getting caught up. I just need one more day to really cram.

But that plan flies out the window when Luke IMs me, e-wheedling me to come hang out.

Bballboy26: r u bzy 2nite? Midterms over. Rents out. Come over.
RachLgirl: Sry. Gotta study. I test 2 go.
Bballboy26: Come on. U studied enuf.
RachLgirl: Math mdtrm! Failure potential!
Bballboy26: We can study here. I'll b good.

Well . . . I could tell my parents I was going over to Jen's to cram.

Bballboy26: Plz :) W/ a cherry on top?

He is so cute when he cyberbegs.

Besides, this might be my best chance to ask him to the dance. I still haven't quite worked up the nerve, unsure what

204

he'll say. What if he thinks school dances are lame archaic rituals, like mistletoe? Every time I've tried to bring it up, I've chickened out, telling myself it would be better to do it in person. Now the dance is only days away, and Jen is ready to murder me.

Besides, there is something I'm dying to show him. . . .

RachLgirl: OK. When?

Bballboy26: 8.

"Mom, I'm heading over to Jen's to study, okay?" I ask in a rush of words as I enter the kitchen. She is sitting at the table, frowning as she sorts through a pile of mail. Even though my dad is a certified accountant, for some reason, it's my mother who always gets stuck paying the bills. "Fine," she says, waving her hand at me distractedly.

Then the doorbell rings. "Who can that be?" She crinkles her nose. "Can you be a sweetie and get that?" When I answer the door, it is Mrs. Goldstein, here to offer my mother her sincerest condolences, and a fruit basket.

I lead her back to the kitchen, where she hands my mother the huge woven basket wrapped in cellophane. "This is too much," my mother is saying, as Mrs. Goldstein holds up her hand and says, "Please. I should have stopped by sooner. . . ."

I stand there, unable to escape as they begin talking about the burden of elderly parents and untimely loss. Then Mrs. Goldstein turns to me and says, "Oh, Rachel, wasn't that funny when I ran into you and your friend at Katz's? What a coincidence!"

I freeze. I am about to be so busted.

"Yeah," I say warily, praying Mrs. Goldstein doesn't get more specific.

"Oh, really?" my mom asks. "When was this?"

"Last Saturday." Mrs. Goldstein turns back to me with a sly smile. "So . . ." she drawls.

BUZZZZ.

We all jump.

"Oh, shoot!" Mrs. Goldstein says, reaching for her hip pocket. "That's my new pager. I'm on call tonight, unfortunately." Already, her tone has turned brusque, and she is pulling out her cell phone. "One sec." She speed dials a number and listens intently, while my mom and I just stand there. "Uh-huh. Uh-huh. Four minutes? Right. It's time to head out. I'll meet you there as soon as I can." She clicks off. "Well, duty calls."

"Thanks again," my mother says as we quickly walk her to the door—my mother out of politeness, me, so I can circumvent any further mention of Luke sightings. And she is gone.

"That was sweet of her," my mother says as she closes the door. "So, you and Jen went to Katz's? You didn't mention that."

"Uh, yeah," I say, relieved at her misinterpretation.

"Isn't Jen a vegetarian these days?" my mom muses,

206

inconveniently remembering a detail of my friend's personal life. "I'm surprised she'd even step foot in Katz's."

"She likes their potato knishes," I say, grabbing my coat. "See you later."

"Be back by ten," she calls.

When Luke opens the door, I can hear a chatter of voices behind him.

"Who's here?" I ask.

"Sully and Mick and the guys stopped by to celebrate the end of midterms," Luke says casually. "We're watching *The OC*."

I feel a stab of annoyance, both at Luke for misleading me, and at myself for being so naive as to think we were really going to "study." Good thing I lugged my humongous geometry textbook, which is thicker than the *Seventeen* prom issue.

"I thought we were studying." I say in a low voice, so no one else can hear. "I still have one more midterm."

"Relax," he says, leading me into the living room. "You have all night." The old, dutiful Rachel would have panicked, but the new, relaxed Rachel just prays he is right. I have plenty of time.

"You guys remember Rachel," Luke says, waving a hand at each of them by way of introduction. "Mick, Sully, Christine, Shannon."

The guys good-naturedly grunt hello, their eyes peeled

to the set. I recognize Shannon as the sexy Santa's helper from the Christmas party, the one who played strip poker with Jen and Matt. From the way she coolly avoids acknowledging my existence, I can tell she has Luke in her crosshairs.

"Hey," I say weakly, trying to inconspicuously shrug off my backpack. I'm still stressed that our private study hall has just turned into recess on the playground: our first public inauguration as a couple.

"Beer?" Sully offers, gesturing at a six-pack on the table.

"No thanks, I've, ah, got a midterm tomorrow."

I turn to Luke. "Where are your folks?" I ask.

"Oh, they're out," he says airily. "Some parent-teacher conference. Come check out my room."

Luke drags me toward the back of the house. At the doorway, I hang back warily. You never know what you're going to find in a strange guy's room. Video game consoles spilling everywhere, like in Ben's room? Beer posters of half-naked blondes all over the walls? Decapitated baby rabbit heads stacked inside a freezer? Anything is possible.

I peek in: the coast looks clear. The room is clean but sparse. Dark wood dresser, blue shag rug, pennants on the wall, gleaming sport trophies—and a tiny wooden crucifix hanging right over the bed.

"Aren't you coming in?" he teases, plopping down on the navy plaid comforter. "I don't bite. Generally speaking."

I sit down next to him and cross my legs. Not too close.

Not too far. I realize this is the first time we've been alone together. Really alone. He leans in closer. His arm drifts across the bed toward my knee, and he begins running his hand up and down my outer thigh. "So . . ." he says, like there is no ending to the sentence. I feel all squirmy inside. Are we about to hook up right here, right now, right on Luke's bed, right beneath this wooden cross? I suddenly feel like I'm being watched: by Jesus, Rabbi Wasserman, and my bubbe above—the holy trinity.

I try to stall, jumping up off the mattress. "Notice anything different about me?" I say flirtatiously, doing a little twirl.

Luke smiles as if to say, *I'll play.* "Hmmm," he says, stroking his chin, inspecting me slowly from head to foot. "New haircut?"

I shake my head. "Lower."

His eyes travel down my body, landing on my chest. "New . . . sweater?" I shake my head again, almost sorry I began this game.

"Is it something I can see?" he asks. "Or something . . . underneath?"

I place my ankle on his lap, as if I were Cinderella and he were my prince fitting me with the glass slipper, and tug down my wool sock. "Surprise!"

He stares down at my foot, his gaze freezing on my ankle. "I can't believe it!" he says excitedly. "You went and got one!" He shakes his head in admiration of the small reddish-brown rosebud tattoo adorning my ankle.

"When? How?"

I am about to tell him, but before I can, he jumps up. "I was just telling everyone about that tattoo place," he says. "Come on, let's show them."

"No, wait," I protest, but before I can stop him, he is dragging me into the living room, positioning me in front of his friends like I am the object of today's show-and-tell, and pointing to my foot. "Guys, check this out."

I'm not sure what to do. This isn't what I had planned. I'd wanted to show him what I had done in private, tell him the deal, get his reaction. But now, with Luke's friends watching, me and my new tattoo have been outed.

I pull down my sock again. Everyone oohs and aaahs.

"Ripe." Sully nods.

"I would have gone with you," Luke says.

"I know," I stammer. "I really wanted to see the look on your face." Which is the truth. I'd been dying to know how he would react.

"You're amazing," he declares, stroking my wrist bone with his index finger.

I squirm slightly at his unbridled enthusiasm. After all, it's not like I actually achieved anything notable. Climbed Mount Everest. Cured cancer. Negotiated world peace. I just have a red rose on my foot. In the grand scheme of things, what does it matter?

"Did it hurt?" Christine, a petite girl with a pert ski jump nose, wants to know.

"Not really." I shrug, trying not to bask in the newfound attention.

"When I got my belly pierced, it hurt and swelled up sooo much," Shannon gripes. "But now it's fine." She lifts up her T-shirt gratuitously so the guys can all take a good look at her flat abs and sparkling silver ring. I want to jab Luke for looking, too, but I restrain myself.

She turns and squints her over-Maybellined eyes at me. "I thought you had to be eighteen to get tattooed," she says suspiciously.

"There are ways," I say airily, trying to sound casually mysterious.

"Fake ID?" Shannon drills.

"I can't reveal my sources," I say coolly. At times, it can be helpful to have a former journalist in your family.

Christine leans in conspiratorially toward me. "My sister promised to lend me hers when she turns eighteen. But that's not for another three months."

The conversation shifts away from my tattoo and turns to the difficulty of procuring quality fraudulent documents to buy beer. "My cousin cooks them up off his iMac," Sully brags. "He does a sweet business."

"Yeah? How much?" Mick wants to know.

"A hundred bucks. But—"

As he launches into an involved story of fake ID procurement, I can't help but think of the juxtaposition: my bubbe's story of how a fake ID saved her life in escaping from

Europe; my friends using them to get butt-wasted and get tramp stamps.

"My cousin was going to make a killing," Sully concludes his tale of woe, "but this guy Jewed him down to fifty dollars each."

"That's totally whack, man," Mick sympathizes.

"I know. He was pissed."

Wait. WAIT. WAIT!

My mind snaps to attention. What did he just say? Did he say what I *think* he said? I try to mentally rewind and replay Sully's last sentence.

"Jewed him down."

I've never heard the phrase before. But even so, I know instantly what he meant. The ugly words echo loudly, angrily, inside my head, like a sudden pounding migraine.

It means we're cheap. Stingy. Skinflints.

Are we? Cheap? I mean, true, my dad hasn't bought a bar of soap for years—he's made pocketing miniature hotel soaps into an art form. And my mom is an avid coupon clipper who always waits for tax-free weekends before she goes shopping for big-ticket items. But I always thought they were just being frugal. Clever. Smart. There's a Grand Canyon gap of difference between craftily thrifty and Scroogily stingy, isn't there? I glance at Luke to see his reaction, but he is engrossed in the machinations of the on-screen bimbettes.

I feel like I've been dropped into some *Teen People* advice column.

Question: One of my new boyfriend's friends just made an

ethnic slur about my culture. Do I stand up and protest? Or do I sit back and let it pass? Please respond as soon as possible.

Answer: Of course you should not sit idly by when someone has made an inappropriate remark. It is up to you to firmly correct the person. Tell them, "What you said is offensive to me, and I'd appreciate if you didn't do it again."

Good advice.

But of course, I wimp.

And every second, the comment scrolls farther back up off the screen into conversation history, and my window of opportunity to speak up slips away.

Instead, I sit there, fuming, the rest of the night—mad at Sully, mad at myself for being so spineless, mad at Luke for not noticing I'm mad, mad at Leah for being right as always, mad at my stupid parents for making me be born into this religion and getting me into this situation.

Eventually, after the last shocking family secret is revealed on *The OC* and the latest adulterous affair is consummated, the viewing party disintegrates. After scenes from next week, everyone "rolls" with a "later," except Shannon, who coos, "Bye, Lukie."

All I want to do is go home, too. Besides, I do have a math midterm tomorrow morning. I only have a few more hours to study, assuming I don't want to pull an all-nighter. "I should go," I say, stuffing my arms into my jacket.

"What's wrong?" Luke whispers, grabbing me. "I thought you'd stay awhile."

"Nothing," I stammer. "I really need to study."

He looks uncertain. "Are you sure?"

I nod firmly.

"Is something wrong? You've been so quiet all night."

"All right." We're finally alone in the hallway. "It's stupid. Didn't you hear what Sully said?"

"Sully? Noooo. What did he say?"

Even though I'm bringing it up, I'm still reluctant to say the words aloud. I feel ashamed, somehow. As if the words are dirty, dirtier than cursing, dirtier than anything.

Luke sees my reluctance. "Rach, he's a moron; he's always talking smack. You can't take anything he says seriously."

Except, I am taking it seriously. Too seriously?

I don't know what to say. Worse, I'm not exactly sure what I want Luke to say. Or do. What I want, I guess, mostly, is to see his reaction.

"He said . . . this guy . . . 'Jewed him down.'" I blurt out.

For a minute, Luke just looks blank. Then it registers. "He did? I . . . didn't even notice. When?"

"When he was talking about selling fake IDs."

"It's just a dumb expression, Rach. He didn't mean it—personally. I don't even think he knows you're Jewish."

"So it's okay to say that as long as no one in the room is Jewish?" I snap.

"No," he says, running his fingers through his hair in frustration. "I mean, it's wrong either way. I just meant, he wouldn't care what you are. He's not like that."

214

I really don't care what Sully is like. What I want to know is, what is Luke like? I scrutinize him, waiting to see what he will do.

"I can talk to him," he finally offers.

"No," I say firmly. The last thing I want is to extract some resentful apology from Sully, something to prolong the awkward situation. Besides, I'm not the PC police. Already, I'm regretting that I opened my mouth. "Forget it. I shouldn't have said anything."

"How about this," he says, grabbing me around the neck and pulling me into a hug from behind. "I'll kick his ass, if you want. Or"—he grins—"I could hold him down while you beat him." He grabs my wrists and simulates little punches and jabs, trying to get me to laugh against my will.

Like when someone tickles you exactly in the right spot and you have to laugh, he's impossible to resist. "No." I smile back. "I don't want to make a big deal. I just felt weird, you know?" I'm vaguely disappointed in his response, although I'm not sure why. "But . . . does it bother you? That we're different that way?"

"Me?" He looks amused at the question. "I'm not into labels. People are people." He blinks at me. "Why? Does it bother you? I didn't think you were that religious."

"I'm not," I say. "It doesn't matter to me at all." And even though we agree, there's a moment of weirdness, like we've just broached a forbidden subject, a door that is supposed to remain locked.

The only way I can end the weirdness is to change the subject. Which is how I finally muster up the nerve to ask him to the Winter Dance. And by the time he agrees to take me, I've almost forgotten about the disturbing parts of the evening, the blown-off study session, Luke's shrine to his Savior, Sully's crude comment—all of it.

Almost.

MY EUPHORIC HIGH over the prospect of taking Luke to the dance lasts about twelve hours, until this morning's ultimate buzz kill: my math midterm. After getting home from Luke's, I'd stayed up until two in the morning, cramming as best as I could. But would it be enough?

"This will be one of the determining factors of your midyear grade," Mr. Diamenties announces solemnly, pacing the rows as he shuffles out the three-page exam. "Good luck."

I push everything else out of my mind, flip over the test, and dive in. The first question practically makes me smile. It's almost like Mr. Diamenties is apologizing to me personally.

What is a triangle with an angle greater than 90 degrees called?

This time, safe in my anonymity, I have no problem filling in the correct answer.

* * *

When I get home from school, mentally fried, Mr. Marathon Man is sitting outside, slowly lacing up his sneakers.

I can't help but frown, reminded of my looming athletic ultimatum. Last week, Mr. Gee had announced that before moving on to our next activity in gym, we'd all have to run two miles in less than fifteen minutes. Then he timed us with a stopwatch, so we'd know how much we each needed to improve.

I had clocked in dead last, at 20:36.

So even though my midterms are finally over, I still have the stress of figuring out how to shave five minutes off my time by next week—short of using steroids or a time machine.

"What?" he says defensively, reacting to the grimace on my face. Or maybe, I realize, it's just that Howard always looks pained to see me.

"Runners," I spit out. "What is it with you people?" I fill him in on my sad state of athletic affairs. "It's hopeless," I conclude, eyeing his reaction. Lately, I never know which Howard I'm going to get: the Buddha-wise one, or the snarky, sarcastic one. "No, you're not hopeless," he says. "Come running with me. Learn from the master." Standing up, he casually adds, "if you can keep up."

Clearly, today is the snarky sarcastic one.

My lazy muscles want to kill me, my lungs chime in "No way," but my pride somehow gets the last word. "Fine," I say, unlocking the front door. "Just let me ditch my book bag." Inside, all is quiet. My parents are still at work, and lately, for some reason, Ben has been spending every free afternoon playing basketball over at the JCC.

I toss my book bag into the entryway, risking my parents' freak-out if one of them gets home before me and trips over it. As if it's *my* fault they're klutzes, when they passed their genetic ineptitude on to me.

When I return, Howard frowns at my sneakers. "Don't you have any real running shoes?" he asks, like I've shown up in stilettos.

"Sorry, my cross trainers are in the shop. Ready?"

But he is twiddling with the adjustment knob on this huge hunk of metal on his wrist. "Wait, let me set my timer."

"New watch?" I ask.

"It's a runner's watch. Chanukah gift. From Tara," he says proudly. "It comes with a pedometer and a heart-rate monitor."

"Wow." Clearly, Howard mistook the fancy gift as a sign that their relationship was getting serious; I'd say she's trying to buy his affection.

"But," he adds, shaking it with a frown, "it's crazy hard to figure out." He looks up at me and smiles ruefully. "Just like all you chicks, eh?" Finally he makes one last twist that sets off a loud beep. "Got it!" he exclaims, turning to me. "Ready?"

"As I'll ever be."

He clicks the timer, and we're off.

We jog along in silence for a few minutes, for which I'm grateful, because I don't think I can handle any casual banter. My chest is burning, my legs are cramping, and it's all I can do to not start wheezing like an asthmatic. Large stains of sweat pool beneath my shirtsleeves. It is agony. I don't know what he gets out of it. After like, a block, I'm lagging behind and Howard has to circle back to me. "Come on, Lowenstein. Can't you hack it?"

I grit my teeth and press to match his strides. I'll work through my pain, like those prepubescent gymnasts who sprain an ankle but go on to finish their floor routine and win the gold.

"Your form's okay," Howard says, breaking the silence. "But your strides are short."

"Can't . . . help . . . it. . . ." I gasp. "I . . . have . . . short legs."

"And you should use your arms more."

I nod dutifully at him, hoping to avoid having to keep the conversation going on my end. All my energy is going into staying on my feet. I can't spare any lung capacity for this casual chitchat.

"Let's head into the park," he booms with ease, gesturing to the wooded trail leading into the park, past the playground where we used to swing on the monkey bars whenever the intimidating junior-high skateboarders weren't co-opting our turf. Under the canopy of trees, a damp, woodsy smell lingers in the air. My lungs hungrily devour the brisk oxygen. Our feet pound down the trail, scattering autumn leaves in our wake.

Suddenly I begin to catch my second wind. I feel a surge of energy. This isn't so bad. I almost feel human again. My chest expands and I tip my chin up toward the sky. My body ripples and hums with newfound confidence. Must be those glorious endorphins Howard had talked up.

Maybe I can do this. Maybe this is, in fact, my true calling. Maybe I, Rachel Lowenstein, should take a crack at running, too. If Howard can do it, why not me? If I started training now, I could be running track by the spring, then marathons next year, and someday, maybe the summer Olympics.

I glance up at Howard, wanting to share my growing excitement with him. "This is—*OOOOFFFF*," I sputter, my legs flying out from beneath me and landing me right on my butt. I twist and stare indignantly at the tree root that snarled my unsuspecting foot. Jeez.

Howard screeches to a stop, races back toward me, panting anxiously. Once he sees there's no sign of blood or broken bones, but just me sitting on my butt, staring at a tree trunk, his concern for my well-being evaporates.

"Walk much, Lowenstein?" he drawls, with a snort of amusement that only further emphasizes what a dolt I am. His perfect Tara would never take a tumble on her ass in front of a guy. Super-coordinated, pep-squad Tara, who does mind-blowing tumbles in front of a stadium crowd, rather than on a muddy jogging trail.

"Clearly not," I say, starting to clamber to my feet, when I feel an unpleasant throb in my ankle. "Ooohh." I sink back down to the ground.

"What?" he asks, finally looking a smidgen concerned.

"My ankle," I yelp.

"Let me see." Howard drops to his knees and probes his fingers around my ankle bone, flexing my foot back and forth. "Does this hurt? How about this?"

"No. No. Yes!!! *Owww*," I howl, half in sheer agony, half hoping this will cut short our track session. "A little," I amend, not wanting to look like a total wimp.

"There's nothing broken; it's probably just a sprain," he says, popping off my sneaker and peeling back my sock. "But let's see if you're swelling."

It's too late to stop him. My feet haven't seen a pedicure since the dog days of summer. They most likely reek of sneaker odor. And what if he sees the primate-like wisps of hair growing on my big toe?

He doesn't seem to notice, focusing instead on something on my ankle.

"Rachel, you're bleeding!"

I am?

"No, wait." He tentatively rubs his finger over a spot on my ankle, then inspects it. Nothing. "That's not blood. What is that?"

Oh, that.

I'd almost forgotten.

"A tattoo?" I say uncertainly, as if it were a question rather than a statement of fact, a habit that drives my parents crazy.

He momentarily drops his medicine man act. "A tattoo?" His eyebrows practically spasm off his face.

"So?"

"So, nothing. I'm just surprised. Whose idea was that?"

"No one's. Mine. What do you mean?" I demand, vaguely insulted. Doesn't he think I can come up with an idea on my own?

"You just—I don't know. Don't seem the type."

What does he mean? Because I get good grades? Don't cut class and get high? Never had a boyfriend before? Besides, he's one to talk. *You don't seem the type to be a jock dating a She-Devil.* I might have pointed out.

"How do you know what type I am?" I say indignantly.

"I know you," he says, giving me a piercing look. "I'm surprised you're being so . . . You usually do your own thing."

"Oh," I say, confused now. It isn't at all what I'd expected him to say. It almost sounds like . . . a compliment.

But he is right. Maybe a tattoo once had some shock value, but now it's so downright common. I mean, when squeaky-clean types like Kelly Ripa have ankle tattoos, you know body art has jumped the shark.

"So what did Herb and Sylvia have to say about that?" he asks.

223

"They don't know," I snap. "Obviously."

"All right, come on," he says, reaching down his hand and pulling me onto my feet. "You're fine. Let's walk it off."

"Wait!" I stand, wincing and gyrating my ankle in exaggerated circles to stretch it out.

Howard watches in amusement. "With your pain threshold, I'm amazed you didn't bolt halfway through."

His insight is eerie. That's exactly the reason I told Leah why I'd never get tattooed.

"Who says I can't take pain?" I ask, limping slightly to keep pressure off my foot.

"That summer when I slammed the door on your finger? Don't you remember?"

That's right. It was the summer after second grade. Howard and I had been having a water gun fight on the front lawn and I'd tried to run into the house to escape his Super Soaker. The door had closed on my finger, and it hurt so bad, I thought my whole hand was going to drop off. Howard had raced inside to find my mom, who'd rushed us down to the hospital.

"You cried for hours," he says. "Over a broken nail. And you wouldn't talk to me for weeks."

It was true. "I still have a scar," I say defensively, showing him the white spot under my pinkie nail. "See?" I shove my finger in his face.

Howard lightly grasps my hand and inspects my pinkie. "You're right," he says, shaking his head in regret.

224

"I'll probably have it forever."

"Did I ever apologize?" he asks.

"Yup. But only because your mom made you."

He looks truly sorry. For a second, I think he is going to kiss my finger to make it better, like my mom did when I was five and had a boo-boo. But I must be having some kind of delusion from the shock of my injury. He holds my finger for an instant more, looking like he wants to say something, but hesitates.

Finally he says, "Well, your tattoo will last forever, too." Then drops my hand.

It had been easy enough to lie last night to Luke and his friends. They don't know me that well. But with Howard it's impossible to keep up the bluff. "If you must know the truth," I sigh, "I didn't really get a tattoo."

chapter 33

HOWARD'S FLABBERGASTED look is so priceless,
I am almost enjoying myself, despite the ongoing ache in my
ankle. "You didn't? Then what's—"

"It's henna . . . You do it yourself . . . I needed a study
break."

He is still staring at me like I am crazy.

"It only lasts a couple of weeks," I explain. "I just wanted
to try it out first."

"Try it out?"

"Luke thought it would look good," I say defensively. "I
wasn't sure . . . It's a very permanent decision. Did you
know it's a serious sin?"

"Where'd you hear that?" he asks.

"Around," I say, not wanting to admit that Leah is the
source of all knowledge about my own faith. Howard's family isn't super religious, but I get the feeling even he would
know basic trivia like that.

We start heading out of the park. I'm still limping slightly, but Howard doesn't even offer me his arm for support. Not that I want him to. But still.

"So did he like it?"

"Who? Luke?"

Howard nods.

"Ummm . . . Too much. He kinda . . . thought it was real, and before I could tell him the truth, he was showing me off to all his friends."

"So you didn't tell him it's fake?"

"What was I supposed to do, look like a total baby with a temporary tattoo?"

"Glad you have such an up-front, honest relationship," he quips. Before I can respond, he starts grinning, at first just a smile, then a chuckle and snort.

"What's so funny?" I demand.

"What are you going to do . . . when it wears off?" He laughs. "Keep reapplying the same one?"

That's a good question. One that hasn't occurred to me.

"It's not funny," I say indignantly, turning the corner heading toward home. I don't know what possessed me to tell him the truth. Clearly he can't be trusted.

"It's sort of funny," he says, still smirking at me. Then, seeing that I'm about to stomp off in anger, he grabs my arm. "Don't go," he says. "Let's stop at the Avenue and get something to drink. Maybe get some ice for your ankle."

I'm still mad, but my throbbing ankle could use an ice

pack. "Fine," I agree. We make our way down the main drag, past the kosher butcher shop and the pharmacy, and enter the local pizza place. Howard heads right to the counter while I eye the room to see who's there.

Immediately I spot Jen and Alissa sitting in a corner booth, their hair still wet and slicked back from swim practice. When Jen sees me standing in the doorway, she freezes halfway through a bite of her salad, looking like I've just caught her in the act. At first I assume she's embarrassed I've spotted her out again with Alissa. Then I wonder, maybe she's ashamed to acknowledge me in front of her new So Very friend?

"Rachel!" Jen waves, quickly recovering. "Over here." I nudge Howard and we head toward them.

Alissa's eyes flash, casually sizing up the situation. "What are *you two* doing out and about?" she asks in a super sweet tone of surprise as we reach them. I can tell what she really means: what am I doing hanging out with Tara's boyfriend?

"We were out running," Howard says, sliding into the booth and casually appropriating Alissa's Vitamin Water, in that way popular guys assume that everything they want is theirs for the taking. I wonder if dating Tara has given him that confidence, or if he'd quietly had it all along. "Rachel twisted her ankle."

"Are you okay?" Jen asks me, and I tell her, "I'm fine," while across the way, I can hear Alissa squealing, "Howard, you stink!" as she pinches her nose and scoots away from him.

"I thought you hated running," Jen accuses.

"I do. But I have that running test in gym."

"So where's Tara?" Alissa pointedly asks Howard.

A look flashes across his face I can't read. "Picking up invitations with her mom," he says simply.

"For the party?"

He nods distractedly. "I'll go get some ice and water," he says, hopping out of his seat and heading toward the counter. "Anyone want anything?" The three of us shake our heads. My aching ankle has killed my appetite, and they're still picking at their salads.

I turn to Jen. "Party?" This is news to me.

Alissa pounces on my confusion. "It's Tara's Sweet Sixteen. It's going to be totally awesome. Much better than the school dance, where *anyone* can show up."

"It's in two weeks," Jen explains. "Tara's handing out invites next week."

"To *select* friends," Alissa adds.

Jen and Alissa begin an exhaustive dissection of who will and won't be invited. Rule number one: no freshmen allowed. Then they begin eliminating half the sophomore class with arbitrary reasons, like too short, or too needy, or once looked funny at Alissa. "And no dorks like Josh Green," Alissa says. I shoot Jen a look. It's not that Josh and I are friends, exactly, but Jen knows the twisted history of our mathlete romance. But Jen just smiles in weak agreement. "Or juvies like Wayne Liu," Alissa adds.

The whole discussion is making me so queasy, the only thing that can cure it would be a slice of greasy pizza. With pepperoni. And sausage.

"Hey, Howard . . ." I call out. "I changed my mind."

I guess the smell of sizzling meat makes Alissa and Jen nauseous, because soon after it arrives, they wrinkle their noses and jump up to leave. Such a pity.

Howard and I linger, gobbling down our slices as I ice my ankle.

"So here's what you're going to do," Howard proposes. His tattoo strategy: keep getting the rosebud reapplied every few weeks, so no one will be any the wiser, and to get it as a real tattoo if and when I decide I really want one. It's so brilliant, I wish I'd thought of it myself. By the time we get up to leave, the swelling has gone down and I can pretty much walk normally again. We hobble home, and when we finally reach my front steps, Howard turns.

"Oh, I almost forgot," he says, snapping his fingers. "Whatever you decide, don't freak about that cemetery thing."

"What?" I say, confused.

"It's a total myth. My grandpa Dave had a huge anchor tattooed on his chest from his time in the navy. And he's resting peacefully at Cedar Park Cemetery, right next to my grandma."

So there, Leah, I think. You don't know everything after all.

"Howard?"

"Yeah?"

"Thanks."

chapter 34

EVEN THOUGH THINGS have been strained between us, I can't resist calling Leah to tell her what Howard had told me.

"So guess what?" I blurt out when she answers her cell phone.

"What?" she says carefully.

"Howard says his Uncle Dave had a tattoo, but he was still able to be buried in a Jewish cemetery!"

"Not surprising. I *told* you it wasn't always enforced."

That wasn't exactly the way she made it sound at the time, but I let it slide.

"So you're going to do it?" she asks.

"Well . . . actually . . ." And I tell her about my total cop-out with the fake tattoo.

"You are so sketchy." She laughs.

"So am I off the hook?"

"Sure, temporary tattoos don't count," she says generously. "They even had them at my cousin's bat mitzvah last year. So I take it things are going well with Luke, then?"

"Completely. We're even going to a dance at my school this weekend."

"I thought you didn't believe in school dances," she says, surprised.

"Don't ask," I moan. "Jen swears this time it'll be different. I think the lack of animal flesh is affecting her sanity. It's like reverse Mad Cow."

We both laugh, tension finally gone. "Actually, I was thinking of going shopping after school tomorrow for something to wear," I continue. "Wanna come?"

"Oh," she groans. "Tomorrow? I can't."

"BBYO?"

"Um. Yeah," she stammers.

"Again?"

"Sorry."

Next I try Jen, but her cell is off and her mom says she's busy party planning with Alissa and Tara. Hmpft.

So I end up going back downstairs and approaching my mom. At least she's always a reliable partner in crime for a shopping excursion.

"Mom?"

"Mmmm?" she murmurs, absorbed in the *Times* crossword puzzle.

"There's this thing at school Saturday. The Winter Dance?"

"A dance?" she perks up, putting down the paper

and rubbing her ink-smudged fingers on her pants. "At school?"

"Yeah."

"Do you have—a date?"

Does she have to say this with a near-gasp of happy disbelief? "No," I say, trying not to care when her face falls. "It's just me and Jen—"

"Jen and I," she automatically corrects.

"Jen and I," I amend. "You know, like last year."

"So there's no one you want to go with?" she prods, looking so saddened by my social insignificance that I am almost tempted to tell her the truth. Almost. But then I think of the inevitable questions that will follow: *Who is he? What's his last name? Where does he go to school?* All unanswerable questions.

"How about that boy in your math class, what was his name? Josh?" My mom knows of him because Josh had been the only boy to send me a flower last Valentine's Day, a wilting white carnation, his lukewarm declaration of friendship. She had found the flower and the accompanying card—*Rachel, Happy Valentine's Day. Yours truly, Josh Green*—stuffed in the trash. She still asks about him, especially after she read he was elected class president in the parents' bulletin.

I quickly deflate her idea balloon. "I think he's going with someone else," I lie, certain that Josh is more likely to be staying home to sketch geometric fractals than showing up at a school dance.

"Oh." Then she perks up. "Maybe you'll meet someone

there. Why don't we get you something new to wear. And new shoes. Maybe a necklace?" All I was hoping for was a new outfit, but I'm not about to turn down a full-fledged shopping spree.

"I know," she says, her eyes gleaming. "We'll hit Loehmann's Back Room tomorrow after school." I groan inwardly. Loehmann's is my mother's own personal mecca. It's this legendary New York discount clothing store, where crazed old ladies snatch up last season's over-beaded evening gowns at half off. The worst part is, you have to stand like cattle in a communal dressing room with blaringly bad fluorescent lighting. Naked.

Too late: I see visions of organza and lace dancing in her head. "Mom, it's not like prom," I backpedal desperately. "A new skirt would be fine."

But she is already laying the coordinates for our seek-and-shop mission. "So why don't we hit Loehmann's, and then we can always try Macy's and Nordstrom's at the mall."

After a fruitless hour of picking through the racks at Loehmann's, I end up empty-handed, while my mother picks out a new silk scarf for herself, to keep company with the quadrillion other scarves she already owns. It's so sad: women my mom's age are always over-accessorizing with pins and scarves, trying to look younger, while tween girls pile on dangly earrings and jingly bracelets, trying to look older.

Even with the labels sliced off, I can tell the designer

duds in the Back Room are the dregs of last season. No dress is worthy of wiggling out of my bra in a communal dressing room.

"Nothing?" my mother asks with disappointment as we head to the checkout area. "Just this, then." She pushes her garments onto the counter.

"Did you find everything today?" The guy behind the register looks like a part-time college student. He's wearing some kind of crystal, hanging on a tight black nylon cord, around his neck, and has tight, curly, yellow hair.

"I did," my mother replies as he runs the tag through his scanner. "That's not on sale, is it?" she asks hopefully.

"Nope," he says, barely pausing to check.

"Well, is it about to go on sale soon?" she presses, smiling winningly at him.

Mom! I want to shout. Sully's words echo back at me. *Jewed him down.* I'd always considered my mom's bargain hunting an annoying quirk. But now I'm seeing it in a different light, the way an outsider would. I swear on the spot that once I get my own credit cards, I'll happily pay full retail, no questions asked.

He pauses and carefully considers the question. "We don't have any sales scheduled," he replies patiently.

I roll my eyes loudly. "Let it go," I mutter quietly to myself.

"You never know," she says to me, sensing my irritation. "Do you know how many times I've bought something and seen it go on sale the next day?"

236

"So true," he agrees, nodding his head in sympathy. "That can be a total bummer."

Somehow, this encouragement prompts my mom to look at him as if she has found a kindred soul. "Can you believe my daughter couldn't find anything?" she asks, as though it is a failing of my initiative and not the store's inventory.

"Is that your daughter?" he asks coyly, like he's working for a tip. "I thought you two were sisters."

Her giggle almost reminds me of Jen's, and she bats her eyelashes at him as she hands him her MasterCard. Oh, yuck. My mother is actually flirting with the Loehmann's check-out clerk.

He swipes her credit card. "I need to see your ID, please."

"Don't worry, I'm over twenty-one," she jokes as she hands him her driver's license.

"Barely," he replies, glancing at it and handing it back. "Here you go, ladies." He winks and hands her the shopping bag. "Have a great day."

"Thanks." She tilts her head coquettishly.

"Mom, let's go!" I manage to drag her out of the store before he can ask for her address and digits, for the store's "mailing list."

She is in such a good mood, I am able to convince her to try the places I really want to hit, like Forever 21 and the mall boutiques with the music thumping and the strobe lights and the clothes that people my age actually wear. My mother tsks-tsks her disapproval at the discolike decor, then fixates on the trendy flimsywear.

"How about this?" I say, picking up a black halter dress off the all-black rack. She snatches it out of my hands and begins scrutinizing it like she's Inspector #403. "Look at the stitching," she says, turning the dress inside out and plucking at loose threads. "It's practically falling apart."

She gazes wildly around the store, hoping to find a more demure outfit. Usually she can turn up the least attractive alternative to whatever I've picked out, but this store has her befuddled.

"It's only $19.99," I wheedle.

"When you wear cheap, you look cheap."

Of course, just then, a perky salesgirl with long blond hair and a short miniskirt materializes.

"Can I help you?" she coos.

"Yes, miss, what is the quality of this dress?"

The salesgirl looks confused, as if she were a Miss America finalist suddenly asked to opine the meaning of life. "The quality?" she stammers.

"Yes, the quality," my mother says firmly.

"Mom," I say sharply, beginning to break out in a sweat from mombarassment. "I'm only going to wear it to one dance. It doesn't have to last forever."

"I just want you to have the best," she says defensively. "That's all. Is that wrong?"

"Our clothing is made of excellent materials," the girl

says, finally summoning up her employee training. "Why don't I start a dressing room for you?" She gingerly plucks the dress from my arms and takes off quickly, before my mother can question her further. I give my mother a "so-there" glance, and trail after the clerk, not looking behind to see if she is following.

Inside the thankfully private dressing room, I kick off my jeans and sweater, and wriggle into the dress. The result is a major disappointment: the halter makes me look totally flat chested, like I'm wearing overalls, and the stretchy polyester gives me a butt like Beyoncé. But it's hard to tell. Maybe it's the sneakers that are ruining the look, I think, so I kick them off, along with my socks, and stand on my tippytoes, like I'm wearing heels.

"Let's see," my mother calls over the door.

"One sec," I say, before cracking the door open.

My mother does a full-body scan.

"What do you think?" she asks diplomatically.

"I look gross." I grimace, and she grins in agreement.

"I didn't say it." She laughs. "Let's try—" Then her eyes widen in alarm. She is staring down at the little red rose. "Rachel, what is that spot on your ankle? Are you bleeding?"

Oh, God. Here we go again. You'd think I would have learned my lesson. All week, after my indiscretion with Howard, I had been diligently padding around the house in thick wooly socks, which hid the evidence—while also satisfying my mother's footwear obsession. But now I've shed my cover in a momentary of lapse of reason.

"Oh, that," I sigh. "It's nothing, Mom. Really."

"That is not 'nothing,' Rachel Claire Lowenstein," she declares, deliberately enunciating my middle name. No good can come of that. "What is on your ankle?"

And that is the end of our shopping excursion.

As we hastily retreat from the store, I consider just telling my mom the tattoo is a fake. It would make things so much easier. But for some reason, I don't. Maybe I'm curious to see what her reaction would be, if I had gotten a real tattoo. But mainly, because her immediate attack puts me on defense.

"I can't believe you made a life-altering decision without even consulting me or your father," she fumes as we stomp out to the parking lot. "You know we never would have given our approval for this."

I want to remain calm and reasonable. To appeal to her better nature. Her sense of individualism. But instead, I'm getting ticked off. I mean, it's the principle of the matter. It should be my decision whether or not to get a tattoo, just like it should be my decision what guy I want to be with. So instead, I begin arguing my case.

"Maybe I don't need your approval for every little thing."

"You do for this," she says, nearly hitting a pole as we swerve out of the parking garage.

"Why are you making such a big deal?"

"It *is* a big deal. Did you stop and think about this? Really think about it?"

"It's my body. Why shouldn't I do what I want with it?" I demand, trying to frame the argument in a pro-choice slant. "It's my life." But she is having none of it.

"Well, your life, Rachel, as you know it, is over."

"But—"

"I'm calling Dr. Drummond tomorrow morning to see if we can get this thing removed." Dr. Drummond is my mother's dermatologist, the one who denies me Accutane for my acne but is happy to prescribe Retin-A for her wrinkles. She grips the steering wheel tightly, her jaw set. "And I don't even want to *think* about what your father is going to say when he gets home." And we ride in silence the rest of the way.

"You're defiling your body," is what my father has to say.

"It's just body art, Dad," I tell him.

"That is not art," he says, running his fingers over his head like he wants to tear his hair—the few remaining ones— out of his head. "It is a slap in the face to many people." He doesn't even mention the desecration or cemetery thing. Instead, he goes into a long rant about how Jews in concentration camps during the Holocaust were forced to have numbers tattooed onto their arms, making it especially anathema for us to voluntarily tattoo our bodies.

241

I can see his point. I even feel a little bad. But I don't see how a little red rosebud is anything close to that.

"I just thank God your grandmother didn't live to see this day," he says bitterly.

For different reasons, I couldn't agree more.

chapter 35

AFTER MY PARENTS finish their ranting and raving, they tell me I'm grounded for two weeks. Grounded! Can you believe it? I've never been grounded before in my life. Obviously, I'd never done anything ground-worthy before in my life. Slowly, it sinks in what being grounded actually means. It means seeing Luke will be impossible. It means they're confiscating my cell phone, computer, and all other methods of communication. It means the dance on Saturday, my public debut as one of the datable, my fantasy of slow dancing with Luke, is off. My life, just minutes after it finally started, is over. The bitter irony does not escape me. More like, the bitter irony knees me right in the solar plexus, wherever that is.

I can't figure out where I've gone wrong. Wasn't breaking the Teen Commandments supposed to make my life better, more exciting, less predictable?

Haven't I kept my end of the bargain?

To review, I:

Got wasted at a party ✓
Cut class ✓
Failed my math test ✓
Got an ankle tattoo. Sorta ✓

So far, it's been working. I have Wayne confiding in me,
Aidan after me, and Luke dating me. So what happened?

"Just tell them it's fake," Jen groans at lunch, after I fill her
in on the whole gory tattoo tale. "You can't miss this dance."

But she's missing the point. "No," I say stubbornly. "It's
the principle of the thing. I'm not giving them the satisfaction. If I did want a tattoo, I should be able to get one."

"But—they're ruining your chances with Luke."

"They don't even know I'm going with him," I sigh. "They
think I'm just going with you."

"So tell them that," she urges. "Maybe your mom will feel
bad about ruining the only time you've ever had a date to
take to a school dance."

"Thanks." I give her a withering look. "That might work
if I were going with someone they actually approved of. Can
you believe she actually suggested I go with"—I glance
around the cafeteria, looking for him—"Josh Green?!"

We both glance over at our wannabe Mr. Valedictorian,
his head buried in some textbook. Or more likely, the ency-
clopedia. I'd heard once he liked to read the dictionary in his
spare time. For fun. "Your mom would just love that," she
agrees.

244

"Almost as much as she'd so hate Luke," I conclude.

"Maybe you can just sneak out?"

"Right. Have you seen the Brink's system my dad turns on every night? Our place is locked up tighter than Fort Knox."

It's hopeless. Unless. . . .

"Wait."

"What?"

"You're a genius," I say, jumping up and sliding my tray with me.

"The fire escape?"

Does she think I live in a tenement?

"No," I say patiently. "There is one person who they love even more than Josh Green. I just have to find him."

I race out of the cafeteria and head straight toward Howard's locker, hoping to catch him in between periods. No luck. And for the rest of the day, every time I see him there, Tara is fixed at his side, sending off invisible deterrent signals like an electronic dog fence, discouraging any bitch other than herself from approaching.

Finally, at the end of last period, I catch him alone. "Howard?" I pounce.

He turns, slamming his locker shut, looking almost happy to see me for an instant. Then he coolly says, "Can I help you?"

The idea that seemed so brilliant fourth period has aged

245

badly by last bell. Still, I have no other choice but to plunge ahead. "So, you're going to the Winter Dance, right? Any way you can give me a ride there?"

He raises his eyebrow. "Sorry, Lowenstein, you're out of luck. I'm going with Tara."

Clearly I am going to have to beg. "I know," I say patiently. "I just need a ride, Howard. I *have* a date. We don't have to hang out or anything. We just need a simple lift, so I can be spared the public humiliation of being dropped off by my parents."

"Don't worry," I add, "he lives really nearby."

"Oh, is this your"—and he puts his fingers to his lips—"hush-hush guy?"

"Yes. Luke."

"Luke. Right. So Herb and Syl are fine with him?"

I forgot that I'd told him I was keeping Luke a secret. "Um, yeah. You were right. They didn't flip out after all."

"Well . . . whata ya know. Yeah, I guess there's room . . . sure." At least he doesn't say, I have to check with Tara first. "Be ready to leave around eight. I'll ring your bell." Just as I had planned, I would be the first pickup since I am right next door.

"And a ride home, too, right?" I add, just to make sure the parameters are clear.

"Home, too. How about some pink champagne on ice?" he says, tipping an imaginary chauffeur's hat.

Just then, Tara strolls up behind me and intertwines her arms through Howard's.

"What's up?" she asks Howard pointedly, not even saying hello to me.

He squirms uncomfortably, all his swagger gone. "Hey, Rachel was just asking if we could give her and her boyfriend a ride to the dance. That's cool, right?"

"I thought we were doubling with Alissa and Robbie," she says, peevishly twirling a piece of auburn hair with her finger. "Why does she need a ride?"

Howard looks trapped, like it hadn't occurred to him that she might object. "It's right on our way, Tara. Anyway, I thought Robbie had a car."

"Maybe they can give Jen and Matt a ride?" I say helpfully.

"Fine," she snaps, although I can tell she doesn't like this idea at all. And just like that, the first part of the plan is set.

When I get home, I throw my book bag on the counter and go directly to my room, not coming down until dinnertime. At the dining-room table, I sit quietly, pushing peas around my plate, while Ben gripes about his upcoming seventh-grade canoe trip up the White River in Vermont, where, he had just learned, all electronic devices are forbidden, leaving him without his Game Boy fix. I wonder if there are any twelve-step programs for Gamers.

Then he comes out with this shocker. "Guess what?" he

says brightly. "I found a chat room of Israeli kids. They all live on a kibbutz, and get to pick olives, and milk goats, and sleep in a dorm room. It's so cool. Can I do that?"

You would think he'd announced he'd gotten early acceptance to Harvard, the way my parents get so gleamy-eyed.

"We could look into teen tours to Israel," my mom says, shooting a look at my father like she always knew she liked her younger child best.

"Or maybe take a family trip over the summer!" my dad cries, already mentally loading up the digital camera.

Great. They want to put all our lives at risk so Ben can go fondle goat teats in Tel Aviv.

I can't believe it. First the Anne Frank book report, then hanging out at the JCC, and now a trip to Israel? The way things are going, Ben is going to end up a cantor, and I'm going to get written out of the will.

"Why do we need to go to Israel?" I gripe. "Why can't we ever go anywhere even remotely cool, like Paris or San Francisco?"

"She's right." My dad turns to my mom with a wink. "Who needs to travel around the world to see the Wailing Wall? We can hear all the wailing we want just standing outside Rachel's room."

Har-dee-har-har.

Once Ben races up to his room to *kibitz* with the kibbutz kids, my parents finally acknowledge my misery.

"Rachel," my mom says, whipping the dishes off the table. "I know you're mad about being grounded, and missing the dance tomorrow, but there are consequences to your actions." But if she thinks she's gearing up for The Great Tattoo Brawl, Round Two, she is sadly mistaken. Instead, I spring my Secret Dance Plan into action.

"Yeah, well, the consequence is going to be that I'm known as my school's biggest loser. The only two people who won't be at the dance are me and Howard Goldstein."

"Oh? Howard's not going to the dance?" she says, cocking her head in sympathy. "How do you know that?"

"Because, would you believe, he actually asked me to go with him?" I snort, like this is the most improbable thing I've ever heard. "I don't think he's ever asked out a girl before. He was really nervous, sweating and stuttering . . . It was painful. . . ." I hold my breath to see if this lie will go over. Like all parents, my mom's comprehension of my peers' social standing has a two-year lag time, which is why she still asks if I've talked to Leeza lately, when I haven't spoken to her since the summer after eighth grade. My mom seems blissfully unaware that plain old Howard has become the Marathon Man, dating Tara Silver—and what that means. I just have to pray she doesn't run into Mrs. Goldstein in the next few days.

"I told him I was grounded, but I think he thought I was just making an excuse. I mean, he knows I've never been grounded in my life. He looked . . . crushed." My parents exchange a look. "It's too bad, it's too last minute for him to ask anyone else." They are silent. I'm not sure if my lying is Academy Award material, but I press on. "Oh, well. I'm sure no one will even notice that he's not there." I turn to go up to my room.

"Wait," my dad commands. I turn slowly, my heart pounding.

My mom clears her throat. "We don't want to punish poor Howard; he didn't do anything wrong."

"There's one boy who could use a little boost to his self-esteem," my dad admits.

"He must have felt comfortable asking Rachel, a girl he's known forever." The two look at each other, coming to some unspoken parental agreement.

"What if we gave you a choice," my mom says to me. "You could stay grounded tomorrow night—or go with Howard to the dance."

It's time for the ultimate bluff.

"What?" I grimace. "You actually want me to go with Howard? I only told you because I felt *sorry* for him. Going with him is, like, ten times worse! I'd rather be grounded!"

"How about this," my dad suggests. "Go with Howard, and we'll cut your grounding time in half." He beams like he's just won a MacArthur award, which is only given to certified geniuses. I sit and stew. I agonize over the decision. I chew my nails and rub my temples. I really should win an

Oscar for this. Finally I tell them I'm willing to make this ultimate sacrifice as part of my punishment.

"You're doing the right thing," my dad says solemnly, taking me at face value. I suddenly realize why my poor, trusting dad has never met a poker game he couldn't lose.

BY MY CALCULATIONS, Howard is running several centuries behind schedule. For all he cares, I may just fossilize by the time he gets here, and a team of archeologists of the future will dig out my bone fragments and deduce that I was a Homo sapien female, fifteen, who died of impatience. Of course, I don't really care when *Howard* gets here, but what if *Luke* thinks I'm blowing him off?

I check the clock. Ten minutes after eight.

Ding-dong.

It's about time. Like racehorses at the starting bell, as soon as the doorbell rings, my parents are off! I can hear their footsteps as they sprint to the front door, my mom coming from the kitchen, my dad from the family room, each hoping to edge out the other. They arrive simultaneously in the entryway, pausing to collect themselves.

I pop my head into the stairwell, looking down at them. "Coming," I call out calmly, and begin heading down the stairs.

"Rachel." My mom urgently waves me back into my room. "Young ladies don't greet their dates." Like only a total hussy would ever open her own front door.

I'm about to say, "Who cares? It's just Howard." But then I realize, for the first time this millennium, my mother is actually right. Somehow, for the next ten minutes, I have to enact my parents' vision of a boy picking me up for a dance—even if it is something I've never actually experienced before. But I've seen it in movies. The girl waits up in her bedroom so she can make her grand entrance at the top of the stairs, with some upbeat song playing in the background. The boy looks up and is struck dumb by her beauty. For my parents to fully buy into this charade, they have to be the ones to answer the door. Besides, since I'm supposedly being forced into this date, any show of enthusiasm would seem off-key.

So I stay upstairs, spying from the landing. My mother begins primping her hair into place, readying herself to open the door. "Mom," I whisper urgently. "Please don't make a big deal out of this."

"Who me?" she mouths, gesturing innocently at herself. "Don't worry."

Now I'm panicking.

In the entryway, I can hear my dad opening the door and greeting Howard with a hearty thump on the back and a "Good to see you." My mom ushers him into the never-used formal living room for some awkward moments of standing.

I wait for what seems like eternity.

"Rachel," she finally calls.

Cue music.

Except in real life there's no audio guy dubbing the sound track, so I glide down the stairs to the sound of silence, trying to exude casual indifference for Howard's sake, and hidden reluctance for my parents'. In my house, you can't actually see the staircase from the living room, so I don't really make a grand entrance until I reach the doorway.

Howard is wearing a pair of black jeans and a dark blazer. It looks like he made some effort with his hair, and when I get closer, I can tell that for once he doesn't reek of gym shoes and locker sweat.

All right, he cleans up nice. So what.

His eyes flicker over me briefly as I enter the room, but I can register no expression. Which is irritating. I mean, I know I look decent. Because I had nothing to wear, thanks to the shopping debacle/temporary grounding, Jen let me raid her wardrobe last minute, turning up the perfect black dress. Even my mother, who always grouses whenever I wear black, was so entranced with my date that she hadn't said a word. I also spent the better part of the day sweltering in our humid bathroom, depilatoring to perfection. I didn't go to that much effort to get utterly no reaction from the male species. Which, technically, includes Howard.

"You ready?" he asks impatiently, his car keys still jangling in one hand, his jiggling foot tapping against the floor.

My parents are going to freak. Howard is acting like he's just picking up a pal, but it has to look like he's madly into me.

I rush to cover for him. "Ready," I say, giving him a dazzling smile and flinging my mom's ivory pashmina shawl around my shoulders.

Fortunately, my mom mistakes his impatience for jittery nerves.

"Howard, you look very handsome this evening," she tosses out, stroking an ego that hardly needs it, in my humble opinion.

He gives her an "Aw shucks" look. "Thanks, Mrs. L."

"Call me Sylvia," she cajoles.

Since when does my mother even have a first name?

"And doesn't our Rachel look beautiful?" prompts *Sylvia*.

Ugh. Like I need some forced compliment. I roll my eyes.

But Howard just looks amused, finally turning and giving me an exaggerated once-over. "A vision," he says, with a tone in his voice that naturally goes right over the heads of my parents, who are both beaming. I want to kill him. A *vision*? A vision of what? But instead I have to smile gamely and grit my teeth.

No one mentions the one-thousand-pound gorilla in the room: the rosebud on my ankle, which I meticulously covered with a clear Band-Aid. I've been carefully taping it up every time I shower so it won't fade away. So far, it is valiantly holding up, although the edges are beginning to flake a bit. Dr. Drummond told my mother it was better to let the skin heal completely before attempting a reversal, so I'm off the hook for the time being.

"We're so glad you're taking Rachel to the dance," I hear my mom gushing.

"It's no problem." He shrugs. "It's not out of the way—"

SHUT UP! I want to scream, before he gives away my whole cover story. "We're late, right?" I tap Howard's arm, trying to change the subject and propel us out the door.

"No corsage?" My dad frowns. I notice he has his camera dangling from one hand, ready to freeze the moment into a photo for Mom's next Hallmark scrapbooking club. Howard shoots me a confused look, like, Why would I bring you a corsage? And I shoot him back a look of, Hey, you know my parents are certifiably insane.

"Dad, it's not prom," I clarify, as if it weren't obvious. Honestly, fathers just have no clue. Even if Howard were my date, corsages went out with poodle skirts and Sha Na Na. "No one does corsages anymore. This is just a random school thing. And we have to go."

But my dad is already motioning us to crowd together in front of the fireplace for "just one picture," which turns into thirty, which turns into Howard and my dad marveling over his new digital camera.

Eventually, mercifully, hallelujah, proof there is a God, we are ushered out onto the porch, where my parents

cheerfully wish us bon voyage, waving like we are sailing off
on a cross-Atlantic oceanic cruise.

"Don't stay out too late!"

"Drive carefully!"

"Have fun!"

But their words, which sound well-intentioned, reek
upon further inspection. By the time I reach the end of the
driveway, I've put my finger on it.

What ever happened to:

"Call us as soon as you get there!"

"Be back by eleven!"

"Don't drink and drive!"

They might as well have counseled us to avoid mixing
hard alcohol and beer, how to dodge speed traps, and to
always use a condom during an orgy.

I can't believe it.

Howard is getting a free pass.

There is NO WAY if I were going to this dance with
Luke—well, I am going with Luke, but you know what I
mean—he'd be getting such preferential treatment. It's like
I'm an Ivy League college, and Howard is a legacy.

I am jarred back to reality as Howard unlocks the rust-
ing, paint-chipped car door for me and heads around to his
side of the Volvo. I pause at the passenger side door. No
doubt my parents are spying, er, peeping out from behind
the venetian blinds. This has to look convincing.

"Aren't you going to open it for me?"

Howard stares at me for a second. "Are you incapacitated in some way I should be aware of?" he asks. "Old ankle injury acting up?"

Clearly, I need a convincing excuse to get him off his unchivalrous ass.

"Nails!" I smile, waggling my fingers at him, as if my fragile tips might break off should I come in contact with something so menacing as a door handle. I'm counting on the fact that he won't look closely enough to realize my nails are, despite my resolutions, bitten to the nub.

"Chicks," he mutters, shaking his head. But he comes around and flips open the door with an exaggerated gesture, adding, "You'll have to move to the back when I pick up Tara."

"Naturally," I snap, sliding into the front seat, pushing aside Clif Bar wrappers and empty Gatorade bottles. God forbid the Queen shouldn't ride shotgun. As soon as he gets in the car, I turn to him. "I can't believe how easily we got out of there," I say accusingly. "My parents think you walk on water."

"Easily?" He snorts. "Only after your dad lectured me for forgetting the corsage and took a million pictures of us." He shoots me a piercing look. "It's like he thinks we're going together, or something."

"Ahem, well, er . . ." I mumble, and start fiddling with the radio dial, which turns out to be busted.

"You have to"—he gives the radio a thump with the

flat of his hand and it bursts to life—"give it a smack."

A minute later, we're stopping short in front of Tara's house, the Volvo's aging brake pads squealing their objection. Howard gets out and pops open the back door so I can switch seats.

"Be right back," he says, strutting like a male runway model up Tara's walkway. I sit in the car alone, trying to imagine how Tara's parents act when her dates arrive. They're probably so jaded by now, they don't bother making a fuss. Certainly, it's not considered a photo op.

Sure enough, they return to the car in less time than my parents took to answer the door. Howard gives me a pointed look as he gallantly flings open the car door for *her*. Honestly. Tara is barely cordial when she glides into the front seat, even though I've given up shotgun for her.

When we pull up at Luke's, he is waiting outside for us, like I asked, and looking adorable in a pair of preppy khaki pants and a deep blue, button-down shirt. To my relief, Luke's parental units also don't feel the need for a first-degree grilling.

Tara, who practically didn't even talk to me along the way to Luke's, twists around in her seat and begins peppering him with questions. Within ten minutes, she gets more out of him than I did during our four-hour date. He has four older siblings—*Luke's mom must be a saint*, I think—one is a pilot for the air force, one is in the police academy, one sells auto parts, and his oldest sister is a nurse; all he knows is that he wants to play hoops for St. John's University. Howard, who hopes to be Cornell-bound, merely grunts, *Uh-huh*, while Tara tilts her head and goes *Really?*, like it's the most fascinating thing she's ever heard. I can't tell whether she's flirting madly or probing for some character flaw.

Suddenly there is a loud pop and a slow wheeze from somewhere beneath the car, and the Volvo jerks to the right. Howard slams on the brakes, and we are all pitched forward and back like crash test dummies, until we stop with a clunk. "Ohmigod," Tara exhales, clutching her chest where the seat belt has dug into her cleavage.

I brace myself, wondering why the air bags didn't inflate, then remember that Howard's dinged-up old Volvo is from the pre–automotive-safety era.

Howard looks shaken. "Is everyone all right?" he says, spinning to see how we are doing in the back.

"I'm fine. Are you okay?" Luke asks me. I nod, still stunned.

Realizing no one is hurt, Howard shifts his concern to his car. "What was *that?*" he says, throwing his hands down on the steering wheel in frustration.

"Sounds like you've blown a tire," Luke answers mildly.

The two of them get out of the car and circle it slowly, looking for the offender, while Tara and I stay in our seats, rolling down our windows and peering anxiously at them in the darkness.

"There." Luke points to the rear tire.

"What?" Tara demands, leaning out the window.

"It's flat," Howard says.

She gives him a death stare. "Can't you fix it?"

Howard looks dubious. "There might be a spare, but I'm not sure. . . ." He pops open the trunk and pulls out a small donut tire and a rusty red jack. He fumbles around for a couple of minutes, even retrieving the manual from the glove compartment and thumbing through it, before finally admitting defeat. "We should probably just call Triple A."

Tara moans. "We are so going to miss the dance."

"Mind if I take another look?" Luke asks. Howard defers with a wave.

Luke rolls up his sleeves and begins digging in the trunk. Finally, he pulls out a small tool kit and pops open the lid. "This might work." I can see he is holding some kind of patch, which he begins massaging with his hands, and a tube of putty.

Howard watches as Luke kneels over, probing the tire for the hole. We all wait silently for a minute while he wrestles with the leak. When Luke stands up, he is up to his elbows in black grease and tire rubber, and the knees of his pants are smudged with the dirt of the road.

"This should get us there and back," he tells Howard. "Just needs a little air. You'll have to go get a new one tomorrow."

"Thanks man," Howard says, clasping his hand.

"Oooh, you're my hero," Tara squeals to Luke as he

261

tosses the spare back in the trunk and slides into the backseat.

"How'd you know how to do that?" I ask.

"My older brother," he says, "the one who sells auto parts.
But everyone should learn how to change a tire. You ladies,
too. You can't always rely on the kindness of strangers."

I can't help glowing. For some reason, I feel vindicated
that Luke came out on top, that Howard looks so inept
compared to Luke and his capable hands. I shoot him a tri-
umphant look, and he blinks in shame.

Take that, Howard.

By the time we pull up in front of the school, Tara's gratitude has faded. "Why don't you two hop out while we go
park?" she suggests to Luke and me, trying to sound sweet,
but clearly not wanting her grand entrance tainted by being
seen with us—me and my grease-stained wretch.

"Good idea. We'll see you in there," Howard says totally
missing the point of her request. As we walk away, I can
just make out her whining, "Why does she need to hitch a
ride from us? Can't her mommy and daddy drive her?"

"Tara," I hear Howard say sharply, like he is annoyed, but
I miss the rest of his response as Luke turns and grabs my
hand, pushing thoughts of Tara and Howard out of my
mind. Who cares? I am here, at a real live school dance, with
an honest-to-god boyfriend, arriving sans parents. Nothing
can kill my mood. Not even the grease he gets all over my
hand.

We make our way inside, past a plastic banner reading, simply, WINTER DANCE, and follow sparkling arrows leading down to the gymnasium. As soon as we step through the door, before my eyes can even adjust to the lack of light, Jen swoops in for the kill, with Matt trailing close behind.

"Finally!" she shrieks, not even noticing Luke's state of disrepair. "We've been here for, like, hours. Where have you been?" She is wearing a strapless red dress and has liberally applied body glitter all over her bare arms and shoulders, radiating bursts of light in every direction, like a walking disco ball. I fill them in on our car troubles, while Luke heads off to the bathroom to try and wash the grime off his hands.

"Where's Alissa?" I ask. Jen and Matt had begged a ride with Alissa and her senior boyfriend, Robbie.

"They've ditched us already." She laughs. "Drinking beers out back, I think. Robbie says school dances are for underclassmen."

Once Luke returns, the four of us cluster by one side of the gym to scope everyone that shows up. Our classmates parade by, looking markedly different from their everyday personas. Everyone has put in extraordinary effort, calculated not to look like effort. The girls wear far more dark eye shadow than they dare during the daytime and far less comfortable shoes; the boys have run a comb through their hair and splashed on too much body spray. The sight of people trying to transform themselves into something else

263

depresses me. It never works. The coolest girls somehow know how to pick just the right outfit, while everyone else just inevitably reveals their fashion flaws.

Jen launches into a commentary on everyone who enters the room, like she's Joan and Melissa Rivers covering the red carpet at the Oscars:

"Here comes Darren Wald, with his muscles practically popping out of his blazer."

"Look, it's Mr. Thinks-He's-The-Most-Eligible-Bachelor-of-Riverdale-High, Aidan Levine—stag!"

"Finally, we have Josh Green. The Big V," she announces. I'm not sure if she is referring to his valedictory aspirations or his certain virgin status. "Wait. He's with a date!"

This I have to see. I had told my mother he already had a date, sure it was an impossibility. Had I somehow willed it so? But what girl could Josh Green have scavenged up? Someone from the Latin Club? Elaine Woo, our class secretary? His mother?

But no.

On his arm.

Is a real live girl.

LEAH??!!

My so-called friend, Leah. Who hadn't even told me she'd been asked out. On a date. TO MY OWN SCHOOL DANCE.

chapter 37

SO IT TURNS OUT that Josh Green was driving
Leah's newfound passion for BBYO, not some slavish devotion to after-school Judaism. JOSH GREEN! I don't get it.
But Leah is practically swooning over Josh's shining intellect
and presidential status. "He's so brilliant, isn't he?" she confides to me in a whisper. I guess power really is an aphrodisiac. For his part, while Josh has taken Latin, French, and
Japanese, he seems all impressed with Leah's foreign-lan-
guage acumen. "Do you know she can read and speak
Hebrew?" he brags, slinging his arm around her neck.

Actually, I have to admit that Leah and Josh don't make
the worst couple on the face of the planet. Leah thinks she
knows it all, and Josh actually *does* know it all. I don't know
why I never thought about getting them together before.

When I pull her aside for a private debriefing, she says
she's been dating Josh for months, but was too embarrassed

to tell me because she knew I thought he was a hyper-competitive scholastic tool. Although, to be fair, she doesn't use those exact words.

"I didn't think Josh did school dances, but then at the last minute he said he wanted to come, and what could I do?" Leah smiles sheepishly, relieved at finally being found out.

Then I tell Leah she's crazy to care what I think of Josh, after all, considering who I am dating. But she tells me that as long as I'm happy with Luke, I shouldn't listen to what she has to say—an all-time first for Leah. Of course, it's not like I've been listening to what she says anyway, but I pretend like I am really touched by the gesture. And we hug. So I guess all is forgiven.

Leah and Josh wander off to chat up Mr. Harvey, the chaperone and college adviser, while Luke leads me toward the polished wooden floorboards that serve as our dance floor. Above us are basketball hoops interwoven with silver and purple streamers, our school colors.

As we head out to dance, a new worry that hadn't even occurred to me before, pops into my head. How am I going to dance with Luke? I've danced plenty with other girls in groups, but rarely with a partner of the opposite sex, when dancing is basically vertical sex on the dance floor. Before I can give it too much thought, we are facing one another, melting into the heat of the crowd. Not surprisingly, Luke is a perfect dancer, holding my hand lightly with his fingers and pressing one leg between mine, not too aggressively but not too meekly, either.

Finally, just as I've mastered the art of gyrating, the mood slows down as the DJ begins spinning a slow song. Luke looks down at me, and it is just like I envisioned at my brother's bar mitzvah, only without all my relatives looking on.

"Ready?" he asks, putting out his hand.

I dissolve into his arms, and we sway to the music for a while as all other fears are erased. It's nice, and after about two minutes, I actually remember to breathe. And after about three minutes, I stop worrying about stepping on his feet. Out of the corner of my eye, I see Tara and Howard sitting way up high on a row of bleachers across the room, observing us from above—far too superior to get out on the dance floor.

Their loss, I think.

Luke and I drift like this for a while. Eventually he murmurs in my ear, "So do you want to give me the grand tour?"

"All right," I say reluctantly, feeling like I've been drugged with a sedative. I really don't want to leave the dance floor, but right now I'll do whatever he asks. We slip out of the gymnasium, past Josh and Leah still distracting Mr. Harvey from his official chaperone duties, and into the deserted hallway. The school looks different at night, abandoned, with all the life pulsing from the gym behind us. It's

267

a little creepy. We wander down the corridor, passing gray metallic lockers and locked classrooms. The music wafts down the hall behind us, but the magical spell of the dance floor is broken as we're slapped with the cold air of institutionalized learning.

"So," I ask, "what do you want to see?"

Now that we're out in the hallway, I'm not sure what we're doing here. After all, most public schools from this era look exactly the same: a cross between a loony bin and a state penitentiary. Seen one, and you've seen 'em all.

Luke doesn't seem disinterested, though. He seems fascinated. At least, in the words coming out of my mouth. Or, maybe, just my mouth.

I press my back against the wall, feeling the chill of the cold tile against my skin. "So the locker rooms are down the hall, and the cafeteria and library are upstairs. Do you want to see a classroom?"

He shakes his head sexily and begins heading toward me. "Not really."

He halves the distance between us, while I keep babbling, certain that if I stop talking, some kind of catastrophe will occur. Desperately, I try to dredge up some point of interest. What can I show him? I'm pretty sure the access to the roof is locked. . . .

"Or, if you want, I could show you the quad, where we hang out before school. . . ."

He halves the distance again, smiling disconcertingly. It

idly occurs to me that even if Luke keeps halving the distance between us, he'd theoretically never reach me, because the distance would just get smaller and smaller and smaller until it reached infinity.

"The quad," he echoes, looking hard at my lips. The distance between us is so minuscule now, I can almost feel his breath.

It occurs to me, belatedly, that Luke isn't all that interested in a tour of the school grounds.

"Or, I know," I say, succumbing to defeat. "The computer lab—"

Mmmffffpphh.

Without formal notice, my lips are being smothered, relieving me of the need to keep talking, to keep thinking of places to show him, to keep every tendon in my body coiled in nervous anticipation. I melt, letting him kiss me, letting the sensation of Lukeness wash over me like the waves of an ocean.

And wash. And wash. And wash it does. There are buckets of saliva, freely flowing between us. I didn't know the human body could produce so much saliva. I am drowning. Someone needs to toss me a flotation device. Then, without warning, Luke's tongue dives into my mouth, like an airplane making an emergency landing in my throat.

Mayday! Mayday!

I can barely breathe.

When we pull away, the whole bottom of my chin is

dripping wet, like I've been bobbing for apples. Luke is looking at me tenderly, but all I am thinking is, is it rude to wipe?
But if so, isn't the sight of me dripping in saliva a bigger
turnoff?

It's a moot point, because Luke has moved back in, this
time kissing around my ear and neck. I bury my face in his
shoulder, nuzzling him back, but really just trying to wipe
away the excess moisture.

"You're so exotic," he murmurs, twirling a strand of my
dark hair around his finger.

Exotic? I feel about as exotic as a wet sock.

My brain is having a meltdown. *Luke. My bussable busboy.*
Great looker. Bad kisser. Error. Error. Does not compute. I can't
resolve the two competing thoughts. There's even a psycho-
logical term for it that we learned in health class: cognitive
dissonance.

Then I realize the truth. Of course it's not Luke. It's me.
Obviously I'm not doing something right. Luke's probably
kissed countless girls, and I've kissed a grand total of two
guys, if you count a late-night game of Spin the Bottle at
camp and those two weeks with Marc Goodman in seventh
grade. Luke doesn't seem to think there's any problem here.
I must need some more practice.

And I get some. For the next half hour, I play defense
while Luke acts as if he has an All-Access Pass to my vocal
cords. It is totally exhausting.

When we eventually come back inside, we find Matt and

Jen over by the doorway. "Come with me to the bathroom," I say to Jen, hoping to get a second opinion. And before she can object, I yank her toward the exit. In the girls' bathroom, we wait until two juniors in fishnet stockings finish their cigarettes, grinding them out on the floor as they exit. Once I am sure no one is in the room, I'm about to ask her what to do, when she casually says, "Matt is so sure we're going to sleep together tonight." I don't know if she is announcing her intent, or lamenting Matt's idiocy, so I just look interested while I wipe away the eyeliner smudges from beneath my eyes. "I'm like, hello?" she continues, powdering oily spots on her face and neck. "I'm not having my first time be in Robbie's Camry during the Winter Dance. Gross! I mean, maybe if he planned something a little more sophisticated . . ."

"Have you told him that?" My kissing dilemma with Luke suddenly seems so kindergartenish by comparison, I'm embarrassed to even bring it up.

She looks worried. "I keep putting him off, but I think he's gonna be really pissed when he realizes I mean it."

"So do you want to or not?"

"I don't know," she wails. "Matt says girls who hold out beyond high school just end up losing it to some drunken frat boy who doesn't even remember them the next day. He says it's much better to do it with your high-school sweetheart, so it will always be meaningful."

I had to admit, Matt was good. You couldn't poke a hole in his dementedly warped logic.

"I can see why he's such a star debater," I say offhandedly.

"What's that supposed to mean?" she says, pausing halfway through reapplying her lipstick.

Suddenly I'm regretting getting into this conversation. "Just that he's very, very good at persuasion," I stammer.

She snaps the tube shut and turns toward me. "What? Are you saying he's manipulating me?"

"No," I say weakly. "Just make sure you're doing it because *you* really want to."

"Of course I want to. I wouldn't do something I didn't want to do." She challenges me with a glare.

Yeah, like the way you became a vegan for Alissa. Or the way you played strip poker for Matt.

I guess she can read my thoughts in my eyes. "I wouldn't," she repeats stubbornly.

"If you say so," I reply.

"Thanks for the support," she snaps, storming out of the bathroom in a huff, not waiting for me, not even speaking to me again for the rest of the night. I head back to Luke, distracted. The evening is not turning out as I had expected. Kissing Luke is a nightmare, and Jen barely acknowledges me when she takes off with Alissa and Robbie. I'm almost relieved when Howard and Tara thumb at us that they are ready to go.

When we reach Luke's house, I get out of the car to say good night, painfully aware that Howard and Tara are observing us like lab specimens. A cheek peck would be fine.

But no, Luke bends over and pulls me into another close encounter of the slobbering kind. I count, like I am holding my breath underwater, until my lungs almost burst.

"I'll call you," he whispers. I slide back into the car, quickly wiping my chin with the back of my hand, hoping that no one noticed my ambivalence.

"What a hottie." Tara whips around and grins, trying to force some girl bonding. "How did *you* snag *him?*" I smile and shrug my shoulders, unsure if her emphasis was more on the you or the him.

When we reach Tara's house, Howard gets out and walks her up to the door, while I slump down in the backseat, trying to give them privacy. I can see their silhouettes from the streetlamp. Howard confidently leans in, cups one hand around her cheek, and tilts her head toward his. From where I am sitting, there doesn't seem to be any excess moisture. And neither seems in a hurry to break apart. How did Howard get game, I wonder. Graphic novels? *Penthouse* letters? Blow-up doll?

Howard finally makes his way back to the car, and I duck my head, pretending I wasn't watching the entire time. As I get out of the back and hop into the front seat, he shoots me the same look of triumph I shot him before, when Luke had fixed the car.

"Nice guy," he says graciously. "Your Luke. Very . . . handy."

"Mmm," I murmur in agreement. "And Tara really

273

is so very . . . you know . . . spectacular. . . ."

He looks a little abashed at my obvious sarcasm, then recovers. "So I guess you two kids need a ride to her party?"

I hadn't even thought ahead that far, but now that he mentions it . . . "That would be great," I say, stifling a yawn.

"Tired?" he asks.

"Exhausted." If only he knew from what.

Finally, Howard pulls up into his driveway. We both get out of the car. "Well, later," he says, turning to head into his house.

"Later," I sigh. Then I remember. We have to complete the illusion of a date through to the grand finale. You never know if my parents are waiting behind the door, just to make sure we get home safely. Well, in my case, I take that back. I do know. Of course they are.

"Oh, hey—" I stop him. "Do you mind walking me to my door? You know, just in case?"

He gives me a look like I am crazy. Our neighborhood isn't exactly known for needing Crime Stoppers.

"Paranoid much?" he teases.

"Easy for you to say," I retort. "You don't know what it's like to be a poor defenseless female, fumbling for your keys in a dark doorway."

He shrugs, as if to say, you win, and accompanies me up to the porch.

"Well, good night," I say.

Do I detect a curtain rustling behind the window? Are

my parents lurking on the other side of the door? Better make sure. I need a perfectly polite display of leave-taking, so I lean up, grab his hand, and peck him on the cheek.

Just for appearances' sake.

That's all.

chapter 38

EXCEPT, MY MOVE must have caught Howard off guard, because he sort of jerks his head at the last minute, leaving us in a lip brush. A near-miss kiss. Mortifying! But then, doubly mortifying, he actually must think I *meant* to kiss him, and he starts hemming and hawing as if he can't get out of there fast enough.

Sure enough, when I open the door, my parents are trying hard—too hard—to look like they've been curled up on the family room couch for hours.

"Oh, is that you, honey?" my mom says drowsily, as if ten seconds ago her eardrum hadn't been suctioned to the other side of the front door. "Have fun?" she asks, feigning a yawn. Unlike me, she hasn't mastered the art of lying.

"It was fine," I say, denying them any satisfaction of their curiosity. "I'm going to bed," I say, feigning a yawn of my own.

As soon as I step into my room, my cell phone rings. Relief floods my system. It must be Jen, calling to make a truce. I'm not even sure what we had been fighting about, really. And I still need to get her opinion about Luke. Not to mention this mortifying moment with Howard. I snap it open and answer. "Hello?"

A deep voice on the other line. "I told you I'd call."

Luke.

"You couldn't wait eight hours?" I can't help but smile. It's sweet, in a stalker-esque way.

"Nope. I wanted to tell you good night. Without anyone watching." Bad kissing aside, his voice still makes me float. We review the highlights of the dance, and groan over the upcoming week apart while I fulfill the final days of my grounding. After we hang up, I drift off to sleep, visions of Luke dancing in my head.

But my dream is a nightmare reenactment of that awkward good night with Howard. Except, in this version, I'm naked and he's wearing his red running shorts. Tara is there in her pep squad uniform and pom-poms, cheering "Don't Go with the *Goyim!*" And Luke is changing the tire on Howard's car. When I wake up Sunday morning, I am relieved, thinking for a minute that the whole evening had been just a bad dream, too. But no, part of it was all too true. Luke kissing me. Howard dissing me.

But I don't have nearly enough time to properly agonize right now. My cousin Julia, Aunt Merle, and Uncle Milt are on their way over for brunch, to show off the pictures from Julia's wedding. I pull on some jeans and Luke's inside-out sweatshirt, for the third consecutive day, and head down-stairs just as the doorbell rings.

"We've got the proofs!" my Aunt Merle heralds, throwing her hands in the air.

My uncle is right behind her, schlepping several boxes of film negatives. "Good name, proofs," he grumbles, kissing my mother on the cheek. "Thirty grand I spent on flowers, booze, and music, and this is the only proof it ever happened!"

"Milt." Aunt Merle smacks him on the arm. "Behave."

"Come," my mother says, ushering everyone into the living room, a room that has gotten more actual use in the last few months than I can recall in my entire lifetime.

Ben wanders in from the kitchen, amazingly detached from his umbilical cord, er, Xbox joystick controller. Instead, he is clutching a copy of Anne Frank. "DoIhaveto?" he mumbles.

My mother tries to herd him into the room. "Don't you want to see your cousin's wedding pictures?" Clearly, Ben has no interest, while I am dying for a peek.

"I was there, you know," he says. "Why do I need to see the pictures, too?"

"Don't be smart with your mother," my dad says.

"But I'm almost finished," he whines, fingering a book-mark stuck near the back of the book. "I want to see how it ends."

They both spy the cover of his book and melt like

microwaved butter. "Just take a quick look," my mom says.

As he goes by, I lean in and whisper in his ear, "She doesn't make it."

I mean, it's horrible but true. Everybody knows that, right? Except, I guess, not Ben, because the little suck-up visibly stiffens and actually looks distraught. "Really?" he whimpers. I feel a huge pang of remorse. I am not just a sinner, I am pure evil. The wild beasts should be along to trample me any minute now.

Any minute . . .

In the meantime, Aunt Merle spreads out the pictures on the coffee table, as we all relive that glorious autumn day. At first, it is a virtual Julia-fest. Julia's veil. Julia's shoes. Julia's dress. Julia getting ready. Julia hugging her parents. Julia signing the *ketubah*, the Jewish wedding license. I begin to feel bad for the groom. Finally, Brad makes a late appearance, nervously peeking out from under his white yarmulke. Then it's Julia and Brad clasping hands under the canopy. Julia and Brad sipping wine from a porcelain goblet. Julia and Brad being raised up on their chairs, separated by a handkerchief. Julia and Brad cutting the white cake.

And finally, a couple of pictures of the rest of us.

"There you are, sweetie." My mom ruffles my hair. I am sitting at the kids' table, glowering. Next to me, Jared has a big grin on his face, and Ben is holding up his fork. I only vaguely remember a photographer coaxing us to cry "Parcheesi!"

"There's Bubbe!" Ben shouts.

Sure enough, the next shot is of our family's table, Bubbe making her last public appearance alongside my parents and Aunt Adelle. Her red cheeks are beaming, glowing with pleasure. Why shouldn't she be happy? After all, Julia was the good granddaughter, the one fulfilling her dearest wish.

"Look at her," my mom says emotionally, tearing up. "At least she had that happy occasion."

My stomach gurgles, and I excuse myself to the kitchen. I'm halfway through pouring myself a glass of Diet Coke, when Julia saunters in.

"Pour me one, too?" she asks, hopping up onto the counter.

"So how's married life?" I ask, pulling out another glass from the cabinet.

"Great," she says. "It's such a relief all that wedding stuff is over. I was, like, obsessed all last year, completely focused on the wedding. Like I couldn't think about anything else. Was I a total bridezilla?"

"You weren't too bad," I lie diplomatically, handing her the soda. I couldn't hold my strapless fiasco against her.

"Thank God it's over," she sighs. "It's like my fever broke, and now I can concentrate on everything else." She pauses to guzzle her Coke and then peers at me. "When it's your turn, you should definitely elope."

I snort in laughter.

"I'm serious," she insists. "Save yourself the headache."

"The way I'm going, I'll probably have to," I grouse.

She looks at me as if I'm just kidding. "Oh, why's that?"

"What ever happened to that guy Finley, that you used to date?" I ask, changing the subject.

"Finley?" She looks thoughtful. "God, I haven't thought about him since forever. What about him?"

"Did you ever think you'd marry him?" I ask.

"Sure, at the time." She smiles dreamily. "He had this little blue moped, and he'd drive me all over campus. And he had the sexiest upper bod."

"So why didn't you?" I press.

"One big reason—" she says.

I knew it! Religious differences had torn them apart.

"—He was a total a-hole. Senior year, I think he was cheating on me with, like, two other girls! Thank God I found out in time."

I am stunned. Finley seemed so classy. So respectable. So in love with Julia.

"So there was no drama?"

"There was plenty of drama," Julia says grimly. "I poured a bowl of Lucky Charms down his pants."

I giggle. I can imagine her doing it, too, although I personally would have gone with Cocoa Puffs—more embarrassing stainage potential.

"No, I mean drama with Aunt Merle." I take a deep breath. "Because Finley wasn't Jewish, right?"

"They were definitely not thrilled," she admits. "But they

were too cool to say so. My mom told me after we broke up she could tell he was an arrogant jerk, and that it was just a matter of time before I figured it out."

"But it all worked out," I say, trying not to sound bitter. "You found Brad, the boy with the Bubbe seal of approval."

It all made sense. After dating her bad boy, Julia turned to a guy like Brad: a nice Jewish boy who was safe, dependable, a good family man. How bourgeois. There was no way I would let that happen to me.

"Is that what you think?" Julia is shaking her head. "I'm not with Brad because he's Jewish. I'd be with him even if he weren't. Well, in that case, I think . . . I would have gotten him to convert." She waves her hand dismissively. "Anyway, the fact that we share the same beliefs? That's just the cherry on top."

She smiles and hops off the counter to put her glass in the sink. "So is that why you think you'll need to elope?" she asks, giving me a piercing look. "Is there some Finley-like guy in your love life?"

"Sort of," I admit.

I don't mean to fess up, but after weeks of hiding it from my family, I need to tell someone. This compulsion to be honest strikes at the most inconvenient times. Oddly enough, never when I'm talking to my parents.

"Well, it's a tough call."

"What would you do?" Suddenly I really want to know.

"I think you have to follow your heart. Don't worry

about what Herb and Syl think. Figure out what *you* think. If he's the one, he's the one. Whatever he happens to be. Unless he's a jerk like Finley."

I guess it's good advice. Unfortunately, I have no idea what I think. But I'm going to have plenty of time to figure it out. Because until next weekend, all I have to look forward to is being grounded.

chapter 39

BEING GROUNDED IS just like being placed under house arrest—like Martha Stewart, only without the ankle bracelet and the sprawling Connecticut estate. No cell phone, no internet, no IM—it's like I'm living in 1986, or something. My life has been reduced to going to class, studying, and staring at my wall. Since Jen has been giving me the deep chill all week, moving to the So Very table to sit with Alissa and Tara, I've spent most of my lunch hour on the phone with Luke, either borrowing a cell phone from a sympathetic soul, or calling on the campus pay phone, using up all the change I could dredge up from my lunch money. Wayne's four-word assessment said it all: "Sucks to be you."

At least my midterms have been trickling in, all of them comfortably in the ninetieth percentile. Ms. Jensen handed back my *Scarlet Letter* paper, which would make up two-thirds of my grade. She scrawled her thoughts across the top in her red pen. *It disturbs me to concede that society has*

*completely lost its moral compass. There is still a difference between
absolute right and wrong, no? Still, A⁻ for originality.*

But even that is little consolation. I'm living for Tara's
party on Saturday, when my week of grounding will be over,
with time served, and I won't have to find Stone Age ways
to communicate with Luke. I'm beginning to seriously consider carrier pigeons, when Ben appears at my door.

"Get lost, cantor boy!" I say, an autonomic sibling reflex.

He looks offended. But does that stop him from coming
into my room and plopping onto my bed? No. "What's that
supposed to mean?"

I have to know what's gotten into him lately. "You've
become this little religious fanatic lately. What is it with the
Young Judaica routine?"

He looks deadly serious, like he's about to give a sermon.
"Rachel, do you know how much money I got from my bar
mitzvah?"

"I dunno. A couple grand?" I guess, based on what I'd
banked from my own.

"And do you know what they said I had to do with it?"

"Yes, Ben, they'll stick it in a college fund for you. Don't
worry, Mom and Dad aren't jetting off to the Caymans with
your U.S. savings bonds."

"It's my money," he says stubbornly. "Why can't I spend it
on what I want? Now?"

*Because they know you're a video-game addict who would lie,
cheat, and steal to get your hands on a copy of Grand Theft Auto?*

285

"What would you spend it on?" I ask.

"There's the new PlayStation coming out next year."

Voilà. For once, the wisdom of my parents wins by a landslide.

"Ben, you're an idiot. You don't want to spend all your money on that junk."

He smiles. "I did. Until they made me an even better offer."

This is news to me. "What?"

"They said they'd buy me whatever games I wanted if I showed some interest in our heritage. But there was no way I was going to go back to Hebrew School, so . . ."

"So the kibbutz?" I demand. "Israel? The teen tour?"

"Do you know they have to get up before dawn to pick bananas?" He wrinkles his nose. "And they have communal showers."

"Anne Frank?"

"All she can talk about is her crush on some Dutch twit named Peter, like some typical whiny female." He shakes his head in dismay. "She should have made some grenades, ditched the attic, and bombed those Nazis! Like Lara Croft!"

I would love to see that ending.

"What about the JCC?"

He stops and considers. "No, I actually like playing basketball there."

I can't believe what he's saying. His religious awakening

has just been a mockery of our faith. A total manipulation of our parents. For material gain.

I guess I can respect that.

Still, as his older sister, I feel obliged to sustain some sense of moral outrage. "I can't believe you're bribing our parents into buying you games," I say. "Do they know?"

"Nope," he says proudly. "And you're not going to tell them."

"Why not?"

"Because I'll tell them about Luke," Ben says casually, but I can tell he's making a pointed threat. "Is he your boy-friend?" he singsongs.

"NO. Shut up!"

"Then why is he programmed into your cell phone?" He jumps up in triumph. "Why do you call him every day?"

"Who said you could touch my cell phone!" I shriek. The indignity! Is there nothing sacred in this world?

"Mom gave it to me to use this week, since she took it away from you," he taunts. "'Cause you're grounded."

Darn it, I'd forgotten to delete all traces of my cellular tryst. I guess I'm still a rank amateur at this sneaking around thing.

"Looks like you call him a lot," he says gleefully. "So does he go to your school?"

"No, he goes to St. Joseph's," I admit, bracing myself for his reaction.

But Ben is oblivious to the intricacies of Catholic high

schools and the Love That Dare Not Speak Its Name.

"Did you tongue kiss him?" he teases, waggling his tongue at me. "Mmmmm."

Disgusting. This is what my religion considers a man? No wonder I've given up faith.

"Did you dump Howard for Luke? I like Howard."

That's the final straw. "Get out!" I roar as he scrambles for the door, barely escaping with his life. *Thou shalt not kill thy little brother*: a Teen Commandment begging to be broken.

chapter 40

AFTER I'VE SUFFERED through a week of social
isolation, the Saturday night of Tara's party finally arrives.
I'm not even sure I'm still invited. Now that I'm not speaking to Jen, it's possible I've been blackballed, too, like Josh
and Wayne. But Howard assured me that my name is still on
the guest list.

When I told my parents he was picking me up for the
party, they took that to mean that we were now an official
couple. My dad even gave me the speech about giving people a chance, and still waters run deep, and how glad he was
that I'd seen the light.

So tonight, when I make my grand entrance, it's just like
déjà vu. My parents start gushing sickeningly all over
Howard, trying to entice him into conversation while I am
trying to inch us out of the room without making a scene.

Meanwhile, Howard keeps a healthy distance between
us, clearly spooked to be around me, scared I'm going to
molest him or something. Honestly, does he think that just

because he is big man on campus, every girl is going to throw herself at him? As if! I'm going to have to make it clear that it was just a polite good-night cheek peck that went astray. No more, no less.

We are halfway to the door when my mom, the master of bad timing, asks innocently, "So, who is this Tara?" Why does she have to choose NOW to revert to her old nosy, overprotective ways?

"She's my—" Howard begins.

"—She's this really great girl in my class." I cut him off. "Tara Silver. On the dance team. Popular, really sweet."

Howard gives me a hard sideways look. I can practically hear his inner voice of disbelief: *Sweet?*

"Oh, yeah, Rachel and Tara are like this," he says, entwining his fingers and giving me this *look*.

As soon as we escape the house, I hop in his car, this time without waiting for him to open the door. But instead of starting the car, Howard just grips the steering wheel tightly and sighs heavily, as if he is trying to summon up the right thing to say. I ready my comeback, sure he is going to give me some prepared let-her-down-easy speech about how he's flattered but not interested.

"What am I?" he finally demands. "Your beard?"

"What?" My stomach clenches like it's making a fist.

"You know, your cover. Your red herring."

This I hadn't expected. I've been so focused on the door-way disaster, I never thought he'd figure out the truth. "I don't know what you're talking about," I say haughtily.

"Your parents think I'm your date tonight," he insists, shaking his head in disbelief. "Don't they?"

I evade the question. "My parents think a lot of crazy things. My mom thinks she should have Katie Couric's job. My dad thinks he'll someday win the World Series of Poker."

Howard just waits patiently. The jig, as they say, was up.

"All right, yes," I sigh, releasing my breath in defeat. "They think you're my date."

"I knew it!" he crows, sounding oh-so pleased with himself for figuring out the truth. "Why?"

I roll my eyes. "Look at how they act around you. They want me with someone like you, not Luke."

"You never did tell them about him, did you?" he demands.

"Not . . . exactly." Now that the truth is out, I just sit there, panting slightly.

"Why not?"

"I've told you why. They'd hate him."

"Because of his religion?"

"Yeah, obviously."

"Maybe that's the point," he mutters.

"What do you mean?" I demand.

"Nothing. Forget it." Then, after a moment, he adds reluctantly, as if he can't help it, "Just that, are you sure you really like him—or maybe, you like it that they won't like him?"

"That's ridiculous," I say. "Of course I like him!" *And why would I want my parents not to?*

"Sure you do. What's not to like?" he says, flipping on the radio dial and giving it his customary whack, abruptly ending the conversation.

But now that he's raised the question, I can't help stewing over it. What is Howard suggesting? Luke is handsome, a decent student, an athlete, a Boy Scout, for God's sake. I like Luke. Everyone likes Luke. If only my parents could like him despite their prejudice, all my problems would be solved.

It was impossible to pinpoint the most objectionable aspect of Tara's Sweet Sixteen.

Was it:

A. The egregious gobs of cash her parents had obviously dropped, renting out Trash, one of Manhattan's trendiest nightclubs

B. The fact that Tara supposedly had her dress, a plunging strapless beaded concoction, custom made by Betsey Johnson herself

C. The way she had personally hand delivered her invites last week at school, sending the entire student body into a pitched frenzy of antici- pation, and publicly humiliating those who didn't make the cut

D. That the whole nauseating extravaganza was being filmed by a reality TV crew from MTV for a future episode of _Sadly Spoiled Schoolgirls,_ er, _My Super Sweet 16_

E. All of the above

It's a pretty easy multiple-choice question. Even Jen, if she weren't so ensnared by Alissa and Tara's evil spell, could get this one right without the help of Princeton Review. But she is otherwise preoccupied. From the minute we get to the party, I've been hoping to catch her and call a cease-fire. But even from a distance, I can tell it's not a good time. Things between her and Matt seem strained. I can see them across the room, clasping one another on the dance floor with more tension than passion. He murmurs something into her neck, and she shakes her head no. And their voices are beginning to get louder.

I'm preoccupied monitoring this awkward dance of intimacy from afar, but Luke doesn't seem to notice. "Don't you think Jen and Matt are acting weird?" I ask him.

"I'm sure they're fine." He shrugs. "Anyway, I thought she was being a total bitch to you. It's not your deal."

"I guess." I feel annoyed. I wish I could get him to focus, but when it comes to something serious, he always dodges the issue. "Back rub?" He begins massaging my neck, but instead of relieving tension, he only makes me feel more stressed.

When I next look up, Jen is nowhere to be seen, and Matt is stalking off toward the other side of the room, disappearing into the crowd.

"Where did she go? Should I go find her? Maybe I should talk to her."

"Stop worrying about her," Luke says, nuzzling me. "You stress too much."

"I do?"

"Yeah. It's kinda cute, though."

It is?

Luke, as always, drapes his arm over my shoulder and begins nuzzling me. It hangs there, heavily, like a stone. When he first did it weeks ago, I felt all aglow, but tonight, for some reason, it makes me feel trapped. Suffocated. Smothered. I need to get away, just for a minute. I should go check on Jen. Maybe try to end our stupid fight.

"I . . . gotta hit the bathroom," I tell him, disassembling his arm from its permanent fixture on my back. "I'll be right back."

I duck away through the throngs of couples and head down the dim hallway toward the bathroom. Inside, it's teeming with chattering girls covering zits, blotting sweaty armpits, borrowing Tampons, praying at the porcelain altar. But no Jen.

I stumble out, still looking for a place I can be alone.

Down the hall, I wander by the coat check at the far back of the club. The counter is deserted. The sultry attendant who had taken my coat must be on her cigarette break. I carefully raise the partition and step into the darkened room, taking in the musky scent of leather jackets and suede coats.

Alone. At last. I sink against one of the racks, leaning my weight up against the cushiony support. What is wrong with me? Here I am, seeing and being seen at one of the most sure-to-be legendary parties in our school's history, with the most perfect dream date, tall, blond, and can slow dance, even. So why am I hiding out in the coat closet?

Down the hallway, Tara's piercing voice rings out louder than the steady bass beat of the DJ. "Well, where is he, then?" Even without seeing her face, I can detect the pissed tone in her voice.

Whoever is with her murmurs some quiet words of consolation.

"He knew we're supposed to dance to that song," she screeches, her words slightly slurred from her private pre-party. "The video crew is waiting." I can hear her heels click down the marble floor, amplifying as she gets closer to the coatroom.

"Howard," she calls anxiously, "are you in there?"

I freeze. What if she comes in and sees me hiding out alone? I mean, it's one thing to be hooking up in a coat closet during a party, it's another to be totally alone, hiding out from your date.

Sure enough, before I can think what to say, Tara sticks her head inside the door, her blue eyes squinting to make out my form. "Is someone in here?"

"Hey, Tara," I say weakly, feigning surprise, as if I hadn't heard her shrieking down the hallway.

"Rachel?" Tara looks surprised, as if I am the last person she expects to see messing around in a coat closet. Which, I guess, at her party, I am. Then she sees it's just me, and a sneer flies across her face. "Are you in here all alone? What are you doing?"

"I'm just grabbing my lip liner from my pocket," I say lamely. Except, I'm not standing anywhere near my own coat. I don't even have any idea where my coat is. So I turn and paw at the nearest jacket, faking a grope for my makeup deep in the pocket.

Tara gives me a suspicious glare. "Isn't that Darren's coat?" I look down at the coat I had arbitrarily claimed. It is a bright purple letterman's jacket, size Extra Large, that clearly reads *Darren* in looping white script right on the lapel.

I drop my hand like a hot potato. "Oh, whoops. This one's mine." I reach for a less identifiable dark blue peacoat hanging next to it. But she's already lost interest.

"Oh. Whatever," she says, flouncing off before I can remove my arm, empty-handed. I listen to her heels click down the hallway.

Great. Now she'll probably start a rumor that I'm stalking uber-jock Darren Wald.

Behind me, I hear a rustling from deep in the second row of racks. Oh my God. There must be a rat in the corner. Rustling. Definite rustling. Except, it sounds way too big to be coming from a rat, even one of those giant mutant rats that live in the subway.

I muster up every ounce of courage in my body. "Is someone there?" No reply. Now I'm getting pissed. Isn't there any place a person can get a little privacy? I mean, what possible insane excuse could someone have for hiding in a coat closet—other than trying to hide from your boyfriend, of course? I stride over to the far rack of coats, spread my arms wide, and thrust the coats apart.

And standing there, totally busted, is Howard.

chapter 41

HOWARD SWAGGERS OUT as if hiding in a coat rack is the most natural thing in the world. "Lip liner?" he says, already recovering his composure. "You barely wear lipstick."

I am utterly confused. Why is Howard, of all people, hiding in a coat closet? More specifically, why is he hiding from Tara, his spectacular girlfriend, in the middle of her spectacular party? But instead of explaining any of that, he is mocking my cover story, which basically saved his butt, too.

"Howard!? What the—?"

Suddenly he steps forward and presses one hand over my mouth and the other around the back of my head. He's lost it, I think. Howard is having a nervous breakdown, brought on by more popularity than his central nervous system can handle.

Then I hear what he heard. Tara's heel clicks, growing louder again.

He purses his lips. "Shhhhh."

We stand there, paralyzed for a split second, like a hunter and his trapped prey. I can feel Howard's large hand pressing right against my mouth, my lips. I try not to breathe too loudly. I try not to drool into his hand. I try not to think. Just before Tara pops her head back into the room, Howard evaporates behind the racks of coats, like a superhero dissolving into the gritty streets of Gotham.

"One more thing . . ."

I spin to face her, semi-aware that Tara, from her position by the doorway, can't see Howard, but when I glance over, I can see him peeping back up at me from behind the jackets.

I quickly lick my lips to give them a glossy appearance. "Found it," I cry, smacking my lips as though I had just reapplied my lipstick, and pretend to slide the tube back into my pocket.

"You came with Howard, right? Maybe he's getting something in the car. Could you run out there and see? Just tell him I need him. Now."

I hesitate. I can't help it. I sneak a peek down at him, trying not to give his presence away.

He nods his head slightly, silently pleading with his dark brown eyes, all bluster gone.

"Sure, Tara."

"Thanks." She whirls around and clicks away, this time, I pray, for good.

Howard steps out of the shadows. "Thanks."

Without asking, I know what's going on. Howard has

finally seen what a wench Tara is, and can't stand to be near her another second. I'm just amazed it took him so long. I suddenly feel super self-conscious of the two of us, all alone in a darkened coatroom.

"So . . . you and Tara . . ." I begin to say.

"She wants me . . . TO DANCE," he whispers, as if in sheer agony.

"Huh?"

"She wants us to do this big dance routine in front of the whole party. For the video crew. But I . . . DON'T . . . DANCE. I'm a wreck. And if everyone sees me try, they'll know I'm just a total loser . . . ." He gulps miserably.

I can't believe it. Howard the Marathon Man doesn't want his girlfriend to know he has two left feet. To think that only a few weeks ago he was the one lecturing me about honesty in relationships.

"So, what, you figured you'd just hide here for the rest of the party?"

"Why not?" he says, crossing his arms defiantly.

Wait. "Is this why you wouldn't dance with me at my brother's bar mitzvah?" I demand.

Howard avoids eye contact with me, hanging his head sheepishly. "Yeah," he admits. "You know I don't dance!"

"No I don't!"

"I haven't danced since fourth grade, since that square dancing class. They called me Howard the Heaver for weeks? Remember?"

"And you've never danced since then?"

"Nope. You knew that." I shake my head. "Well, the way you asked me at your brother's bar mitzvah, I thought you were mocking me. I didn't think you really wanted to dance with me."

I don't bother telling him that, at the time, I hadn't actually wanted to dance with him. What would be the point?

We just stare at each other for a second. A long second.

If this were some sappy Hilary Duff movie, I guess I would say, "I'll show you," and the music would swell and I'd take his hands and give him a two-minute instructional speed dance course, and he'd go dance with Tara, and the crowd would cheer while I stood on the sidelines, smiling, and he'd give me a wink, acknowledging that it was all because of me.

But something stops me. Maybe I don't want him to go dance with Tara and wow all her friends.

"What about you?" he asks, suddenly realizing I'm hiding out, too. "Where's Luke? Did something happen between you two?" He cocks his head faux sympathetically, like he knew it was just a matter of time before Luke dumped me.

"He's fine," I say. "We're totally happy. Never better."

"Oh, really?" he challenges, with a tone that suggests he doesn't believe me. "Then why are you standing in a coat closet talking to me?"

Bing! Bing! Bing! Very good question. "I'm . . . I . . . have no idea," I snap, turning on my heel and stomping out.

When I return to the party, Luke is wearing a neon

necklace and is pounding a Red Bull. "For you," he says, taking it off and looping it around me. Sensing my distance, he tries using the necklace to drag me closer. I shut my eyes tightly as Luke bends in to kiss me, blocking out all other thoughts. Quietly, a little niggling voice in my head finally blurts out what I'd never admit to anyone, except maybe Jen. Luke really is a bad kisser. World-class bad. In fact, the thought of kissing him for one more minute practically makes me want to gag. Jen's words ring in my head. *If the physical isn't good, the rest doesn't matter.* I'm dying to tell her that she'd been right, until I remember we're still not talking.

I open my eyes to take a peek, and see that Howard has reemerged from the coat closet. He stands across the room, arms crossed, staring at us. Tara stomps up to him and peppers his chest with her fists. I can practically read her lips from across the room: *Where have you been?* The two of them stand there arguing for several minutes. Howard looks like he is pleading with her and she is shaking her head. A film crew circles them like vultures, snapping up the raw footage. Howard abruptly strides over to us, and I jerk away from my lip-lock with Luke. "I'm leaving now," he says curtly. "Are you coming?"

This party is jinxed, I think. First Jen and Matt are fighting, now Howard and Tara. We'd better leave before Luke and I are the next casualties. "Let's go," I say, taking Luke's hand.

On the ride home, Howard is quiet, while Luke holds up his end of the conversation as though nothing is wrong. "Man, did you see those dancers they hired?" he gushes. "Do you think we'll really be on TV?" My head aches, and I just nod numbly.

After we drop off Luke, Howard and I head for home. Finally I can ask what I've been wanting to the whole car ride home. "What happened?"

"I told her."

"And?"

"She didn't take it well." He shuts his mouth, and it is clear he doesn't want to talk about it. He pulls up into his driveway, and the two of us get out of the car, quietly, quickly.

"G'night," I say, heading toward my house. I've never seen Howard in such a dark mood. I don't even want to be around him.

This time, Howard is quickly by my side. "I'll walk you up."

"That's okay."

"Oh, but we have to play out the charade, don't we?" he says grimly. "For your parents?"

He is right. At the door, I avoid meeting his eyes, not even wanting to give him a quick cheek peck. But this time, Howard leans in, cups my cheeks in his hands, and firmly kisses me on the mouth.

Before I can respond, before I can process what is

happening, before I can kiss him back, it is over. I stand, dazed and confused, a million thoughts exploding in my head, like a blender without the lid on. What does he think he's doing? What about Tara? What about Luke? I gaze at him woozily, no words coming to mind.

He looks at me strangely, then jerks his head toward my porch, indicating my parents inside. "That should convince them," he says quietly, then turns on his heel and heads off into the night.

Right. So of course. It takes me only a beat to realize that Howard was just kissing me to keep up the act for my parents. I am the biggest fool who ever lived.

The house is pitch black and quiet when I enter, still off balance. After all that, everyone seems to have retired for the night. I can't believe my parents didn't stay up to demand the full reenactment of my evening. I sprint up to my room, just in case they wake up, and barely reach the door when my cell phone vibrates. It must be Luke calling like last time to say good night. Except I don't want to talk to him right now. What if he hears something funny in the sound of my voice? What if he can tell I've been technically unfaithful in the ten minutes since I saw him last?

But when I check the caller ID, it isn't Luke.

"Hello?" I say happily. But all I can hear is the sound of weeping. Then a gasp. A sob.

And before she can say a word, my best friend's heartbreak breaks my heart.

chapter 42

IN TIMES LIKE THESE, all petty squabbles are automatically called for rain. Like we'd never fought, Jen tells me what had happened: the jerk dumped her ten minutes after Tara's party. I knew all along he was pond scum, and it is satisfying beyond belief to finally get to tell her so. It's too late to go over to her house, so I lie on my bed, in the dark, cell phone attached to my ear, trying to give solace from afar.

Jen tells me they had barely made it to the party when Matt began pressuring her again to have sex. They slipped out, taking a long walk down the lower half of Manhattan, and ended up on a pier at the South Street Seaport, viciously arguing.

"All he would say was, 'It's just not working out.' But I know the real reason," she says bitterly. "It's because I wouldn't sleep with him."

We both knew it was true.

"And you want to know the really sad, pathetic part?" she

continues. "I was thinking of doing it, on Valentine's Day. It would have been so romantic, you know? I can't believe I was this close. Two weeks away. And he couldn't stick around to wait."

We each take a moment to shudder at Jen's near-sex experience.

"I can't believe after dating someone for three months, I won't even have a boyfriend on Valentine's Day," she laments. "I've been waiting to have a real boyfriend on Valentine's Day my whole life."

I know exactly what she means. "Yeah."

"And *you* will," she accuses.

"Oh. Yeah." I hadn't even thought about it, to be honest.

She takes in a big breath. "So, about the night of the dance . . ."

"Forget it."

She pauses. "I hate that you were so right about him."

"I didn't want to be. Honestly."

We sit there in silence for a while, just breathing on the line. Partnered suffering.

Then she asks me the painful question. The one almost too awful to contemplate. "Rachel?"

"Hmmm?" I'm getting drowsy.

"Do you think if I'd slept with him . . . maybe . . . we'd still be together?" she whimpers.

"No," I say truthfully. "I think you'd be sleeping with a jerk who eventually would have dumped you for some other stupid reason. And then you'd have lost your virginity to a known a-hole. This way is better. You're done with him. This way, he won't be able to hurt you again."

It sounds convincing, even to me. So why can't I kick the gut feeling that we haven't seen the last of him?

IN THE MORNING, I meet Jen at the bus stop so we can walk onto campus together and she doesn't have to risk facing Matt or any of his friends alone. As soon as we step into the courtyard, Alissa and Tara practically sprint up to Jen, bursting with faux concern. Both of them ignore me, not even commenting on our reunion; I wonder whether Jen had told them about our fight.

"We heard about what Matt did, it's so awful," Alissa blurts out, giving Jen a big hug.

"Yeah, thanks," Jen mutters from somewhere in Alissa's shoulder.

"You must be really upset," Tara says, tilting her head sympathetically.

"I guess."

Jen's lack of emotion only makes Tara more bloodthirsty. "I don't know how he could do that to you," she huffs, itching for drama. "Dumping you. And then posting those pictures."

Pictures? Just like last night, when I told her everything would be fine, I feel an oncoming sense of dread tingling down my spine, the same creepy feeling that I used to get when we played Light as a Feather, Stiff as a Board at junior high slumber parties and pretended to levitate off of our sleeping bags.

Jen looks confused. "What are you talking about?"

Tara leans in conspiratorially. "You poor thing," she says. "Hasn't anyone told you?"

Jen is visibly alarmed at this point. "No. What? What pictures?"

Tara and Alissa exchange knowing glances. Alissa looks sincerely appalled, but I can't help but detect the smallest smirk around Tara's plumped lips.

"There's pictures of you on a Web site. Topless. From some New Year's party," Tara exhales in a burst of disclosure. "It looks like you were playing strip poker with a bunch of guys."

"One of them must have had a camera phone," Alissa explains nervously, glancing at Tara for approval.

I'd never noticed before how Alissa seeks Tara's approval almost as desperately as Jen seeks Alissa's. An analogy pops into my brain: Alissa is to Tara as Jen is to Alissa.

"What?" Jen stammers.

"Don't you remember?" Tara asks incredulously.

I replay Jen's words from that night in my mind: *I don't remember much, I was pretty wasted.*

309

"No. I don't know," Jen moans. "Why would Matt do that?"

"Men are dogs." Alissa shrugs.

"What's the Web site?" I demand.

Tara whips out her cell phone. "I'll text you both the link," she says coolly, as if she is forwarding me a homework assignment and not Jen's crumbling reputation. With a few punches on her keypad, we receive her message. "Do you want to see it?"

Jen shakes her head violently. "I think I'm going to be sick," she says, slumping against the wall.

"Don't worry, it'll be okay," Alissa says sympathetically, giving Jen another hug. I notice a small frown crossing Tara's lips, as if Alissa's undivided attention were her divine right.

"Yeah. Matt's dead to us," Tara says. In her world, there is no greater form of vengeance than cutting someone out of their social circle.

"Maybe you guys could . . . go talk to him?" Jen pleads. "See what he says? Convince him to take them down?"

"No way," says Tara. "Why give him the satisfaction that you care?"

"It's better this way," Alissa agrees.

"Trust me," Tara says, squeezing Jen's arm winningly.

But that's not good enough for me. Matt needs to repent. To make things right. If Alissa and Tara won't do anything, no one else will.

"I'll talk to him," I hear myself saying as Jen's swivels

to me with a glassy-eyed look of gratitude. "Come on."

As we walk away, I overhear Tara say, "She shouldn't have let herself get that drunk and sloppy. What do you expect?" And Alissa, saying nothing in Jen's defense.

I squeeze Jen's hand, hoping she didn't hear, and pull her after me. Jen follows mutely along behind me, still in shock, as we enter the cafeteria. I scan the room, looking over to where Matt and his friends typically cluster around the soda machines.

"There he is," I say, spying him across the room, already mentally rehearsing his tongue-lashing.

"I don't think I can do this," she pleads.

"Fine. You stay here," I order, placing her against the wall. I march over to Matt and his buddies, who all quiet down as they see me approach. Matt, instead of looking stricken, just sneers at me. "Can I help you?" he asks, mock politely.

"Take them down, Matt," I demand.

"I don't know what you're talking about," he protests, raising his hands innocently in the air.

"The pictures. Take them down." I try to sound confident, but I suddenly realize that I have no power to get him to do anything.

"What makes you think I had anything to do with it?" he asks, changing tactics, tacitly conceding he knows exactly what I'm talking about. "I can't control what other people do, can I? If someone has a camera and takes pictures, that's their right. It's a free country."

"I'll tell Mr. Dean," I bluff, naming the school principal. Like all preplanned speeches, this isn't going the way I'd planned at all. How come people never respond the way they're supposed to?

"This has nothing to do with school business," he says smoothly, deflecting my amateurish attempts to debate the master. "The same thing happened at Rockville, and their principal couldn't do anything about it."

Now he's citing case law. He clearly has all the angles covered.

"I hope you rot in it," I finally spit out, retreating across the room, wondering why I thought I could try confronting someone like Matt.

This level of wrongdoing goes well beyond the scope of the Sin-O-Meter. This is Pure Evil Incarnate. Being trampled by wild beasts would be too good for him. I can finally see the appeal of stoning.

I think back to Ms. Jensen's comments on my English paper. *There is still a difference between absolute right and wrong.* It finally rings true. If breaking the Teen Commandments puts me in the same league as Matt, I'm ready to repent now.

I whirl around and return to Jen, pulling her out of the cafeteria and outside the building as I try to decide what to tell her. "Well?" she says anxiously, leaning against the stone wall. Hadn't she been watching the conversation from afar? How can she possibly be holding out hope?

"No luck."

Jen suddenly looks around, like a paranoid schizo-phrenic, as students stream past us into the building, heading for class. "Do you think everyone has seen them?" Is it my imagination, or are we getting second glances? Or are the strange looks because Jen is having a public meltdown?

"No," I lie. "I'm sure just Matt and his friends."

She slumps down to the ground, clutching her knees, moaning catatonically, rocking side to side. "What if my par-ents see?" She sobs. "My dad will kill me."

I don't know what to say. It is wretched beyond belief. The first bell rings, sounding like a death toll. I turn to go inside, but Jen remains frozen to her spot. "I have to go to gym, for my running test," I say. "But I'll meet you at your locker before lunch. I promise."

Jen nods numbly.

I head for the clammy girls' locker room and quickly throw on my sweatpants and T-shirt, tossing my clothes in my locker. I hesitate, and reach back into my jacket pocket for my cell phone. Feeling completely disloyal, I sit on the wooden bench and punch up Tara's text message and click on the link. I'm compelled to see it for myself. Maybe it's not that bad, I think, squinting at the screen in the dimly lit room. Maybe everyone is overreacting.

On my screen, I can only barely make out the stamp-sized image of Jen, holding a beer in one hand and a pair of cards in another, grinning sloppily and proudly flaunting her assets, like one of those Girls Gone Wild on late-night TV.

At least she has assets to flaunt, I can't help but think. I can't imagine the mortification of having the whole school see my nada-tributes.

But then, something else at the top of the screen catches my eye. A T-shirt, faded blue jeans, a shock of rumpled blond hair. I'd know them anywhere. The boy standing in the background of the picture. It's Luke.

chapter 44

THUMP.

Pound.

Wheeze.

I can feel the thump of my feet on the pavement, the pound of blood rushing through my temples, the wheeze of my breath as my lungs circulate the ice-cold air. But for the first time, in some weird way, the pain feels good. Empowering. Bring it on.

A sea of anger and confusion roars in my head. The track rushes by, a blur as I go faster, faster, faster. All I can focus on is the guilty parties flying around my head.

Like Matt.

Thump.

How does he live with himself? How did he fool Jen into thinking he was a good guy? How could he betray someone he wanted to be with a day ago? How could someone do something so evil?

I'm even mad at Jen.

Pound.

How could she let herself get into this situation? Why did she have to do whatever Matt said? Whatever Alissa says? Whatever anyone says?

Then there's Luke.

Wheeze.

What was Luke, my Luke, doing there, watching other girls, skanky girls like Shannon, get naked, when he was supposed to be into me? Wasn't it a little suspicious that he'd never mentioned it? Worse, did he play a part in posting the pictures?

Thump.

Pound.

Wheeze.

I power past the finish line, still aching to keep going. Today I want to run until I collapse, I want to run past this school, this street, this city. I no longer care about the stopwatch, my time, passing gym. I just want to move. I *need* to move. Who needs a personal trainer or a coach? My fury is all the motivation I need.

I barely process Mr. Gee's sarcastic, "Hmmmm . . . just under the wire," as he clocks me across the finish line.

14:34.

Maybe I won't be setting any statewide track records, but it's good enough to pass. Whew. But I'm almost too wound up to celebrate, as one more guilty party clicks into my mind.

Howard.

What was his deal, kissing me like that, then passing it off as fooling my mom and dad? What was his deal, kissing me like that, when he has Tara Silver as a girlfriend? What was his deal kissing me LIKE THAT at all?

chapter 45

TEN MINUTES LATER I slide into my seat in Room 401, still dripping with sweat. I can't help but hear Aidan snickering to someone on his cell phone. "I'd like to play Hold 'Em with her." He laughs. He listens then guffaws even harder at what he hears back. "Yeah, she's got a pretty big pair." My jaw clenches.

"Phones away, or I take them away." Mr. Diamenties frowns at Aidan, who clicks his Motorola shut just as the bell rings.

That doesn't stop him from turning around and leering at me. "Hey, Rachel," he whispers. "You were at that party. Were you feeling lucky, too?"

I want to kill him. I want to run over him with a Hummer, back up, and run over him again. I am seething with road rage, and I don't even have my learner's permit yet. "Who told you?" I demand.

"Tara's been e-mailing the link all over school." He shrugs carelessly. "You've seen it, right, Wayne?"

"Yeah," Wayne says flatly, as if the novelty of naked chicks on the Internet had peaked in the late '90s.

"Tara?" I choke. Tara. Forget killing Aidan. I am going to murder Tara, the little backstabbing—but before I can question Aidan any further, Diamenties interrupts us. "I know you're all eagerly awaiting these," he announces, standing in the aisle with the stack of midterms in his hand. "So let's get right to it."

I'm so distracted by everything going on, I'd completely forgotten he's handing back our midterms today. When he reaches the back of the room, Diamenties puts my test deliberately facedown on my desk, trying to look all stern. But then he can't help himself, and gives me a sly wink as he turns away. It is a dead giveaway. Good thing he never applied for the CIA or anything. Beside me, I see Wayne get his test, glance at it, and causally slip it inside the cover of his textbook.

I venture a peek at my grade. Sure enough, I can see the bright red *A* peeking back at me.

Triumph shoots through my veins. But outside, I remain the essence of cool.

I should just slip the test inside my notebook, safe from prying eyes.

But I don't.

For some reason, I just sit there and wait. Mr. Demented is not the only predator who likes to trap his prey.

Predictably, in less than thirty seconds, Aidan whips

around. "B minus," he crows, snatching my test off the desk with his typical So Very presumptuousness. "How'd you do?" As he turns my test over, his wide leer freezes on his face, like the Joker's grotesque carnival grin. He stares speechlessly at the grade circled on the top of my exam.

A big fat ninety-eight percent.

"I thought you were failing," he says, almost accusingly.

I should just shrug and say that I must have gotten lucky. Or that I offered Demented sexual favors to pass me (which Aidan and his gutter mind would easily believe). Or that Wayne had slipped me a stolen copy of the test.

But I don't.

Something set in motion this morning has finally snapped within me. Why should I care what a jerk like Aidan thinks of me? Why should I care what anyone thinks? I've seen what happens when you care too much—you end up like Jen, a vegetarian naked on the Internet.

So I just smile sweetly, slip my test into the front pocket of my binder, and say, "I guess geometry's just incredibly easy. At least, for me it is." Then I pull out a fresh piece of loose-leaf paper. "Oh, and if you ever need someone to tutor you after hours?" I pause suggestively. "Try Josh Green. I hear he's really good."

chapter 46

THE MINUTE I GET out of class, I whip out my cell phone. I have only ten minutes to walk to English and try to reach Luke.

"Hey," he says smoothly, answering his phone. "So are we still on after school? My place?" He sounds so happy to hear from me, I almost feel guilty ambushing him.

"What happened New Year's Eve, after I left?" I demand, without greeting him back.

"Wha—?" My question catches him off guard.

"You said you'd make sure Jen was all right. I want to know, what happened to her?"

"Rachel, calm down. What's going on?"

"There's pictures of her, naked, on a Web site. And you're in the picture, too, Luke!"

Even over the phone, I can hear his Big Gulp. "Oh that. Yeah, I heard about that."

"Who took the picture?"

"Why are you accusing me? I was *in* the picture. How could I have taken it?"

"Then who did?"

"I dunno," he says. "I only got there near the end. Anyway, what's the big deal? It's just a dumb prank." And he laughs. "Honestly, she should almost be grateful—she's getting more hits than Janet Jackson and her wardrobe malfunction. She'll have another boyfriend in five seconds. It could be the best thing that ever happened to her. Right?"

I can't believe he can be so cavalier about this.

"It's a big deal to her—and to me," I snap, flipping the phone shut. When he calls back, I refuse to answer, letting his rings go to voice mail.

After English, I head downstairs. I expect to find Jen at her locker, but instead she is sitting in the cafeteria with Tara and Alissa, all three picking at their rabbit food. I storm up to the table.

"I need to talk to you. In private." I say.

"What?" Jen asks.

"Yeah, what's going on?" Tara challenges.

I turn to Tara. I hadn't planned on confronting her, but I have no choice. "I heard you've been e-mailing that Web site all over school." She looks at me as if I'm crazy. So does Jen.

"Says who?" Tara challenges, although she doesn't look me in the eye.

"Doesn't matter who," I say. "Is it true?"

"Maybe I forwarded it to some people." Tara shrugs.

Jen squeaks. "You did?" I'm not sure her system can take any further shock today.

Tara turns to Jen. "It's better this way," she says quickly. "Everyone is going to find out about it anyway. This way, it'll blow over fast. In a couple of days, people will forget about it. Trust me."

This time, her *trust me* sounds hollow, even to Jen.

Jen and I just look at her in disbelief. "I can't believe you would do that," Jen says quietly. I notice Alissa squirms uncomfortably in her seat, but doesn't say a word.

"Why is everyone making it into such a big deal?" Tara says blandly, as if we are all crazy. So this is what it means: the banality of evil. Tara personified it to a tee.

"I can't believe you would DO THAT," Jen repeats, her voice getting loud enough that a few people glance over at us.

"Can you please not make a scene?" Tara says calmly.

"A scene?"

"It's bad enough you put yourself in this position. Frankly, it makes us look like skanky-by-association. Right, Alissa?"

We all look at Alissa, who has been conspicuously silent until now. "Right?" Tara repeats warningly.

Jen looks at her with pleading eyes. *You know Tara is wrong. Take my side. We're swim teammates. I've let you copy my French homework. I've given you Luna Bars.*

But Alissa's loyalties were claimed long ago. I don't

expect much. And I'm not disappointed. "You shouldn't have pissed Matt off, Jen," Alissa finally says. "He's a great guy."

Jen's mouth falls open. I want to come to her aid, but there is no comeback in the universe good enough for a moment like this. So all I say is, "Nice," as witheringly as possible, and then to Jen, "Come on," pulling her up from her seat.

The two of us stumble out of the cafeteria, up several flights of stairs, and motor down the long corridor, so we can take refuge in the bathroom at the far end of the fourth floor, the one hardly anyone uses. By the time we get there, Jen has passed through the first stage of grief, denial, and has moved on to the next one: anger.

"Why would Tara do this?" she demands, pacing back and forth on the pink tiled floor.

"I don't know," I say. But I do. I've known since this morning, when I saw the frown of displeasure when Alissa comforted Jen. Tara is jealous of Jen and Alissa's friendship, too. In that respect, she and I actually have something in common. Only, I would never trash another person's life to hold on to a friend.

"I thought Alissa and I were friends," she storms, pacing the room. "But did you see how she just went along with Tara? Like a zombie."

"They're total androids," I agree. "Completely soulless."

"What am I going to do? I'm talking major revenge." Her voice crackles with spunk, the first sign of life I've seen from her all day, all year, practically. It's the old Jen, the brave Jen, the one I thought was gone forever. "First Matt. Then Tara."

"First, we should try to get those pictures taken down," I say. "Before the whole school sees them."

"But Matt won't do it."

"Who needs him?" I realize there's one person who can help. And I know exactly where to find him.

chapter 47

JEN AND I SLIP OUT of the bathroom, down the staircase, and out the side door. Sure enough, our target is just where I knew he'd be, in the parking lot behind the gymnasium, slouching over a PDA with his motley assortment of fellow slacker hackers. Their heads all swivel in disbelief as we approach. Now that I'm here, I almost lose my nerve. Jen looks at me, confused, and I just give her a look that says, *play along.*

"Wayne?" I say, summoning up my courage.

"Present," he says, not bothering to turn his head as he absorbs the general approval of his buds, who smother their snickers in their sleeves.

"They need you in the computer room," I say frantically. "One of the iMacs is having this total meltdown, and Mr. Taft thinks you're the only one who can unfreeze it. He sent us to come find you."

His entourage is impressed. "You the man!" they hoot, pounding him on the back. This he likes. Wayne gets to his feet and thrusts out his chest. "At your service," he says, spinning his wrist and bowing over his arm like a manservant. He all but swaggers as we fling open the door, entering the building. Then, as if something has just occurred to him, he whirls around. "What's the real deal?" he says. "Taft doesn't even teach comp sci this period."

Busted. I'm not sure whether to begin begging or continue with my bravado. "We need your help," I plead. "You're the only one I could think of."

"Help with what?" He crosses his arms as he coldly scrutinizes me.

"This Web site, with my friend's picture." I gesture to Jen, who smiles weakly. He barely glances at her before turning back to me.

"And I should care, why?" He looks ready to head back to the parking lot.

I stare at him, unsure what I can say that would move him. Emotions, passion, sympathy don't affect someone like Wayne. Reason, logic, strategy—that's all he responds to. "Is this really what you think computers should be used for? Humiliating people?"

He looks at me as if I am an imbecile. "No. Of course not." He waves his hand dismissively. "But lovers' spats? It's none of my business."

"So you don't care that her reputation is ruined?" I

challenge as he turns to go. "Seems to me you care a lot about your own."

"What are you saying?"

I can practically see the steam rising from his nose. My knees begin to quake. Why oh why had I picked a battle with Wayne Liu, who, if angered, could wipe out my entire existence? Literally. I'd heard he once hacked into the New York State Birth Records and made it so this kid who crossed him had never been born.

"Just that I know you wouldn't want certain things about yourself broadcast on the Internet. Private things. Would you?" I smile sweetly, to balance the threat of the message. Jen has no idea what we are talking about, but Wayne knows exactly what I mean. He stares me down, a more intense version of that elementary school game of Chicken, seeing who will blink first. But I know even before we begin that Wayne will ultimately win.

A funny looks passes over his face. He has made a decision. But what? He steps close enough to snap my head off. He grabs my arm, like he is taking me into federal custody, and murmurs "Follow me" in my ear. It is clearly an offer I can't refuse. I trail after him, afraid to say no, gesturing for Jen to follow. Wayne leads us to Mr. Taft's third-floor computer room, which, sure enough, is empty this period. The door is locked, but Wayne punches the code as fast as if it were on speed dial. We slip into the deserted classroom.

"So what are you—" I stammer nervously.

He ignores me. Instead, he strides over to the closest iMac and signs on. "The address?" I give him the link. He types rapidly, talking while absorbed in the screen. "You're right."

"What?"

"It's messed up," he mumbles, his fingers flying over the ergonomically correct keyboard. "What?" he says curtly, in response to my stunned silence. "You think I don't know right from wrong?"

I am tempted to ask how he justifies hacking into corporate and government Web sites, but I decide to stay quiet. On the screen, all I can see are green digits and letters flying by, far beyond my Intro to HTML class.

"Name?" He turns to Jen.

"Jen Mackler."

"And the guy?"

"Matt Wallen." He gathers Matt's e-mail address and other more basic information. The minutes fly by, and Wayne seems to finish up what he was doing.

The computer hesitates. ARE YOU SURE?

Wayne clicks yes. He turns to me solemnly. "You're all set."

I'm still not sure what has just happened. "What did you do?"

"The pictures are gone. And the people that posted them just had their computers frozen and their hard drives erased." Jen gasps in gratitude. Even I can't help but be touched.

"Thanks," I say simply. He nods serenely.

"Wait." Jen steps forward, finally summoning the courage to address Wayne directly. "Can you do one more thing?" She leans down, and their two heads confer over the computer screen.

I can see Wayne typing something else quickly, then says, "Done."

Jen flings her arms around him. "Thankyouthankyouthankyou," she gushes, not realizing what a huge mistake this is with Wayne. His body stiffens.

"What did he do?" I ask, as Wayne grabs his book bag and makes a beeline for the exit.

Jen turns to me and arches an eyebrow. "Let's just say Matt Wallen has just sent everyone in his address book an e-mail that says, 'I've been a complete and total butt nugget to Jen Mackler. I'm not worthy of her forgiveness.'"

"Wayne," I say, just as he is about to reach the door. He turns. "You know I wouldn't really have . . ."

He holds up his hand. "I know."

"Then why?"

He is silent for a second, as if it so obvious it needn't be spoken.

"We're even," he says stonily. "You don't owe me, I don't owe you. Besides"—he looks back at me—"this'll make a great personal essay. Hacker does good."

"Really?"

"Yeah," he grins evilly. "Admissions officers *love* that shit."

chapter 48

" I DON'T KNOW how you did it," Jen is babbling. "I still can't believe it. If I hadn't seen it with my own eyes . . ." We slump down onto the floor of the deserted computer room, this time in relief.

"It's over," I say, even though it's not really. The whole school still will be buzzing. There will probably still be snide comments when she graduates. But at least the immediate indignity is erased, and at least Jen has gotten some form of vindication, her e-mail being the modern-day version of a public stoning.

She laughs somewhat bitterly. "Yeah, except that my reputation is permanently trashed. I should go to that alternative school, downtown. The one for dropouts and screwups."

"You are not dropping out," I scold her. "You're going to hold your head high. And deal. You didn't do anything wrong. Matt did. And everyone knows it."

Jen looks at me quietly. "This never would have happened to you."

"Yeah," I snort. "Because I'm too much of a prude to take my top off in front of random guys."

"No," she corrects. "Because you don't care what anyone thinks. What some guy wants."

I consider her words as I finger my ankle. Jen is so wrong. All I've done the last few months is try to have it both ways: Hiding my math skills so guys like Aidan would approve of me. Hiding my tattoo's fakeness so Luke would approve of me. Hiding who I was really dating so my parents would approve of me. All I've done is create a gigantic mess. But the truth is, it's impossible to please everyone—my parents, my bubbe, Leah, Jen, Luke, Aidan, Mr. Diamenties. All I can do is please one person: myself. And it's time to start doing that.

Jen turns to me. I see that old familiar gleam back in her eyes, and I know that she will somehow live this day down. "You know what I could use?" she asks.

"What?" I shake my head.

"A Taco Supreme."

I shudder with relief. The reign of terror, er, Tara, is officially over.

At the end of the day, I casually swing by Howard's locker, wanting to tell him I passed my gym test—and that I hadn't read anything into last night's awkward encounter. But instead, standing there, looking lost, is Tara.

When she sees me, her expression sours. "Looking for

Howard?" she snarls. "Sorry, he can't give you a ride anywhere. He's gone."

"Gone?"

"He just got all Moral Majority on me. He told me off for
passing the link around. Said he couldn't be with someone
'so cruel.' Can you believe that?"

I am too stunned to reply. I also can't help but note the
difference between Luke's casual reaction and Howard's
moral stance.

"Happy, Rachel? Now you can play poor defenseless
female some more."

"What?" I honestly have no idea what she is talking about.

"Oh, Howard, I don't know how to run, can you teach
me? Oh, Howard, I sprained my ankle, can I lean on you?
Oh, Howard, I need a ride to the dance, will you drive me?
What guy can resist that act?"

I think back. Tara has it so wrong.

"Please. He's always been a complete jerk to me."

"Save it," she snaps. "He's had a thing for you forever. It's
so obvious."

Now I know that Tara has lost it. How could she be
insanely jealous—of me? It didn't make sense. Was it another reason she'd tried to hurt Jen—to get back at me?

"Whatever." She shrugs. "I don't know why I was so into
that loser. I can't believe he was hiding out at my party
because he couldn't dance. What a tool."

I can see it already: Tara is going to spread rumors about

Howard and trash his reputation, just like she helped trash Jen's. I can't let that happen.

"Actually, that's not true," I say casually. "He danced with me all night at my brother's bar mitzvah. He's the best dancer I've ever seen." She looks incredulous. "And another thing," I continue. "The two of us *were* hiding out, together, in the coat closet during your party. And you want to know why? Because he said he didn't want to dance—*with you.*"

The smallest part of me is glad to see the unhappy look register on her face. It's almost a shame I no longer need to break the Teen Commandments. 'Cause this one last time, being bad feels oh so good.

chapter 49

I SLIP THE KEY into the front door of my house, praying no one is home yet. I've been on so many highs and lows today, I feel like I'm suffering from mental whiplash. I'm still reeling from the fact that Howard broke up with Tara. And processing Wayne's heroic hack. And celebrating that I aced my midterm and don't care who knows it. And realizing that maybe I'm not the world's biggest wimp after all—physically or otherwise. Now I have one last thing to deal with. Maybe the toughest. There is someone I need to talk to. I just have no idea what I'm going to say.

As I turn the key, the door suddenly pulls open from within. "Rachel." My mom pounces like she's been hovering in the doorway for hours waiting for me. "Good. You're home."

"Hey, Mom," I say, trying to push past her. She's not the one I need to talk to right now. "I really have to—"

"Wait," she says, blocking my way. "We need to talk. Now."

"Can't we do it later?" I plead impatiently.

"Not really. It's about . . . your boyfriend." She drops this bombshell calmly and waits for me to react.

I stop, confused at what she means. "Howard?" I ask weakly.

"Nooooo . . ." she says slowly, relishing my anguish. "Apparently, your *other* boyfriend. Luke?"

Oh God oh God oh God. Busted. Big time. How did she find out? I thought I'd covered all my tracks. There is no way she could know about Luke. Unless. Unless Ben sold me out. The filthy stool pigeon. I am already planning how I will cement his feet together and throw him into the Hudson River, when she adds with a dark smile, "He popped by for a visit." Clearly, she is enjoying my torment.

"He's here?" I panic. It never occurred to me that Luke might brazenly just show up. Then again, I'd never specifically told him he should keep us on the down low.

"In the living room," she says, hooking her thumb in that direction. "Go ahead. I'll be in the kitchen."

I peek around the corner. Sure enough, Luke is sitting there. On my couch. In my living room. Sipping one of my mom's Diet Dr Peppers. It is more than slightly surreal.

"Hey, Rachel," he says, nervously jumping to his feet and almost knocking over the empty can.

"What are you doing here?" I ask bluntly.

"What was I supposed to do? You wouldn't even pick up your cell. You never gave me your home number. I wanted to tell you what I found out."

I sit next to him on the couch, and he quickly tells me what he learned: sure enough, Sully had taken the photo as a joke during the poker game and Matt posted them out of spite after the breakup.

"It's juvenile, but what can you do?" He shrugs.

You could crash their hard drive, like Wayne, I think. You could refuse to hang out with anyone involved, like Howard. But Luke won't do any of those things, I realize. And it doesn't really matter. He is still a nice guy. He just isn't *the* guy.

"Don't be pissed." I can hear him pleading as my mind races, wondering what to tell him. I glance down at my ankle tattoo, relieved I didn't use permanent ink.

"So, uh, your mom seemed kinda surprised to meet me," he says, taking my hand in his. "Haven't you mentioned we're going out?"

Um, er, well. Not exactly so much.

I shake my head.

"My parents are dying to meet you sometime," he continues.

"Maybe," I say politely, knowing it's never going to happen. I squeeze his hand, then worm my fingers free. My lust for Luke has fizzled like a chemistry experiment gone wrong. Then I hear myself voicing the cliché I never thought I'd have to use. "You know, I really think we should talk. . . ."

When I enter the kitchen, I find my mom noisily washing up dishes.

337

"Did I hear him leave?" she asks, shutting off the faucet and wiping her hands on a dish towel.

"He had to go," I say simply.

"So . . ." She gestures for me to sit at the table as she lowers herself into a chair across from me. "What happened to Howard? Did you two break up already? And why haven't you told me about this Luke?"

I have no choice but to tell all. "Mom," I say, cutting her off. "Howard and I were never dating. I just thought he was someone you'd let me take to the dance. And Luke was someone you wouldn't."

"Why not? He seems like a nice young man."

"He is!" I spit out. "And he's gorgeous and on the basketball team and volunteers to coach underprivileged kids on the weekends. But," I continue, "he's not Jewish. He's Catholic. He goes to St. Joseph's. Not that it should matter."

"What?" She looks so overwhelmed by my outburst she's uncertain what point to make first. "What matters is that you're dating some boy and you didn't tell me about it."

"You never would have let me date him," I accuse. "You and dad are totally prejudiced."

"Because he's Catholic? Is that what you think?"

"I heard you and Aunt Merle talking at Julia's wedding, about how relieved you were that she didn't marry Finley 'cause he was a different religion. And then Bubbe, before she died"—I gulp, trying to fight back tears—"she tried to

338

make me promise not to date someone who wasn't Jewish. And you and Dad are so loving Ben because he's hanging out at the JCC and wants to go to Israel, while Leah says I'm just a big traitor to my religion and you and Dad are going to disown me and won't let me be buried in Flushing."

My mom looks like she doesn't know whether to laugh or cry. "Oh, honey." I can tell she is picking her words carefully. "Of course we would like to see you married— someday—to someone of your own faith. Your dad and I believe it makes sharing a life much easier. And we'd like to see our heritage continued. But you'll have to decide for yourself how important that will be in your life. We've just tried to give you the foundation to make that decision. Maybe not always so well." She pauses, probably thinking of our spotty attendance record at Temple Beth Shalom. "But if you come to me and tell my you've met the love of your life, and there's no other man in the world for you, do you think I'll care what he believes in?"

I shrug, too upset to fully grasp what she's saying.

"What I believe in is you. And if you love someone enough, that's good enough for me."

"Really?" I look deep into her eyes for the first time during the conversation, probing for the truth.

"Really. I just want the best for you. That's all I always want."

She starts giggling at my serious expression.

"What?" I demand.

"The other thing, sweetie, is frankly, I'm not expecting you to end up with anyone you date in high school. You've got college, your whole life in front of you, and it's a long shot that the boy, this Luke, who you happen to like today, will be the one you settle down with. These things typically aren't . . . permanent."

"But what about what Bubbe said?" I whisper.

My mom sighs. "You have to understand, Bubbe came from a very different place. Half of her family didn't make it out of Europe in time. Also, she wasn't exactly censoring what was on her mind in those final years. That stroke loosened up her tongue. She never should have said that to you."

I consider that. I'd always admired Bubbe for her strong will. Elderly prerogative, I'd figured. But her sharp tongue had become pretty blunt in the last years of her life, come to think of it. "Are you calling Bubbe a mega-biatch?" I ask.

My mom looks shocked. "No, no, no." Then she chuckles. "Well, sorta. But you never heard it from me." We both collapse in laughter.

News flash: Bubbe won't be tossing and turning in her grave over who I went out with my sophomore year of high school. The Jewish mafia won't be putting a hit out on my goyish guy. My parents won't disown me.

"Really, honey, she'd just want you to be happy," my mom assures me. "That's what I want, too. For you to be happy."

"No, Mom," I correct. "You just want me to be happy *your way*. Not my way."

"Who says I don't know what will make you happy? I am your mother."

"Exactly. You're my mother. You're not me."

She pauses to consider this. "Maybe you're right," she says slowly. "I'll try to remember that the next time. But you have to promise you'll give me a chance and not keep secrets from me."

"You have to trust me when I'm at a party, and don't make me call you and Dad every ten minutes."

"Agreed." The sap level is rising quickly, like we're in an episode of *7th Heaven*. But then, totally breaking the rare reverie of the Hallmark moment, my mom just has to try to bond like she's my BFF. "So when are you planning on seeing this Luke again? I'm sure Dad would like to meet him, too."

As usual, she's *so* three weeks ago.

"Mom," I groan. "Luke and I are history. Get with the program."

Giving up Luke was one of the hardest things I've had to do in my life. I still can't believe I told him it was over. I still can't believe I told my mother the whole sad story, saliva kisses and everything, before I even told Jen or Leah.

The one thing I couldn't give up was his sweatshirt. Even though it was sitting upstairs on my bed, I conveniently "forgot" to give it back to him. Whoops. I just wanted a little memento to remind myself of my first boyfriend. I guess, technically, it's wrong, but I'm sure he'll forgive me. And *He—or She, for that matter—*will forgive me, too.

I bend over to grab my sneakers.

"Where are you going now?" my mom asks, now totally confused.

"Just next door," I say. "I'll be back soon."

Right now, the only person I still want to talk to, no, need to talk to, is Howard. I'm not exactly sure what I'm going to say.

I'm so sorry you and Tara broke up. Or the truth: *I'm so not sorry you and Tara broke up.*

So what if my parents approve of Howard? It was so beside the point. More importantly, I approve.

As I quickly lace up my sneakers, I notice something different on my foot. My tattoo. It has faded away. Gone. All that remains is a clear patch of skin. I feel free, glad that this marker of my first relationship won't show up on my permanent record. I wonder how long it will take my mother to notice.

When I'm almost out of the room, my mom casually adds, "Oh, Rachel, one more thing."

"Yeah?"

"About Ben. Dad and I are well aware that he's just milking us for free video games. You didn't think we actually bought that kibbutz story, did you?"

When I get outside, sure enough, I find Howard stretching

342

on his doorstep. It suddenly occurs to me that Howard does *way* more warm-up stretching outside my front door than is strictly necessary. Maybe Tara was right.

He nods, like he is not surprised to see me. "So, I guess you heard? About Tara?" he asks warily.

"Yeah," I reply.

"Coming to gloat? Say, 'I told you so?'"

I shake my head. "No," I say. "Coming to . . . run."

He smiles. "All right, then, Lowenstein. Let's see it."

We jog along for a while. We start out silently, going through the same route, past the playground, through the park, past the tree with the errant root. As I begin to breathe hard, he glances over at me.

"I thought you hated this," he says.

"Yes. No. Well, I did. Maybe . . . it's grown on me."

"Oh, really?" He arches an eyebrow at me. "What changed your mind?"

I shrug and avert my eyes. "Well, you know. Sometimes, the things you always thought were awful can actually be . . . not so bad."

"Things?" he asks.

"Running . . . people . . ."

We slow to a walk as he digests my meaning.

"And," I add, "the one thing you thought was so great turns out to be . . . not for you."

"Not for you?" he says slowly, tentatively, scanning my expression. "You mean—"

"Uh-huh." I nod, not wanting to Go There when it's time to Move On.

He smiles. "Too bad you're so into running now. I was going to say maybe, next time, we could do something more your speed."

"My speed?"

"Sure. That would be like, hmmm . . . two miles an hour?"

I punch him in the shoulder, like I've done a hundred times before. But this time, he grabs my hand and pulls us to a stop. "No seriously."

"Do something?"

"Yup."

"Together?"

"That's the idea."

"Well . . . you know"—I smile mischievously—"how much I like to dance."

He slumps his shoulders in mock defeat. "Dance?" he says wearily, but his eyes crinkle. "Uh-uh. No way."

"Maybe you just need the right partner."

"Maybe . . . I've had someone in mind . . ." he says turning slowly to me. "But there's still a problem."

"What?" I ask, clueless.

"You know what. I don't know how."

And just like that, I take the plunge. "I'll teach you," I whisper, as he smiles and steps toward me. "You go like this—"

Acknowledgments

This book officially began a lifetime ago, as a piece in the glossy pages of *GQ* magazine. But it would never have come into being without my amazing agent, Steve Malk, who plucked me from those pages and changed everything with one innocuous little suggestion. A hundred and one thanks to my wise and patient editor, Alessandra Balzer at Hyperion Books for Children, for her faith in a first-timer and for keeping me from horribly dating myself. A special shout-out to the capable editorial staff at Hyperion, for all their inspired diligence.

Thanks to my beta readers: Lauren Schorr; the entire Kaufman clan; Erin Krawiec; Tina Headley; Emily Kaiser; and Alan Deutschman, who reassured me I was on the right path. Special thanks to Fran Silverstein, for her elephantine memory, and to Austin Handler, for his discerning eye.

None of this would have happened without the love and support of my family. To my parents, Thelma and Seymour, who almost ruined my writerly aspirations by providing a loving, happy, and (relatively) normal childhood: thank you for never discouraging me from pursuing the improbable. To my daughter, Alexa, who doesn't even know her ABCs yet: thank you for sharing your first precious months of life with your mom's other life-altering project. Finally, to my husband, Gary, who always has more faith in me than I do. Thank you for letting me go first.